Kim,

Thanks for reading my book, hope you like it!

~Amanda Beyer~

Reilly, Angel of Darkness ~ Vol I

Book One - Inferno, Book Two - Angel of Darkness

Amanda R Boyer with Ellen Ritchie

authorHOUSE®

AuthorHouse™
1663 Liberty Drive
Bloomington, IN 47403
www.authorhouse.com
Phone: 1-800-839-8640

© 2009 Amanda R Boyer with Ellen Ritchie. All rights reserved.
No part of this book may be reproduced, stored in a retrieval system, or transmitted by any means without the written permission of the author.
First published by AuthorHouse   5/7/2009

Printed in the United States of America
Bloomington, Indiana
This book is printed on acid-free paper.

ISBN: 978-1-4389-1955-3 (sc)

This book is a work of fiction. DeSoto, Missouri is a real town, but locations listed in this book are fictitious. Any resemblance to actual events, locales, or persons, living or dead, are coincidental.

Dedication

I dedicate this work to my family, for supporting me. To my parents, for encouraging me. To Ellen, for helping me. To my grandpas, Howard and Harvey, for all you have ever done for me, may you rest in peace. And to Katie, for being my friend whether I cheer, play soccer, write, read, or am just plain insane!

Acknowledgements

First of all I'd like to thank Ellen, for allowing me to branch off and give Reilly her own story. Second, I'd like to thank my parents, with out you I never would've went ahead with this. Also, I'd like to thank Kirsten, for listening to me talk about a story that you really didn't know anything about. I'd like to thank Meleah, for your flawless editing and for putting up with my questions. I'd also like to thank my little brother, Trey, for putting up with me and for reading the story even if you didn't understand what was happening. So thank you guys, and to anyone I forgot, you know who you are and you know where I live. Rock on!

Inferno

By: Amanda Boyer with Ellen Ritchie

Inferno
'I thought I knew what was coming,
   turns out that I was wrong.
Now those from whom I've been running,
   are singing my death song.
Lives I thought I'd lost,
       Are found once again,
I now know love,
   I now have friends.'

                          -Amanda Boyer

Contents

The New Girl	1
The truth (Sort of)	7
Old "Friends"	9
The Truth (really, it is).	15
What the Hell is He doing here?!	19
The Order (Again…I hate them!)	21
She's Baaaaaack!	27
RESCUE?!	32
Sacrifice	41
Jezaba's Return	46
Empathy	52
Did I hear that right?!	63
They're fighting…Again!	65
Keira's Boyfriend, Edward's Jealousy.	69
The Ship	71
Humanity Sucks	79
Voices	87
The Past. *My* Past!	93
Jezaba's Plan	100
Plane Ride from Hell	103
Oh No!!!	110
The End…I Think	115
Nightmares	117
Goodbyes	120

Chapter 1
The New Girl

It was too early when I woke up. Only five o'clock. I had had another nightmare. My long, black, blue streaked, hair was soaked with sweat. I noticed that the pair of black track pants and black band shirt I'd worn to bed were also soaked. I got up and went to the mirror to check my reflection. My bright green eyes looked tired. Of course, being a demon, they usually did. (That's right, I said demon. That's why my eyes are not only green, but so bright that they almost hypnotize any mortal that looks too deeply. I can control both fire, and the dark energy that can be found just about anywhere.) I live in the small town of Desoto, Missouri. (It's easier to stay off the demonic radar that way.) I don't live with my real family, (because both my parents are dead,) but my step-parents try their damnedest to make my life hell like any real parents would. You see, they're devil-worshipers who were obsessed with my father, (I don't want to talk about it). As a matter of fact, that was who my nightmare was about. He was an abusive, evil, satanic, bastard and my step-parents were trying to follow in his footsteps, (And not doing too bad a job, either).

My goal this morning was to be dressed, downstairs, and gone before they ever got up. They were sleeping off a major hangover, so I thought I'd be ok. I was wrong. Something came flying out of the kitchen and I had to back up to avoid getting hit. I looked into the other room to see that my 'mom' and 'dad' were sitting at the table, laughing.

"Oh, yeah, that's hilarious. Say, couldn't you wait 'till after school to attempt to kill me?" I asked, politely.

"Well we could, Mutt, but that wouldn't be nearly as fun!" my 'mom' yelled.

"I may be only half demon, but I'm still way more powerful than you! Do you really think that keeping me here will impress Jezaba that much to make you two idiots demons? You haven't heard from him in so long, are you even sure he's still alive?" I mocked, I knew they had their doubts. Their eyes widened, and I bolted for the door before they could have time to react. By the way, Jezaba is a very annoying evil dude bent on destroying anything and everything, just so you know. (Yes, you read right, I'm only a half demon, but an unusually powerful one. The only thing stopping me from killing them both is that I'm trying to stay undiscovered).

But anyway, I had just closed the door when the point of what looked like a very large butcher knife came bursting through it. "You missed!" I called. I heard more laughs, followed by my 'dad' shouting,

"That's ok, you've got to come home eventually." I could take comfort in the sole fact that they were my step-parents and I could only pretend that my real parents were any better. They died "mysteriously" when I was like five or something. My dad was a **very** powerful demon and my mom was, I think, an Angel. They some how fell in love, and I was born. All I'm sure about is that my dad killed my mom (which I was forced to watch,) about a month or so before he himself died, but I don't know how.

☆ ☆ ☆

When I arrived at school, the gates were still locked. I was way early. I didn't know if anyone was inside and I sure as hell wasn't going to wait outside, so I started to pick the lock, within seconds, the gate was open.

"Yes!" I whispered.

I waited in the hall until, finally, the janitor came wheeling his trashcan down the hall. He smiled and I nodded in acknowledgement. (Seldom, if ever, do I smile).

"Hi, Uh…Reilly, isn't it." Again, I nodded. "well, would you like to wait in your room or in the hall?" he asked.

"Room." I said, looking toward my homeroom.

"Ok." He pulled out a huge chain of keys and began looking for the right one, I sighed impatiently.

"Got it." he mumbled, I looked up to see the door swinging open.

I walked in, mumbling a quick thank you as I did so. Then I settled in for a long wait.

✧ ✧ ✧

At about seven-thirty, the other students started filing in. I pretended to be interested in a book, I wasn't in a talking mood. (Not that I ever am).

Not that 'reading' lasted long. I heard a thunderous crash and jumped up to see where it was coming from. (I tend to gravitate toward strange occurrences, it helps me gain information on the demonic government so I know where *not* to go. In this case, however, it wasn't what I would've hoped for. I was about to enter a nightmare). I looked out into the hall and didn't see anything, so I raced to the stairs.

It didn't take long for me to reach the crowd on the next floor. I got to the front and saw, to my horror, that Edward had a new girl pinned up to the lockers. For those of you who **don't** know Edward, (you're lucky,) he's also a half demon, (although a whole lot dumber than me). He's got serious issues and won't admit them. He also **thinks** he can kill me, but he's not actually brave enough to try. And that's about it.

Any way, he had her pinned to the wall and was either having an episode, or was going to seriously injure her in front of everyone. Exposing us all. And even though I noticed all of this, I could still see that she looked surprisingly familiar. But it could've only been the fact that her brown eyes were frozen in terror, (being a half demon, I see that a lot). "Uh, Edward? What are you doing?" I said, trying not to kill him. I sounded amazingly calm, considering the way I felt.

He let her go, still glaring. "Reilly, would you butt out of this!?" Ok, this was seriously not helpful to my whole, 'trying not to kill him' thing earlier.

"Dude, you're about to kill the new girl, I think I get to knock you out before you do." I said angrily.

"But look at her," he shouted, as he shoved the scared girl in front of him, "she's **her** reincarnated!" Then it hit me, Kara! (Who is, incase you don't know, a very annoying holy woman). That was why she looked so familiar, her brown hair, her bone structure, everything was identical to Kara. Edward had been in love with her but she tried to kill him. Needless to say, things went a little, 'down hill'. That also explained why he was now trying to kill her. Jezaba, (whom I mentioned earlier,) killed Kara a while back, (Next time, I'll have to make sure it's final).

I glared at Kara, but some how, kept my voice calm, "Yeah, and I could change and kill you all at any minute. What's your point." I asked. The 'change' I was referring to was into my full form. That, may I add, I can't control. Edward knew that, unfortunately. He seems to have some idea that I'm evil, which I kind of *was*, but so *was* he so we're even. (That would be why I'm trying to stay under the radar, I kind of betrayed the most powerful evil being there was, (Jezaba). Now, though, I'm good. Or at least, trying to be).

"And I should kill *you* too." He added, I just glared at him.

"Try it." I said, through clenched teeth.

"Nah, I pass." he said, shaking his head.

"Chicken." I challenged.

"I have to get to class." The, now, completely terrified girl, Kara, said.

"Then go." I said, impatiently. I was concentrating on Edward, daring him to try something.

Did I mention how stupid he was, because he *did* try something! "She's not escaping yet." He said, as he grabbed her arm, "So Kara--"

"That does it!! My name is Keira, (Oh, big difference,) K-E-I-R-A!! I'm not Kara, whoever that is!" Keira said, with surprising anger.

"You have to be her because...no one smells this disgusting 'cept you." Edward said. I was trying not to laugh.

"How is that possible? I take showers!!" that did it. I laughed quietly, for fear of anyone hearing, no one did.

"Not that kind of smell, your *scent*!"

"Hey dumb ass, too much info!" I spun Edward around to face me, "Go to class." I told Keira. I watched her hurry off and the crowd dissemble. Then I faced Edward.

"Are you nuts!? She's getting away!" He said.

"Aw, poor wittle Edward. Did it ever occur to you that she has absolutely no idea what you're talking about?!" I shouted, no longer calm.

"No..." He muttered.

"Go to class, and if she's there, I swear, if you touch her, I will kill you." I turned then added, "slowly."

"Uh...fine!" He hurried off in the same direction as Keira. Uh-oh, not good. I followed.

As I was approaching the classroom Edward had gone into, I heard a loud, "No!!" I hurried faster.

"Miss May, control yourself!!" I heard the teacher say.

"But this guy tried to kill me!" Oh crap, that was Keira. Time to freeze the room, (one of the many perks of being a demon, or half demon, in my case. The only down side, I can only freeze humans, which kind of sucks really). I snapped my fingers and fire filled the room, (though too fast for human eyes to see).

"Keira, you can't say that." I said, "You'll expose us all."

"What do you mean, 'expose'?" she asked, I was about to reply, but Edward interrupted.

"Never mind! Now's my chance." Oh, you bastard, I thought. But I saw that Keira wasn't moving. Edward said something about Kara, but I was distracted. He began to charge.

"You idiot, move!" I shouted.

"I don't want to move." she shouted back. Stupid reincarnation. (Because that's what she must be if she's isn't the real Kara. Thank God, reincarnations are so much more easily disposed of if that's necessary.)

"Why not?" I asked, Edward was getting dangerously close.

"I'm too scared!" she screamed.

"Edward, stop!" I commanded. To my surprise, he listened.

"Who's gonna make me?" He asked. Technically, I just did, but I'll let it go.

"If you don't stop harassing her, you'll wish I **had** stopped you, permanently." I threatened, he gulped.

"Who said I'm harassing anyone?" He asked, innocently.

"Edward…" I said, my eyes flashing with anger.

"Fine, but she'd better stay away from me." He said.

"I accept your term!" Keira agreed.

I sighed, "you two are impossible."

"And you're a bitch." I thought I heard Edward mumble.

"What!?" I shouted.

"Aw, did I call you a bad name?" he asked in a baby voice.

I tried to stop myself, (not as hard as I could've though,) but…my claws came out and went right across Edward's face. (Not that it helped much, he was still ugly).

"What was that for?" he asked. Stupid demon. I just shook my head and left the room. Out in the hall, I snapped my fingers again and released my hold on the room.

First hour went by quickly, but second hour was another story.

Chapter 2
The truth (Sort of)

When I first heard the singing, I thought some freshmen was getting made fun of, but when I looked up, I froze. Keira was running, no, *skipping* down the hall.

"You've cheered up a bit since first hour." I noticed, annoyed.

"Yep. Because no Edward until the end of the day!" She said, happily.

"Yeah, but that still doesn't explain why you're skipping down the halls like a two-year-old." I said, not really interested.

"I'm so HAPPY!" She shouted, practically in my ear.

"Yeah, I'm sure you are." I said, as Edward came up behind her. When he came in, I could see she was upset. "Wow, you were happy for a whole, thirty seconds, that's a record." I said.

"Why are *you* here?" she asked, still not looking at him.

"That's none of your business." He angrily said.

"Aw, how cute, the old married couple is fighting, *again*." I said, shaking my head, "this is your," I began to count on my fingers, "your eighteenth, going on nineteenth, fight today."

"What? How could you even suggest that?!" Edward exclaimed, too quickly. He definitely liked her.

Lunch time! Oh, lord.

"What is your problem?!" I heard Keira's angry voice shout beside me.

"I don't have a problem, you do." Edward said, calmly. That only made her yell louder.

"What the hell are you talking about!" She screamed, at least half of the cafeteria turned in our direction.

"Temper, temper. Would you quit attracting so much attention?!" Edward asked.

"No!" Whoever wasn't listening, was now.

"Would you shut up!?" He snapped, "You're being too loud."

"You want to hear loud, I AM NOT BEING LOUD!!" she screamed, God help me. On second thought, scratch that last request.

Edward just covered his ears as he said, to my complete dismay, "Are you sure you're an Apostle, you sure don't act like one." Oh no, please don't listen to him! (An Apostle is a weapon of God used to store a virtue, there are seven, unless you count the hidden virtue. Keira, is hope. And I know this, because I can sense it).

"I'm a what?" Well, shit.

"Nothing, never mind." Edward said quickly after I glared at him. (Nice save, dumb ass).

"Please tell me!" Keira was begging now, but Edward said,

"Nope! Never mind." Then as she began to say something else, he covered his ears and said, "I can't hear you!"

"Oh real mature." Keira rolled her eyes, I did too. Luckily, most of the cafeteria had grown tired of their conversation.

"Bravo! You two are great. First, I have to freeze first hour, and now the whole cafeteria knows that you're in love." I said, clapping my hands.

"We are not!" They shouted.

"Really, point proven." I said, matter-of-factly.

"Reilly, do you know what an Apostle is?" Keira asked suddenly. Damn it Edward.

"Damn it Edward, big mouth!" I glared, then I turned to Keira. " No, I know nothing."

"Really, you just called Edward a big mouth."

"I don't know anything." I said, annoyed.

"I'll find out eventually." she called as I walked away. I heard Edward say,

"No you won't." I wasn't sure he was right. She was very smart, too smart for her own good.

Chapter 3
Old "Friends"

I walked around for about an hour before I finally decided that I had to go home. I dreaded the thought of re-entering that hell hole but I had no where else to go.

As I approached the house I heard a too familiar voice, "Where is she?" It asked.

"She'll be here soon, I assure you." My `dad' said.

"She'd better be." The voice, (bitch) said.

"Looking for me?" I asked from the doorway.

"Why, Reilly, how great it is to see you again." The voice (asshole) said, as a figure stepped out of the shadows in front of me.

"Violante. How has hell been treating you?" I asked, Violante is a full demon whom I absolutely despise, and she loves that fact. It's a very long story involving her being *extremely* jealous of me. She wasn't actually in Hell, it was technically the Underworld. But in my opinion, they are one and the same.

"Why don't you come back and find out?" She asked seriously, she was tempting me. (In case you couldn't tell).

"Or, here's a thought, why don't you go back empty handed so they can kill you." The 'they' I referred to were the upper level demons that ruled the Underworld. That is, they ruled after Jezaba disappeared.

"Well, I have better things to do just now. Like get the Apostles. See you soon." She smiled, then was gone. I had about ten minutes to get to Keira.

As I approached the tree line I could hear Keira's voice. "What now?" She yelled.

"Look--." Edward, (what the hell was *he* doing there,) said.

" What? Hey, retard, hello?" Keira said, Edward knew.

I ran through the trees, grabbed both of them by the arm, and pulled them away from the forest.

"Time to go!" I shouted.

"Wait, what's going on?" Keira screeched in my ear.

"Never mind, shut up and stop asking stupid questions." Edward said.

"How many times do I have to hear that!?" she yelled.

I let go and said, "You two play nicely. Edward, refrain from killing Keira. And Keira, keep your voice down." I said, I wasn't about to die just because loud mouth couldn't listen.

"She's back isn't she?" Edward asked.

"What? Who?!" Keira piped up.

"Yeah, and now, I *really* have to leave." I said, and then turned and sprinted for the trees, within seconds I was back in the forest. (Being a demon, I have enhanced speed).

"If you think you can hide her from me, you are deathly mistaken." Violante cackled as she appeared.

"Who says she's hiding? Either way, you have to go through me, and we both remember what happened the last time you tried to do that." I smiled at the memory. But Violante's face twisted into a distorted expression of annoyance and anger,

"I don't have time for this!" She yelled. And then I saw her head toward the street.

"Bitch! Coward!" I shouted in frustration, (I do that a lot. You would too if you had to live like I do). Then I ran back to where I'd left Keira and Edward, (what was I thinking?!)

"No! Don't you get those ideas in your head." I heard Edward shout.

Ugh! "That's it!" I ran up the street. "I TOLD YOU TWO NOT TO ATTRACT ATTENTION, BUT YOU JUST HAD TO ARGUE!!" I screamed. Edward said something, but I was watching Violante emerge from the trees.

Sure enough, they started to argue again. Together, Violante and I rolled our eyes.

"Do they do this all the time?" She asked.

"Yep," I replied, "everyday."

"Do you want to come to the top of a volcano with me?" She asked. That was random, how dumb is she? I smirked.

"Nice try." I remarked, "I still hate you."

"Bitch!"

"Well, you know, I try." I said, coolly. She was mad.

"I'm going to kill you Reilly Scara!" She yelled, I rolled my eyes.

"You know, you keep saying that and yet…here I still stand." I said, still calm.

"How do we get those two idiots to stop fighting?" Violante asked, ignoring my sarcasm.

"Well, I would tell you, but you're after Keira. As long as their arguing, she's safe." I said calmly. I could handle Violante if I had to.

"I'm what?" Keira asked. Oh, now she listens to me and doesn't argue.

"Get down!" Edward shouted as he pushed her down then leapt himself.

"Ashelin! Now, take the Apostle!" Violante shouted, and a frog looking thing came toward Keira.

"Yes, Vio!" It shouted.

"It's Violante! Capture the Apostle!" She shouted.

"Yes ma'am! Um, what's an Apostle again?" It asked.

Violante was about to reply, but I couldn't hold it in any longer. I burst into laughter as I managed to choke out, "Hey, look, a talking frog!" I laughed harder.

"Ha, ha. Very funny." Violante said, un-amused by my remark.

"Um, ma'am?" Ashelin asked.

"What?" Violante replied sharply.

"I'm kind of afraid of her." She said, pointing at me.

"I'll deal with her." Violante said, indicating me. Then she charged. I countered her attack, hoping she wouldn't go into full form, then I'd have to. (Full form is when we embrace our full powers, but, because I'm only a half demon, I can't fully control mine for long. It's the same with Edward. Only, *he'd* never admit it).

Out of the corner of my eye, I saw Itasis appear. (He's another one of Violante's lackeys. But he's not as annoying as Ashelin, who is new).

Suddenly, Violante shouted, "Where the hell have you been!?"

"I was busy." He explained, with a smirk.

"Fine, kill Edward! Or else you'll have to deal with Jezaba." She threatened. Jezaba? Wait a minute, he's supposed to be gone...this is very bad.

"No!"

"Fine, then kill the half demon."

"Oh, so it's a fight huh?" I heard Edward say. Uh-oh.

"Edward don't get carried away!!" I shouted, "we have to make sure Keira stays safe." I wasn't finished, but Violante kicked me in the ribs so hard that I flew backwards into the trees. She followed and we were soon out of the others' sight.

"So, I had a nice chat with your parents. Telling them what we have planned for you." She smirked.

"They aren't my parents!" I yelled, still out of breath from her attack.

"Oh, you're right aren't you? Your dad is with Jezaba now, because he killed your mom and then somehow got himself killed. By the way, I have plans for *that* as well."

"For what?" I asked.

"Getting Jezaba back...and your father, of coarse. Why exactly do you hate him again?" she asked, even though she knew that answer.

"Shut up." I said, my voice shook with anger. She knew I hated my past, but I had to control myself.

"Temper, temper. Are you going to kill me?" she asked mockingly. She knew to do that I'd need my full power.

"Don't push it, I just might do that." I lied.

"Oh really? Why don't we test that statement?" Oh, shit. Please don't.

"Let's." I said, trying to keep calm.

"Alas, as much as I **would** like to put your statement to the test. I didn't come here for that, this time." She smiled, hinting that she'd be back.

"Then you're not going to get what you came for." I said, my blood rising.

"Wanna bet?" She asked, suddenly racing past me. She did, however, have time to claw down the left side of my face.

"Ow." I said, involuntarily. She hesitated, big mistake. Before she could say, oops, I was back in front of her. Right in front of her.

"It won't be that easy." I grinned, as my claws came fully out.

"Fine, but you asked for it." She said.

"No, you did." I said, in reply. Then I dug my razor sharp fingernails into her arm. She screamed and backed away, but she was smiling.

"That's it, Reilly, let your true instincts take over. You know you want to kill me and-."

"*You* shouldn't tempt me." I interrupted her. I couldn't lose control, not now.

"Why? Are you worried about someone?" She seemed to remember something, "Oh, by the way, I saw Charlie. He didn't see me, but I know exactly where he is right now." As She smirked something caught my eye.

I smiled, "so do I." Suddenly, Violante was all the way on the other side of the clearing and Charlie was standing next to me. Charlie is a devil...and there's really not much more to say. Oh, he's one of my best friends and, unfortunately, Edward's too.

• "You're welcome!" He called as I chased after Violante, who had headed back to Keira.

"I didn't need your help." I said, but I was smiling.

"Fine, see you at school." He waved, then was gone as suddenly as he'd appeared. (what did he mean by that?)

"Thanks." I whispered.

I got to the street just in time to hear Violante shriek, "I'll beat you Reilly, and I'll get that Apostle too!" (Who did she think she was, the Wicked Witch? Well, ding, dong, the witch will die).

"Whatever." I said coolly. I had seen Charlie again, but my face hurt really bad.

"That's it! What the hell are you?! And what are these Apostles?! AND WHAT'S GOING ON!!" Keira shouted.

I looked at Edward and could tell he was thinking the same as me. We had to shut Keira up. I walked toward her and knocked her out.

"What'd you do!!?" Edward asked, alarmed. Keira dropped like a ton of brick.

"I knocked her out." I replied, calmly. "she'll wake up, eventually."

"EVENTUALLY?!" He yelled, "she'd better wake up soon, or I'll--."

"You'll what? You don't care, remember?" I asked, my hands on my hips.

"Well no, I don't. But if she doesn't wake up then…then…" he couldn't think of an excuse. I laughed.

Chapter 4
The Truth (really, it is).

I was sitting on the window sill, Keira was laying in her bed, (still unconscious,) and Edward was sitting in a chair in the corner. (He refused to go near me. Not that I cared).

Finally, (after at least an hour of Edward and I glaring at each other,) Keira woke up. She looked confused.

"So, you're finally awake." Edward noted, (glaring at me). She tried to get up.

"You might not want to do that." Edward warned.

"Why not--?" she began, then she crumpled to the ground.

"Whoa, head rush." I said. My mouth hurt badly and I **would** have a black eye, (though Violante hadn't done all of it,) but I was smiling.

"What the hell did you do to me? And don't think I've forgotten about last night!"

I let out a sigh, "not this again." I begged.

"And we have all the time in the world, because it's Saturday." she continued, I rolled my eyes.

"Shit! I was hoping you wouldn't have remembered!" Edward exclaimed.

"Where's my explanation? You owe me! Especially Edward since **he** tried to kill me." Keira yelled, I tried not to laugh, but I don't think I was very good at it.

"What? I have to! What about Reilly? She's the one who knocked you out!"

I cringed, "Edward! You weren't supposed to tell!" In truth, I didn't really care, but if she found out about me, then she'd be in even more danger.

"You what?!" Keira yelled as she faced me.

"I…well…ASK EDWARD!" I said, and we both turned to face him.

"Edward?" Keira said, patiently.

"What?" he asked, calmly. (For once).

"What's an Apostle?"

"Why me?" Edward asked in a whiney voice.

"You've put it off too long!" Keira accused.

"That's right Edward." I said, unable to hide the smirk in my words.

"I hate both of you!" he exclaimed. It was directed to me. "An Apostle is someone with powers!"

"Powers?" Keira asked.

"Yes. Powers."

"There's more to it, I know it!" Keira said. She *was* right.

"Nope, that's it." Edward lied.

Suddenly, Keira jumped up and grabbed Edward by the collar, "TELL ME!" she shouted.

"I just did." he said, shaken.

"Tell Me!"

"Fine, ok." Keira released him.

"Really?"

"Nope."

"EDWARD!" she began to strangle him. As much as I would've liked to just sit there and watch, I had to stop her, (though now, I'm not sure why).

"Keira, as much as I don't want to spoil this, you have to stop." I said, calmly.

"Why?" she asked, (like I said, 'I don't know.')

"Just let go of him." She did, reluctantly. "An Apostle is someone who was chosen by God and is entrusted with his powers." I explained. (There now Edward, was that so hard? You could've done that).

She looked confused, "why me, though?"

"Not sure, God's weird. There are seven; they represent a virtue such as joy, faith, courage, hope, charity, wisdom, and love. You are Hope," I said. Edward made a weird face but I ignored him.

"Why are these people after me?"

"Demons, devils, and even devil worshipers can gain great power from you seven. That's why you have to be protected." Edward explained, (That's why she couldn't kill Edward, because then *I'd* have to protect her. I knew that!) I cringed when he said 'devil worshipers'. Those were my 'parents' all right.

"Ok, then why did *you* try to kill me?" Keira glared at Edward. I smiled. Try to talk your way out of *that* one Edward!

"Edward, want to answer that?" I asked him, knowing what he'd say.

"No!" Man, I'm good! Then I glared at him,

"Just tell her." I said, icily.

"Fine, in the year 1874..." he began, but Keira interrupted. I didn't listen to his story, I knew what happened, basically, Kara had betrayed Edward and tried to kill him...and me...I'm sure *Edward* deserved it, but I never touched the evil hag, I mean, holy woman.

"Ok..." Keira said, when he'd finished.

"Yeah, she wasn't exactly what *I* called a good friend either." I added. (You know, considering she tried to kill me, multiple times. Because of some unknown reason I can't figure out).

"You make her sound evil." Bingo, I thought, but kept my mouth shut.

"So what if she was a stupid "Holy woman," she's evil in my book."

"Edward," I began, annoyed, "everyone's evil in *your* book."

"Especially you." he muttered.

"Guys, would you two stop fighting?" Keira said. She stood up, and walked to the door.

"Where are you going?" Edward asked.

"Going to see if my mom is roaring mad at me!" she said. I had forgotten about the massacre downstairs. When we'd gotten Keira to her house, she was still unconscious, so *she* hadn't seen the carnage downstairs and her mom's dead body...it looked like a wild animal had attacked...a wild animal named Violante that is. Keira's annoying sister, Brittany, was missing.

"I wouldn't do that if I were you." I warned her, remembering the body.

"Why?" she asked, walking out the door. Not ten seconds later, we heard an earsplitting scream. We got up and ran to Keira. Just as we got to her, she fainted.

"It wasn't me!" I exclaimed.

"Help me pick her up." Edward snarled. We got her back to her bed and then there was nothing to do.

"I'm watching you." Edward said suspiciously.

"Oh dear, you've figured out my plan. I was going to deliver her to Violante, my worst enemy, but you caught me." I said sarcastically.

"You probably were." he said, stubbornly. I rolled my eyes.

"I'm not evil you dolt!" I hissed.

"Oh no, excuse me, but weren't *you* the one who sunk Atlantis?" He said, I laughed.

"*You* and *Charlie* helped, remember?" (it's a long story).

"No! And another thing--"

"Shhh, She's waking up." I interrupted him, Keira had opened her eyes and was now looking at us.

"We should've told her that her mom was dead!" Edward shouted, I gave him a look, wondering how long it would take me to burn him with my eyes. Too long, I decided, so I just glared at him instead.

"My mom is dead!" Keira screamed. Man, she could yell!

Well here's pretty much how the rest of the conversation went, I told Keira that, yes her mom was dead, and no she couldn't yell any more. (I didn't mention that if she didn't stop, I'd probably kill her, but I figured it was implied.)

I don't know how long we sat in silence but finally I couldn't take it anymore. I jumped through the window without another word and was soon running through the trees.

I was pretty far away from the house when I heard a crash of glass. That made me smile and I hoped she'd actually hit him with something... hard.

Chapter 5
What the Hell is He doing here?!

"Screw you!" I shouted at my 'parents,' this time they had actually managed to slice my arm. Luckily it would heal before school since it wasn't that bad. (Another demonic perk, I can self heal, and the shallow cuts don't take long).

I wasn't early, actually I was late. I ran through the doors and almost fell over, guess who, Charlie!

"What the Hell?"

"Hello, to you too." he said, smiling.

"What are you doing here?" I asked.

"I was in the neighborhood, and I said I'd see you at school."

"I wasn't listening, now, what are you really doing here?" I asked again, calmly. He avoided my eyes, and I think he blushed.

"I...uh...was checking on the Apostle." he said, still not looking at me.

"Sure, why?" I asked persistently.

"Because Violante almost killed you earlier and--."

"What?! Correction, I almost killed HER!" I said, in his face.

"Whatever, either way, you might need my help." he said, a little too quickly.

"Fine, I'm late." I said, as I headed toward class.

"So am I." He said, then walked with me.

"You didn't, did you?" I asked, horrified.

"If you're referring to me being in all of your classes, then no, just most of 'em." he said, then hurried off before I could smack him.

My morning classes passed quickly even though Charlie had somehow managed to sit next to me...in *all* of them!

Walking to the cafeteria, I could hear Keira and Edward arguing, again.

"This is about Kara, isn't it!" I heard Keira scream.

"Maybe…" Edward said, what the hell was he doing now?!

They kept arguing and finally, we reached their table.

"I told you they fight like an old married couple." I said to Charlie. I had told him something like that earlier.

"You're right Reilly." he said, and we took our seats.

"Charlie!!" Edward exclaimed. (for some odd reason that I can't comprehend, Charlie is his best friend, as I mentioned before).

"Yep," he looked at Keira, "and you must be Keira May. You're the Apostle of Hope." Great, now she's going to freak out 'cause he knows her.

She looked shocked. I told you. (Why is she not at all confused about why I hang out with a half demon and a devil? She should be asking me a whole shit load of questions right now, unless…)

"So, Edward when did it become your business to tell Keira that I'm a half demon?" I asked, before Keira could freak out. He gulped.

"Uh…she…kind of, figured it out." he said. I rolled my eyes.

"Next time, let me handle it, ok?" I asked, he nodded. Then we looked at Keira, she looked either extremely pissed off or else just scared out of her mind. Either way, it was obvious that she hadn't heard us.

"Keira, are you ok?" Edward asked. Then she reached for something in her purse and all Hell broke loose.

Chapter 6
The Order (Again…I hate them!)

"OK, WHAT THE HELL ARE YOU!?" Keira screamed as she came back to reality.

Oh God! I snapped my fingers, freezing the room, as Keira pulled out a gun. Then I glared at her.

"You have a gun!?" Edward exclaimed, more angry then surprised.

"Wow, a gun toting Apostle." Charlie said, amused. I rolled my eyes.

"Keira, put the gun down," I snarled. "*Now!*" She threw it back into her purse and sat there, seething. I unfroze the room, and glared at her.

"So, what are you?" she said, quietly. I was debating on whether I should *strangle* her or not.

"I'm a devil." Charlie said, (well, at least he's honest).

"A WHAT!?" Keira yelled, but lowered her voice when she glanced at me.

"A devil, you know, an evil being sent forth to kill all of humanity, that sort of thing." he said, I tried not to laugh at Keira's expression. Her eyes had widened to the size of my fist and her mouth was wide open.

"All…all of humanity." She stuttered. I was pretty sure she was remembering her mom, so I shook my head 'no' slightly, she noticed.

After lunch, I walked to my class, which Charlie wasn't in, and then walked home.

As I was walking I saw Keira and her annoying as hell cousin, Isabella.

"Hi Reilly!" Isabella was shouting. I can't *stand* her! (Its not so much a personal thing, as she's just *really* annoying! I'd dealt with her briefly during my time posing as an actual high school student.)

I turned off into an alley that I knew would lead me to my house. Unfortunately, Edward and Charlie were coming down the street and saw me. I was trapped. Why me?! Can't they find some other demon to mess with, (and no, Edward doesn't count).

"Where are you going?" Charlie asked.

"Hell." I replied.

"Ha, ha." he said, what he didn't know was that by going home, I really was entering Hell.

"I'm serious." I said, I forced a smile.

Edward piped up, "going to destroy another city again?" he asked.

"Yeah, would you and Charlie like to help me again?"

"Yes, I'd be glad to." Charlie said, laughing.

"No! *I'm* not evil!" Edward yelled, then quietly to Charlie he added, "You'd jump off a bridge for *her,* wouldn't you?"

"Yes." was Charlie's reply, then he smiled. Lately his behavior had been odd.

"Hey, Edward!" Isabella's voice came booming across the street. Damn it, it was closer that time!

He looked up at them, "What?"

"I brought your girlfriend!" she shouted, I laughed at his expression, which turned to a glare when he heard me.

"HE IS NOT MY BOYFRIEND!" Keira screamed.

"Right." I said, skeptically.

Keira was about to reply, but a voice saying, "Step away from the Holy Woman!" stopped her.

I knew that voice. I didn't know the monk's name, but I'd heard his voice a lot. He was from the order. I rolled my eyes, "not them…" I sighed. The order is basically just a bunch of monks and nuns who…well I'm not exactly sure what they do. But I do know that they hate us (meaning anyone who isn't either a nun or monk, or anything holy,). Which is fine, because we hate them too. We'd had a couple of run-ins in the past.

"Put your hands up!" commanded the monk.

"Reilly, what's going on?" Keira whispered.

"Shhhh. Just stay calm and--," I began. But Keira must've realized what was happening, because before I could finish, she shouted,

"I'm too young to go to jail!"

"So much for being calm…" I said.

"Whatever happened, it's Edward's fault." she continued.

"WHAT!!?" Edward shouted.

"I agree with that." I said. Hey, as long as I don't have to deal with those monks again. (It turns out that they don't like it when you kill people).

"Into the cars, now!" The man shoved Edward, Charlie, and I into the nearest car. I saw them usher, (more gently,) Isabella and Keira into the other.

"Hello, Reilly." Said the monk in the passenger seat.

"Mathew." I said, I hated him! (Hey, you would too if he helped to try to kill you…not to mention he was my uncle). Now do you see why I hate the order?

"You know, just because you're a demon, doesn't mean you have to act like one." He said, turning to face me.

"You know, just because you became a monk, doesn't mean that you're no longer a demon." I replied, he turned away.

"Demons." The two monks in the front seats mumbled.

"Monks." Edward, Charlie, and I said.

✫ ✫ ✫

We arrived at the Order's main building, and they dragged us out of the car.

"Follow me." Commanded a monk I didn't know.

Mathew grabbed my arm tightly and leaned forward, "You're going to stay with me for a while."

"Fun, fun." I groaned.

I noticed Charlie keeping a close eye on Mathew. Hmmm, I wonder why.

They took us into a room that was barely big enough for us to stand in. It was made of metal and would be difficult to escape. Hard, but not impossible.

"Be good, and I might come let you out for a while." Mathew said, (What was I, a dog? Don't answer that!)

"Aw, you promise!?" I said, sarcastically. He left without saying anymore.

I walked to a back corner, (which wasn't too awful far from the front ones,) and sat down.

"Who is he?" Charlie asked, as he came toward me.

"Old family friend." I mumbled, again, sarcastically.

"Really, you're not going to tell me, are you?" He asked.

"Maybe later." I said, (much later).

"Hey! Someone's coming!" Edward, who had been watching out the door since they closed it, shouted.

"Who?" Charlie asked, as we made our way over to him.

"Some nun." Edward said, disappointedly. (What was he expecting, an armada of demons and devils sent to our rescue by the supreme overlord of the underworld (who, by the way, hated us for turning 'good.')? You know what, I'm not even going to go there, because he probably was).

"I-I was sent to give you food, what do demons eat anyway?" She asked.

"Fish food." I mumbled.

"Same food as you." Edward said. Suddenly I had a brilliant idea.

"Edward." I called.

"What?!" he said.

"Flirt with her to get the keys." I said. (Ok, so maybe it wasn't **brilliant** exactly…more like a shot in the dark, but at least it was *something*).

"What!? What about--?"

"What about who? Keira doesn't matter to you, remember?"

"Fine." he said, giving up.

"H-here." The nun said shakily.

"So, what's your name?" Edward asked.

"A-Angela, sister Angela."

"That's a pretty name. You're pretty." Edward mumbled, I laughed. He was *really* bad at that, and he was turning bright red.

"What is he doing?" Charlie asked.

"He's flirting…I think." I said, then I explained to him what was happening.

"This ought a be good." He said.

"H-he's really bad at that." I said, echoing my thoughts. I was laughing so hard, I almost didn't get the words out.

"So, do you have the keys to get us out of here?" Edward was saying. Great, now she'll catch on.

"Yes." She seemed enchanted with him, I still can't figure that one out.

"Can I see them?"

"Oh, I don't-."

"Please?"

"Oh, ok." She handed them over, Yes!

"Thank you. You can go now and I'll see you later."

"Bye." she said, then she left.

"Yes! It actually worked!" Charlie said.

"God, you really *suck* at that whole flirting thing!" I laughed.

"It worked, didn't it?"

"Yeah, but nuns are stupid, I don't think it's gonna work on Keira." I said, ignoring the glare he gave me.

"C'mon!" Charlie shouted, he already had the door open.

We walked down a long hall and found that the door at the end was open, we went in and saw about twenty surprised faces looking at us. One of them was Mathew, but I didn't know any others.

"Reilly!" Mathew screamed, he seemed angry.

"Yeah?" I said.

"Don't throw your life away again. You can stay here! You can be saved!" He continued.

"Oh, so now you're a priest, too? Did it ever occur to you that I'd rather die then see you *ever* again?! You helped him, you think becoming a monk will erase that?!"

"No, but he was my brother!"

"He was *my* father, and I still turned against him!" I yelled before Charlie pulled me out of the room. He gave me a look that said, 'we'll talk later.' I nodded in agreement, and we kept running.

We came across another long, dark, hallway and found that that door, was locked. But we could hear voices inside,

"Sister?" Came a meek voice, just inside the door.

"Yes."

"The demons have escaped." We didn't wait to hear anymore, we shimmered outside the windows. (By the way, shimmering is another 'demonic perk' that I mentioned earlier. It means that we kind of, disappear, only to reappear in another place just seconds later. Some demons and devils are different then others, Edward and Charlie, for example, kind of glow until they disappear, but I'm surrounded by a whirl of flames).

"Now Edward, don't do anything stupid." I warned, I was about to say more, but a crash interrupted me. Edward had jumped through the window, "like that." I sighed.

"No!!!" Keira shrieked. "what've you done, Edward!?" I was highly confused, but a band of soldier monks, (Now there's something you don't see everyday,) came running around the corner. Mathew was among them, and he looked as if he was out for blood. Mine.

"Guys, we have to go!" I shouted in through the window. Or rather, the hole where the window used to be.

"But if these people know what's going on with Violante, they have to know something about my sister!" Keira shouted.

"We're leaving!" Edward grabbed her and leapt back out of the now shattered window. Things just kept getting better and better, didn't they?

Chapter 7
She's Baaaaaack!

Keira was silent during the car ride back, but good things don't last forever.

"Edward, stop it!!" She yelled after Edward kept looking at her funny, "Stop giving me those looks." He glared at her, "What, do you have a multiple personality disorder?" She asked, glaring back.

Isabella began to say something, (I don't listen too much when she talks,) but Keira interrupted her.

"I could've found out where my sister is!" That's not all she said, but I won't bore you with details.

Mostly the rest of the conversation was Keira denying her feelings for Edward. (if you haven't been paying attention, SHE LIKES HIM!)

Finally, I couldn't take it anymore, "GUYS JUST SHUT THE HELL UP!" I yelled. Then I thought of something. "And that goes double for **you,** Ed."

Edward glared at me, "Evil bitch!", he mumbled.

I stopped the car, then turned to face Edward. If the look on my face showed the way I felt, he should be terrified.

He gulped, "Uh…I meant…well, is this the part where I get out and start running?"

I nodded, (because I couldn't speak yet,) and Edward took off.

I grinned evilly. "And this is the part where I go after him." I said. Within seconds I was gone. With trees flying past me, I followed Edward.

"Don't hurt me," I heard him say from in front of me.

"I won't." I lied.

"What if I give up?" he asked.

"You'd be a *very* stupid demon." I said, then, using my demonic powers, I tied him to a tree. (Ok, so I wasn't actually going to **hurt** him, but scaring the shit out of him was hilarious).

"Hey, I wasn't ready!"

"Too bad." then I headed back to the car.

As I approached, I heard voices, (and no, not in my head). one of them was Violante's.

"See, no one will save you now! So come with me!" Violante was saying. I got right behind Keira,

"Oh yeah, you want to bet?" I asked, stepping away from the darkness.

"Geez, I thought you were chasing after Ed." Keira exclaimed.

"Yeah, about that, he's a little 'tied' up at the moment." I said.

"What do you mean, 'tied up'!?" She shouted. I was about to explain, but Violante interrupted me,

"Hem, hem. So if you two are done now, I'd like to kill Reilly, if you don't mind." Hello!! *I* mind!

"No, you'd like to try." I said.

"You know, I'm just going to leave you two alone." Keira said, backing away.

"You're not getting away ***this*** time!" Violante shouted, as she leapt toward Keira with her sword. I jumped in front of her and caught it. Unfortunately, I caught the sharp edge. It dug into my hand, which started bleeding.

"What? You didn't have to do that." Keira said.

"Oh yeah I did, Edward would **kill** me if you died!" I said, smiling at the thought of Edward actually trying to kill me.

"WHAT!!" she asked.

"Never mind, you need to get to safety, NOW!" I shouted.

"Excuse me, are you two finished?!! Reilly has to fight me now." Violante broke in, (notice how she assumes that I **have** to fight her, am I ***that*** predictable? That was a rhetorical question!)

"Fine, but you asked for it!" I yelled as Violante jerked her sword out of my hand. It hurt like hell but I didn't say anything. I did, however, glare at her.

"I was always the better fighter, Reilly." she shouted, clearly she was delirious.

"Did you hit your head, because you are hallucinating. You may *wish* you were the better fighter, though." I said, then I lunged toward her, knocking the sword out of her hands.

"Bitch!" she shouted.

"I know, it's what I do best." I said, grinning demonically, (did you catch that? Demonically).

Suddenly, a bolt of lightning shot out of the sky, knocking me backwards. She loves that attack, (but, frankly, I find it more annoying than anything else).

I shot fire out of my hands and it did the same to her. (It knocked her backwards, and probably annoyed the hell out of her, but that was the point).

"We'll finish this later!" Violante shouted, (coward!) then she left.

"Ah!! She's gonna kill us all!!" Edward shouted, (I had forgotten all about him!)

I turned to face him, "if I wanted to kill you, you'd be dead." I said, matter-of-factly.

"Reilly." I heard Charlie whisper. I looked over to see him motioning for me to follow him.

"You have some explaining to do." he said, when I reached him.

"Oh, what ever could you mean?" I asked, innocently.

"Ha, ha. Now, you explain while I bandage your hand." He said, moving toward me.

"It's just a scratch. It will heal soon anyway." I said, pulling my hand away.

"Don't tell me the bad ass demon is afraid of a little cleaning alcohol." He said, laughing. (I didn't find it funny, at all).

"I didn't say that! Do you want me to explain or not?" I said, as he began to clean the cut.

"Fine, explain." he said.

"His name is Mathew. Ouch!" I said, wincing.

"And…" he said, ignoring my pain.

"He is my uncle. And that's all you need to know for now" I said. he pushed on the cut, making it sting even worse, "Ouch! You did that on purpose!" I accused.

"Did not." He grinned.

"Did too." I mumbled.

"Fine, but seriously, Reilly, you could've gotten hurt really badly." He continued.

"Yeah, but it was worth it! The look on Violante's face was priceless!" I was actually smiling.

"Why are you so reckless?" He asked, he was being serious.

"I don't know, it's just the way I am. So Mr. Ex-Sinner, where the hell were you?" I laughed.

"I, um…uh, saw that you were doing good, so there was no reason for me to help you."

"Right…"

"No really, I had you covered." He said, smiling.

"Wait," I knew there was someone listening, so I turned to see Keira. "were you listening the *whole* time?" I knew she wasn't, for if she had been she would've been a bit more upset than she was.

"Yep, the *whole* time." She said, (she only thought so,) then she winked at me, I smiled back.

"Hey, don't think I didn't see that!" Charlie said.

"See what?" I asked innocently.

"Lady Keira, you must come with us!" a monk exclaimed, (whoa, where'd they come from? Don't answer that either. (you'll find that I ask a lot of rhetorical questions).

Edward, Charlie, and I stood protectively in front of Keira, preparing for a battle.

"We go with her or else she doesn't go at all." Edward said defensively. Very brave, Edward. Protect the girl you *aren't* in love with, from the people who *don't* want to take her.

"What?!" Keira, Charlie, and I asked simultaneously. They, too, clearly thought he was acting strange.

"I guess we have no choice but to take you with us." the monk sighed. "Sister Elizabeth is going to blow off her haystack when she finds out."

The car ride there was weird. Everyone was all cheerful and laughing. It made me sick! (I mean, it wasn't like we were going off to a birthday party or something like that…we were probably going off to freaking prison…actually, I'd *wished* we had been going to prison, it would've been easier to deal with.)

Finally, after what felt like endless hours, (of trying not to puke,) we pulled up at the order. Isabella begged to be left in the lobby, and I was glad they let her.

On our way down the hall, the monk said something about the *demons* who wrecked her office.

"Correction, demon. Not plural, I had nothing to do with it." I said.

"Whatever. You all can go, but first she wants to talk to you." the monk said.

"Great…" Keira mumbled.

They led us up some stairs to a room that I expected to be the father's office.

Sister Elizabeth looked up; "this is the first time I have allowed demons into my office. It is these times when we must ally ourselves with the enemy in order to destroy some things sometimes. I'm entrusting you four with a very special mission." Stupid nuns, they always speak in verses. Whoa! Did she just say, *mission*!?

"Isn't that what you have your nuns and monks for, why us?" Edward asked.

"This is about the Apostles! There are two more if you count the hidden virtue! In this case it's the Apostle of Charity. So your assignment is…"

Chapter 8
RESCUE?!

"A rescue mission!?" I yelled as we were being driven back to our homes. I was pissed, I *never* signed up for a stupid rescue mission, (actually, I didn't sign up at all).

"Reilly, the girl's twelve and very defenseless." Keira explained, (well you're seventeen and very defenseless but I haven't had to rescue you. Oh wait, never mind). "I hear she's also a very good singer."

"Good, then she can sing her way to freedom." I said.

Keira rolled her eyes, "Why are you so grumpy all of a sudden?"

I just glared at her for a minute. "Because, I DON'T DO PARTIES," I yelled. It turned out that **Charity** was being held somewhere where there was this fancy house party that night. Which was the only reason we were going, it made it easier to sneak in.

"Neither do I." Keira said, meekly.

"Yeah, but there's a difference between you and me. You're a klutz and I'm not." Well I was right. She's a freaking Apostle of God. I'm so the opposite of that!

"That's right for sure!" Edward said.

Keira smacked him, "Shut up Edward! Who said *you* were in this!?"

" I did, so there!" their bickering was going to be the death of me, (not that Edward would care).

"Don't worry Edward, if Violante shows up, I'll get to kick her ass… again!" I said, cheerfully.

"Great, Violante showing up is the last thing I need." Charlie sighed.

"Why's that?" Keira asked, (you mean besides the obvious?)

"She likes Charlie, and he doesn't feel the same way back." I explained. I meant to sound like I was making fun of him, but I sounded bitter instead. (Well that was weird).

"Why are you so angry *now?!*" Edward broke into my thoughts. "Don't tell me: you like Charlie!"

I felt my face turn red, (why was I blushing!?) "N-no, really he's just a friend. It's nothing like what *you* think!"

Charlie looked at me funny, but I just glared at Edward. How could he suggest that I….well you know!

Isabella looked completely confused now, "who's Charity?"

"No one special." I said, I was still pissed off.

We dropped Keira off, then Edward, and Isabella, until it was just Charlie and I left in the car, (don't you just *love* how that one worked out. I hate irony).

"So you like me, huh?" Charlie began, his eyes shining.

"Yes, I'm madly in love with you." I said, not looking up.

"I knew it." he declared.

"Guess you called that one." I noted. Then we both laughed.

"Get out." said the driver. We had pulled into Charlie's driveway.

"See you later." he called from outside.

"Bye." I said, lazily.

"Is this the one?" the driver asked.

"What are you talking about?" I called, we were no where near my house.

"Yes, Reilly." Uh-oh, Mathew.

"What do *you* want?" I asked, putting as much acid into my voice as was physically possible.

"You to listen to me," He said, turning to face me. His eyes shone in the light, his demonically, red eyes.

"Thought you gave up those sorts of powers." I noted.

"I have, but when I get angry, I just…well." he pulled out a knife and held it out in front of him, too close for comfort to me.

I gulped, as he moved the knife even closer.

"I'm listening." I said, keeping my eyes on the metal object that was now just below my chin.

"Good, your father is going to return, and he's going to look for you when he does. If you stay with them, he'll find you within seconds of his resurrection. But if you come with me, you'll be safe." he paused, and I saw my chance to speak.

"How does he plan to come back?" I asked.

"I don't know that much yet." he said. I nodded.

"So, let's just say, that I choose them and he does return and find me." I said. "Then what?"

"Ugh! Do I have to spell it out for you? HE WILL TORTURE YOU!" He shouted.

"You didn't spell it." I noted, he moved the knife slightly.

"Make your choice." he said, through clenched teeth. Then he pulled the knife away all together. Which was incredibly stupid, because as soon as I could, I screamed, "I choose them!" and leapt through the window, (shattering it, I might add). then I shimmered home.

I arrived on the porch only to find that my 'parents' weren't home. (Yes! Some good luck for a change!)

I raced upstairs, cleaned the blood off of my hands, (you don't shatter a window without getting a few scrapes in return). and put on the *only* dress I own. (I'm not even sure why I had that one. I think it had something to do with some party that my 'parents' hosted in which they wanted to make me as uncomfortable as possible. But I'm not sure).

Edward pulled up about an hour after I got home. I was in my room and had just gotten my hair done, (what, I *am* female).

I got into the car and had to endure several looks of hilarity from Edward, "say one word, and I swear, you'll wish I'd killed you before", I threatened.

"Fine." he said, putting his hands up in surrender.

"And not a word from *you* either", I said to Charlie as he opened his mouth. He shut it quickly.

We pulled up at Keira's house and she came running out to us. She was wearing the same black dress that she had worn to her mother's funeral.

"You look um…uh…" Edward muttered.

"Smooth move, Romeo." I noted.

"Shut up!" he said. Keira didn't hear us.

"What!? Stop staring at me!" she shouted at Edward.

We drove for what seemed like years before arriving at a huge, MANSION!

"How are we supposed to find her in *that*?" Keira asked.

"Trust me, we'll find her." I said. It already reeked of Apostle and God. But there was something else too.

We entered the main hall and the smell became stronger, and I realized what was mixing with it. (The smell I'm referring to is the scents of everyone around me. Each individual gives off a certain…aroma. Being a demon I can pick up on each one and, if I know them, I can tell who it is. I can tell *what* it is no matter what.)

"Damn it." I said.

Charlie looked at me and mumbled, "Cool it."

"Why should I? That bitch is here!" I said. Violante stunk *really* bad!

"Keep your voice to yourself" Charlie said, as he glanced over in the direction where we knew Violante stood.

"So, what's this girl's deal?" Edward asked. (haven't we already explained this?!)

"She's twelve years old and already a well known soprano. Her name is Charity Sims, she was singing with the orchestra and got separated from them. So, some guy named Lerajie adopted her." Charlie explained, (again,). Edward tensed up at the mention of the name Lerajie.

"Edward, you ok?" Keira asked.

"Yeah, sure. Lerajie is a devil, though." Edward answered. I should have guessed. (this kind of thing is *never* easy, is it?)

"An Apostle of God in the hands of a devil, huh? Sounds like an explosive combo" Keira said. Yeah, if you're referring to us blowing up the mansion to get her out of here, maybe.

Suddenly, I had an idea. (but it could have just been the nauseating smell getting to my brain).

"Keira, you take Lerajie's private floor, where Charity most likely is. Charlie, keep post here. Edward, you go outside." I said, I was calculating how long it would take me to kill Violante.

Edward glared at me, "and what about you?"

I narrowed my eyes, "I'll be busy." I said with hatred.

✲ ✲ ✲

It didn't take long to find Violante, all I had to do was follow my nose.

"You're wearing a DRESS!?" she exclaimed when she saw me.

"So are you!" I said angrily.

"Yeah but, I actually look good."

"Do you own a mirror?" I asked, but I guessed she didn't.

"Well….did you really come here to ask me that?"

"What do you think?" I asked.

"I think you shouldn't have come to find me because you're not leaving this room alive", Violante said. I heard a whirring and then a click. With sudden horror, I realized that the doors and windows were covered with metal.

"Is that *really* necessary?" I asked.

"Yep." she grinned, then she went into full form. (remember how I explained what that was? Well, as you may have guessed by now, if she attacks me when I'm *not* in my full form, there's a good chance that I'm screwed).

"Is *that* really necessary?" I asked again.

"Yep, I'm going to make *sure* you die."

"Not that again. You know, you're like a broken record." I sighed, I was trying to distract her, (in case you haven't figured that out yet).

Anyway, in the middle of these thoughts, I realized I was being thrown against the wall, but Violante hadn't moved.

"Mathew!" I screamed, as he pinned me to the wall.

"Oh, he can't hear you", Violante said from across the room. Great, she had now taken control of my uncle. In case you don't understand, let me explain. You see, Violante can do this thing where she takes control of people and makes them, kind of like her puppets for a while. Usually she kills them first, but I guessed she had just skipped that step this time. The only problem is that if she doesn't kill you first, there are side affects. Not to mention that any time I try to touch one, or one touches me, it burns that spot of my skin.

"You are really starting to get on my nerves!" I screamed at both of them.

"That's kind of the point!" Violante shouted back, Mathew just kind of looked at me blankly, (that would be one of those side affects, I was talking about earlier).

"Ugh! I can't stand you!" I screamed, then I threw Mathew out of the way. He hit the brick outer wall, and stayed where he fell.

"That wasn't very nice." Violante noted. By now, I was seeing red.

"I'm going to make you wish you hadn't locked me in here!" I said. She must have guessed that she was in big trouble because she decided to make the first move. She dived foreword, sword out in front of her, and sent me flying back! Which, of course, only pissed me off more.

I caught my self just before I hit the solid metal. But Violante was still on the offensive. I dodged her blade and it got stuck in the wall. (Yes, it actually pierced the thick metal. Now, put *me* in between the two. Can you say ouch!?)

"I am going to kill you!" she screamed, (broken record!) then she back handed me so hard that I flew to the opposite end of the room, through the door, and…right into Charlie's arms!

"Nice catch." I muttered.

"Thanks, where are you going?" No one else heard that, but then to the others he said, "I guess she didn't get to finish her off."

My claws sprang out and I headed back to the door, but Charlie caught my arm, "We're leaving!" he said, as he pulled me back.

"Fine." I growled.

After Charlie drug me out of the mansion, we all went home. I didn't talk much on the way back to my house.

"See ya" Charlie mumbled. I barely heard him. I just froze, the lights in the living room were on.

"Bye." I muttered, not looking away from the glow. I ran to the back of the house and jumped through my window, (after I unlocked it, making me feel like I was breaking into my own house, which, I guess I kind of was).

"REILLY!" that was my 'dad.' I figured he'd seen Edward's car drive away.

I didn't see anyone in my room, so I got ready and went to bed.

✧ ✧ ✧

The next morning, I awoke to see both of my 'parents' standing over me.

"What the hell--ow!" I screamed. I was so startled by them that I jumped up and hit my shoulder on the headboard of my bed.

"Where were you last night!?" my 'mom' screamed.

"I was busy. Since when do you care where I am?" I asked. My whole arm hurt and they were pissing me off even more by screaming.

"We care now because you have to be here for the--."

"Shut up, you can't tell her now, she'll find out!" (Uh, duh! Of course I'll know if you tell me. But I actually don't really care right now).

"I have to get to school." I said, anxious to get away. I tried to sit up but something hit me in the forehead and forced me back.

"What the? What was that?" I asked, blinded temporarily by the blood in my eyes.

"That is what will happen to you if you're *ever* late again!" My 'dad' spat in my face.

"Whatever...can I go now?" I asked, once I could see. (ok, I know I should've probably paid more attention, but I didn't think that *they* were smart enough to be a threat to me. Next time some idiot tells me to 'come right home.' I'll listen more to what they *aren't* telling me).

"Yes, get the hell out of here!" my 'mom' yelled.

I washed my face off and got ready quickly. I was out of the house in a record, ten minutes. (I probably could've shimmered, but that might look a little suspicious to an unsuspecting mortal strolling by school, now wouldn't it?)

"Heal, damn it, heal!" I was saying to the nasty gash on my head. If anyone saw it, I was doomed. (do you remember how I said I can self heal? Well, it only happens quickly for small cuts and bruises, not for gashes or wounds like that or worse. I'm not invincible after all, only powerful. So I can still die from stuff like that. I'm just not as likely to as you would be).

I had just made it to first hour when Keira came into the room. Well crap, I'm screwed.

"Hey Reilly---Oh my God!" she exclaimed when I turned to face her.

I just glared at her. (Maybe if I look her straight in the eye, she'll lose her memory and I can heal before she notices again. Hey, it's a possibility isn't it?)

"Wh-what happened?" she asked, which was the exact question I had dreaded. (It figures she'd ask the one question I couldn't answer).

I sighed, there was no point in denying what happened, "I got hit in the face." I said.

"With what?" she asked.

"Don't know, didn't see it."

"By whom?" Damn it!

"Uh...um..."

"It was your parents, wasn't it?" she said. how'd *she* know!?

"Uh...um...uh..." Honestly, what was I supposed to say to *that*?!

"Are you abused?"

"Yes."

"Oh my God!"

"Shhhh! I don't want you to tell Charlie!"

"Tell me what?", came a voice from the doorway. Well shit. (Yeah, so he just *happens* to be walking by at *that* particular moment!)

"Nothing." I quickly said.

"What happened!?"

"I...uh..."

"She fell." Keira stepped in, I glared at her for a minute before saying,

"Uh...yeah, I fell." I said, not looking away from Keira. (I fell!? What kind of an excuse is that anyway?!) Charlie wasn't buying it. "I fell down the steps this morning." I elaborated.

"Fine, see you later." he said, leaving the room. It was pretty obvious that he didn't believe me or my paper thin excuse. (Though can you blame him for the second one? I fell!? Honestly!)

"That was a close one." Keira exclaimed, when he was out of earshot.

"I fell?" I asked, angrily.

"It was the first thing I thought of." she said defensively, (clearly).

"But I don't fall, *you* fall!" I exclaimed.

"I'm sorry you're abused." she said, seriously.

"Don't be, I hate it when people feel sorry for me." I explained.

Later, when we were in class, and I had healed completely...

"Reilly! Keira!" Charlie came storming into the class room. "You two were lying!" (Wow, how'd you figure that one out?)

"Why do you say that?" I asked innocently.

"Because Edward says-" (since when are we taking advice from Edward?!)

"Edward is an idiot. Haven't you figured that out yet?" I asked angrily.

"Anyways, he said you can't get a gash like the one Reilly had this morning from falling down stairs."

"How does he know?! Has it ever happened to him?"

"I don't know." he stammered.

"See, there we go. For a proven fact, you don't know!"

"Well that and, Reilly has good coordination, Keira has none what-so-ever." he said, Keira stuck her tongue out at him.

"Keira, stop being immature."

"I can be immature if I choose to be!" she said.

Suddenly, Keira turned to me. "Good thing he doesn't know you're abused." I, too, thought Charlie had left the room, but a thunderous,

WHAT!?" proved otherwise.

We looked up to see Charlie standing in front of us, looking horrified.

"Oh shit!!" I said, then glared at loud mouth. "Thanks a lot Keira!" I said. Then I ran.

I didn't know where I was going, but anywhere was better then school at that moment. I didn't stop until I was half-way home. I couldn't believe what had just happened. I sat down for a while, then headed back.

After school I went straight home, I didn't even notice when I opened the door, I felt numb.

I walked in and nothing could have prepared me for what happened next.

Chapter 9
Sacrifice

In one corner of the room, there was a giant cross. In the other, was a metal pentagram. In the middle, (you're gonna *love* this,) was a stand with chains on it. Guess who's going to stand there.

"Welcome home", came my 'mom's' voice.

"What the hell?" I said, but I was roughly grabbed from behind and thrown onto the stand.

"Hey, let me go!" I struggled, but it did no good.

"We have waited for this since we got stuck with you," my 'dad' said.

"Waited for what?" I shouted as something sharp was shoved into the palm of my right hand.

"You're father's return!" They shouted as the roar of a machine grew louder. I felt like a part of me was being ripped away. (Which, if I truly was bringing my father back to life, was true).

Soon it was over. And I was unhooked from the chains and thrown onto the couch.

"My dear daughter, how nice to see you again." said a voice I will never forget.

"Dad?!" So if you haven't already guessed, I don't exactly get along with my father. (But that's another story entirely). I'll explain more later.

"Getting to be more like me everyday, I see. I can feel your hatred."

"I *do* hate you, but I'm *nothing* like you!" I screamed.

"Aren't you? Your powers are fueled by hatred, same as mine. You're my daughter, you can't help but be like me." my dad shouted back.

"Oh yeah, what about mom, did you forget about her. I only have half of your power. The rest is hers!" I said. I saw a flash of anger in his eyes, but it was quickly replaced by calmness.

"And what, may I ask, *did* you inherit from her?" he asked, amused. Uh-oh. I didn't know exactly, I just knew I was different.

"I...uh...I..."

"Exactly! I could kill you now and no one would care! You're worthless," he said, as his hands enclosed on my throat. "No one loves you."

"Mom did." I chocked out.

"Your mother was stupid," He smiled, "So I got rid of her just like I'm getting rid of you. I still don't see how I could've loved her," He shook his head, "but there is hope for me yet, because...I never loved you." his hands clenched tighter and I could feel consciousness leaving me.

"So you admi-t th-at y-you lov-ed her" I managed to say, and he actually let me go!

"I *will* see you again, my child, and you *will* regret everything you have said to me today" he said. Then he was gone.

"Ha-ha!" My 'dad' shouted. Apparently, him and my 'mom' had been in the room the whole time, but I hadn't noticed. I *was* a little preoccupied though.

"You brought him back!?" I hissed.

"No, you did." my 'mom' replied.

"You forced me!" I screamed.

"Well, of course. We can't kill you, but he can!" my 'dad' said.

"You will regret that!" I said, my rage overwhelming me.

"I doubt that!" my 'dad' said.

"That's too bad, because I know how you hate to be wrong." I hissed, my voice sounding more and more like a demon's.

"Uh, her eyes are glowing." My 'mom' noticed. They were probably considering how close I was to changing. (Into my full form).

"Kill her?" My 'dad' suggested. (didn't he just say that they couldn't do that?)

"You can't." I grinned.

"But we can *try* like hell." They came at me with their weapons. All the while taunting me about my past, and now, my future. (You know, the one they took away by bringing *him* back).

What happened next was so fast that I didn't even mean to do it.

What happened was this: my 'parents' continued to advance forward, still saying their insults. But as I scrunched myself into a ball and covered my ears. I heard them begin to scream. I opened one eye, and saw that they were being swallowed by flames. (I knew that meant that *I* had something to do with it).

Suddenly, my 'dad' reached out and backhanded me so hard that I heard my head snap sideways. He sent me flying into a glass cabinet.

Of course, it shattered upon contact. Then the whole stupid thing fell over, landing on my shoulder.

"Reilly!" I heard Charlie's voice faintly.

"GET OUT!" I cried. I still sounded scary. They practically launched themselves back through the door.

I concentrated on my 'parents.'

"You deserve to die with us, Reilly." my 'mom' shouted.

"Leave me alone!" I shrieked, then a great rumbling started, followed by a crash and then a loud BOOM!

"Oh, God." I groaned.

"Reilly!!" Charlie shouted, (hasn't this already happened?)

"I…they were…and I." I said, I realized I had been crying.

I nodded to the place where my 'parents' had been but where now stood two piles of ash.

"Reilly, you had to do it. They gave you no choice, they were going to kill you." Charity said softly, I couldn't make myself look up.

"No I…they…but." I only faintly realized I wasn't making sense.

"Reilly, it's ok." Charlie said, I heard him move closer, then I heard more movement as Keira and Charity did the same.

"Edward!" Keira hissed. To be honest, I didn't even know he was there.

"Uh…s'ok Reilly." he mumbled. That *almost* made me smile. ALMOST. It was kind of hilarious to see him try to make me feel better.

The next day, I decided against going to school. I really didn't want to answer all of Keira's questions, which I knew she'd ask.

Instead, I decided to go and see if there was any surviving information of my past. I knew where my 'parents' had kept all of that information, so I was going to see if I could find the safe. (But apparently, when it says, 'durable through all kinds of disasters,' it doesn't mean demonically enhanced sonic blasts, because I didn't find any remains of the safe, or even my house, for that matter).

I was very careful to keep an eye out for my dad. But he didn't show up, luckily. I wasn't in a 'fighting mood.'

I had been digging through the rubble, with little hope, for about an hour, when the wind picked up.

"Shit." I mumbled when Violante materialized in front of me.

"We had a visitor yesterday." she said with a smile.

"Oh, yeah, and who might that be?" I asked, standing up. I already knew who, but I had to keep her talking. (Because not only was I not in the mood to fight, but I was so weakened from the night before that I wasn't sure I would live if we fought).

"Why, your father, of course." she said, still smiling. (I would've loved to wipe that smile off her face, but like I said).

"Of course." I agreed.

"He's going to help us kill you." she said.

"Is that so? Well, if you came here to tell me that, you wasted your energy, 'cause, I already knew that." I said.

"Did you?" she asked, generally amused.

"I did, and I figured it out all by myself too!" I said, sarcastically.

"You're not scared?" she asked, raising her eyebrows.

"After what he's done to me, killing me would be a blessing." I said, truthfully.

"I'll be sure to let him know." she said.

"Yeah, you do that!" I called, before she departed.

"What was *that* about?" Came a familiar voice.

"Damn it, Charlie. Don't do that!" I shouted after I jumped about ten feet in the air.

"Sorry, now tell me what happened last night." he said.

"I blew up my house, and killed my step-parents, you were there." I answered him.

"I meant before that." He said.

"Oh, uh…nope." I said, matter-of-factly.

"Why not? I think I have the right to know!"

"No you don't. Besides, you don't *want* to know", I warned.

"Try me." he said, (well, don't say I didn't warn him).

"Fine, let's just say I have issues with my father." I said.

"That's it, that's all I get!?" he yelled.

"That's it." I said.

"Liar." he accused.

"I am not. I told the truth, just not all of it. Or, if I really am a liar, then I could be lying at this very minute, couldn't I?" I said.

"Maybe, but you're not, are you?" he smiled.

"No, I'm not. Or am I?" I asked, smiling back. (This is weird).

"You're not going to tell me, are you?" he asked.

"I might, maybe later." I said.

"How come I never get a straight answer out of you?" He asked.

"Because I think it's fun to watch you figure them out." I smiled.

"Where are you going to stay?" he asked, this question caught me off guard.

"Not sure." I admitted.

"Well...I...uh..."

"I'll find someplace." I said, trying to keep the laughter out of my voice.

After that day, I stayed away from school for another. But on the third day, I went back. I tried to act as normal as possible, but I don't think I was very good at it, considering I was waiting for my father to come and kill me.

But I'd made up my mind, I wasn't going to let him hurt my friends, too. If he was sending me to hell, I was taking him with me.

Chapter 10
Jezaba's Return

"Hey, Reilly!" Keira greeted me when I came back. I just glared at her.

"Don't worry, Reilly, we all hope you feel better soon----not!" Edward remarked.

Ok, now before I go on, you have to know that I was thinking a lot about my dad. And what Edward said, and the way he said it, reminded me of him, so **without** thinking, I took out my claws and drug them across his face.

"Ouch! I was only joking!" he said, but I wasn't really listening. "Damn it!" he finished.

"Edward, stop antagonizing her." Charlie said, I didn't even know he was over here.

Suddenly, it began to rain...*blood!* and that meant that Jezaba was about to return. (Jezaba has many signs that warn us of his arrival, why he warns us, I have no idea).

"Ewwww!" Keira screamed. Edward moaned something (probably, 'damn it, blah, blah, blah.' but that's just a guess). Then ran Keira inside. Charlie, Charity, and I followed.

"I can't feel his presence anywhere," Edward snarled, "damn it!" (anyone else noticing how often he uses that word?)

"Edward, stay with her all day, you know he's after the Apostles." Charlie said.

"Who?" Keira muttered. Did he have to get her started?

"Jezaba!" Edward shouted.

"Jeza-what?"

Charlie glare at her, "No one. I'm going to shadow Charity. Reilly, make sure they play nice," then he left. (why couldn't *I* get Charity? At least *she* doesn't talk!)

As soon as we got to first hour, we noticed that the cross that was in the corner was all burnt up.

"Reilly." Edward growled.

"What?! It wasn't me, I swear." I whispered.

Keira gasped, there was no need to look out the window, I knew what was now burning in fiery numbers in the grass outside, (6-6-6). I waved one hand toward the numbers, making them disappear.

"Attention all students: school has been canceled due to the mishaps this morning. Thank you and have a safe trip home." Came the nasally voice over the intercom. Everyone but the three of us rushed out of the room.

We walked slowly outside, (the rain had stopped,) and met Charlie and Charity.

" He's at the park," Charlie said.

"Who?" Keira asked. (Honestly, how dumb was she?!)

"Keira, Charity, stay here, you have no idea how Jezaba can be." Edward commanded.

"That's right, and he's after the Apostles so we have to protect you" I added. Keira looked absolutely horrified.

"Well, maybe I'm tired of being protected all of the time! I want to fight for myself!" she yelled, Edward's eyes were huge.

"You can't be serious!" He said.

Charlie and I exchanged glances, I could tell he was thinking the same as me, so I sighed, "Get in the car."

I drove as fast as the car would allow to the park. But when we got there I wished I would've gone slower. What if Jezaba had brought my dad along? In the middle of this fear, I realized that Keira had jumped out of the car, "oh God." I sighed.

"Damn it!" (told you). "you idiot!" Edward shouted, getting in front of Keira as some black smoke appeared. "You're cocky, the miasma would've killed you if you stood in it!" Miasma is the cloud of energy that usually surrounds a demon or devil when they either re-awaken, or first appear. Its pretty much deadly to anyone...or any*thing*...that gets close enough to be affected. Keira had been *dangerously* close.

I looked up, "shit." I muttered, "we've got Legion heading our way." If you don't know, Legion are lower level demons. They're even below half demons, especially Edward and I. (You see, we both had especially powerful demonic fathers, giving us even more power that some upper level demons. The demon side of us almost makes up for the human side, in other words).

Edward pulled out his sword and said something about action. What an idiot, I thought. Then we began to fight, which was fine with me because I could get all of my anger out. Keira and Charity hid somewhere.

When we were done, they came out, but I wished they wouldn't have because it was too late. Jezaba was here!!

"What?" Keira asked, at our terrified expressions.

"He's here." Edward muttered. (could he be *anymore* vague?)

"What?"

"He's here, right now!" (wow, I guess so).

A light must have went on because Keira grabbed Charity and ran!

The ground split and Jezaba flew out as a raven, (an ugly raven).

Then he turned into himself, (which was worse).

"I'm the Alpha and the O- the, oh what the hell was it?" he demanded. "Aw forget it! I am the beginning and the end. You know, the start to finish!" he finished, I'd forgotten how dumb he was.

"Jezaba." Edward snarled.

"*I saw your daddy, today.*" a voice in my head echoed. It was Jezaba's. "*We have big plans for your demise!*"

My hatred overwhelmed me and I sprung at the evil creature before me. But he carelessly flung me out of his way.

"What a shame, you've lost your strength over the years." he said, shaking his head.

"*You haven't seen my strength yet!*" I thought angrily. He got the message.

Then he sent sharp rocks over at Edward (for no apparent reason) who fell to his knees in pain. Then, Jezaba grabbed Edward by the throat and sighed, "your dad could at least put up a good fight. I'll spare your life if you join me."

"Sorry, I'm not like you." Edward said, looking Jezaba in the eye.

"I see." He sighed, then threw Edward off to the side.

"Edward!" Keira shrieked, running out from her hiding place.

"Oh, dear Keira May, you've grown into an attractive young woman." (I just threw up a little in my mouth). Jezaba exclaimed when he saw her. Then I noticed Keira's gun, (oh God, take cover!)

"Bastard, where's my sister?!" she shouted.

"And if I don't tell you, will you shoot me?" he asked, generally amused by the idea. Then he mentioned that *he* was the only one who knew where to find Brit-what's-her-face.

"Keira…" Edward said weakly.

Jezaba extended his arm, making Edward scream. "You're so predictable, Kara."

"Huh?"

"But that's enough; I'm here for something else…Charity, come on out." he called. "The disasters that have occurred today are my way of 'welcoming' you. Keira, you're so mistaken. The truth is that my actions *saved* Brittany." So that's her name, I knew that!

Keira was giving in, "saved?" she asked, lowering her gun.

"Don't listen to him!" Edward yelled.

"Listen everyone…" Blah, blah, blah. I'd heard his speech before. Mostly, he just blames God for everything evil in the world and credits himself for everything that's not.

"Keira, you mustn't listen!" Edward begged. Then Jezaba held out his hand and Edward came flying toward him.

"EDWARD!" Keira screamed.

I was beginning to get extremely annoyed. Who did he think he was anyway, God? Besides, he didn't need to be suggesting to my father ways to kill me. I got out my claws and let my powers slowly come to life. But Keira stopped me, "If he dies I'll never find my sister!" she screamed.

I glared at her, "what good would that do?!" I hissed.

"Please," she begged.

Jezaba laughed, "isn't this fun? Even at a time like this the one you believe in will not speak *one* word to save you." Again, more God bashing, big surprise. Then he moved on to say that the Apostles were cursed. Then he talked about God's 'inflated ego!' When he finished his hands tightened around Edward's neck.

"And Charity, what about your goals?" Here I listened, he wasn't leaving here with anyone, especially Charity, (whoa, did I just say that?) "and Reilly, *you* were getting abused by your step-parents, until they died a fiery death you caused." He put his hand over the black hole that was where his heart should have been. "I'll miss them. They were such good minions. And you killed them. But why did you kill them? Oh, I know, it was because--."

"Shut up!" I screamed at him.

"Very well, later then. Any way, Keira, your mother has died and your sister is missing. Isn't it painful? But I can save you all from the curse of the Almighty God!" More God bashing, big surprise! "Don't you see? It was from this that I saved Brittany."

"Stop saying that, you bastard!" Keira exclaimed. (what a colorful vocabulary you have Keira).

"You're pointing your gun at the wrong person. The one you need to defeat is up in Heaven. But, of course, being like yourselves, you can't kill him. But I can, right Charlie?" He turned toward Charlie, who was glaring at the ground.

Jezaba sighed, and began to beat the shit out of Edward, (again, for no apparent reason,) when he was finished, he tossed him aside and Keira ran to him.

"We should work together, Apostles. It is for this reason that I need your powers." Jezaba said.

Then it hit me; he wasn't talking just to talk, (though I'm sure that was *one* reason,) he was distracting us so he could take Charity! Keira realized this too, because she ran back to Charity's hiding place.

"Desist, you're not going to shoot me and you know it." Jezaba said to Keira.

Keira actually looked like she had every intention of shooting him. There was a moment of silence, and then she really *did* shoot him! But, as I knew it wouldn't, the bullet didn't phase him.

"I won't let you take Charity!" Keira screamed, in tears.

Jezaba moved toward her. "But you gave me your sister." he smirked.

Keira must have been weakening, because she completely lowered the gun.

"Keira…" Came Edward's voice again.

"Poor, poor Keira May, but I can save you." Jezaba grabbed her. "Give yourself over to me, Kara." he said, Then he (get this,) kissed her! (ok, now I'm seriously going to throw up!)

Keira just froze there for a minute.

"GET AWAY FROM HER!" Edward's angry voice came charging over to us. He was changing, and this time, I wasn't going to stop him. I would've changed myself if Jezaba's voice hadn't been roaring in my head. (when I said, 'I wasn't going to stop him,' I was referring to the multiple times when Edward has lost his temper and I had to threaten to kick his ass if he didn't calm down).

"That's right, Edward, let your demon blood take over your pathetic human blood." Jezaba taunted as he pulled away from Keira. (Our demon blood is like our demonic energy, if we're not careful, it will completely take over, which is what Jezaba was hoping for).

"JEZABA!" Edward screamed, beginning to lose control.

"Oh, so you have feelings for Keira May…" He noted. (Well duh!) "Hmmm, maybe I can use this to my advantage."

"Stop this, please!" Charity screamed, running toward us. That's just all we need, now he has them both!!

"That's a girl," said Jezaba, like she was a puppy, "so willing to sacrifice herself for her friends." he continued.

"Save her, Reilly, before I kill her!" Jezaba's voice came crashing through my thoughts. I covered my ears, (though I don't know why, it was **inside** my head). but (of course,) it didn't work.

Suddenly a blinding light cut down Jezaba's voice until it faded away. I looked over at where the source of the light was, and saw a winged Keira in the air,

"The Apostle of Hope, *finally* awakens." this he said out loud…I think.

The light faded away along with Keira's wings. Jezaba laughed, "now I have both of you!" He said, reaching toward them. Then he jumped back, howling with pain. He went up into the sky. Whatever hit him, also hit me. Suddenly, my mind erupted with pain. I flinched and the pain subsided.

Everything was going back to normal, and Keira almost collapsed when Edward caught her. "Is it over?" she asked.

"For now," he said, setting her against a large rock. "That thing wasn't the real Jezaba." (Yeah, I figured as much, no wonder we couldn't sense him. That also explains why I could hear his thoughts, because they were meant for me to hear).

Keira's eyes popped open, "What!?" she struggled to get up, but fell back down, "No!" she cried, pounding the ground with her fists.

Chapter 11
Empathy

I woke up to find Charlie looking at me, I shut my eyes again, "what do you want?" I asked.

"What was going on last night with Jezaba?" He asked.

"What do you mean?" I asked.

"I mean, you know better than to attack Jezaba like that." he said.

"Ok, but don't laugh." I started, "I think I can hear Jezaba's thoughts." I sighed, and waited for him to laugh any way.

"Really?!" he asked with a straight face.

"Yes." I said, confused.

"This is good, now you'll know when he's about to attack!" he shouted.

"Uh, I don't think it works quite like that. I think I can only hear them when they're about me," I admitted.

"Oh, so you're a selfish mind reader," he laughed.

"Ha, ha. Now be serious, because it's not only his thoughts. When he felt pain, so did I." I said.

"Great…" he muttered.

"I'm pretty sure it was a one time thing any way." I sighed, wishing that I really *could* read minds. "So-." I began, but then I sensed something that silenced me.

"What….oh." he mumbled, when he caught on that I was sensing Jezaba. "We should probably go to Keira's house," He suggested.

"Yeah, probably."

We got to Keira's and leapt through the window in time to see Edward leaving her side. Charlie and I looked from Keira to Edward, and I commented, "I don't even *want* to know."

Charlie found that funny, then he was serious again. "He's made another appearance."

"Great, just great." Keira muttered.

"And Violante's with him too…" he glanced at me and I glared back.

"What!?" I snarled.

"What does *she* want?" Keira asked, (honestly, even a rock would've caught on by now).

"What else, me." I said dryly. I knew what I'd have to do in order to beat her because, clearly, she wasn't playing around about killing me anymore.

"Aw, don't worry Reilly, you've only been stabbed, electrocuted, and ditched in an exploding building because of her." Edward said, (where did he get the 'exploding building?' I don't remember--- never mind. That was a long time ago, though).

"EDWARD! That's not what I'm worried about." I said. The last part was to myself.

"This is the time when we must do our best to protect Charity and Keira." Charlie said, (and cue hero music). "And so, Edward, I have taken the liberty of switching around all of your classes so that you're with Keira all day." (I'm sure *that* will go over well).

"Wait, don't *I* get a say in this!?" Keira asked, or rather, shouted. (yeah, that's what I thought).

"No!" I said, firmly, "just listen and do as you're told," because you're screaming is pissing me off!

"NO! NO! NO! NO!" Keira screamed, which was starting to get on my nerves.

"God, can you scream any louder?" Edward asked, awarding him a glare from Keira.

"Yes." she commented.

"So, where's Charity?" Edward asked. That was the question I had been waiting for, considering I didn't want to leave her where we did.

"We left her with the order." Charlie said. (No *you* did. *I* tried to talk you out of it, but you wouldn't listen to me).

"And they are going to take care of her?" Keira asked. Probably not.

"I think so." Charlie said. Ha, yeah right!

"Ok." she sighed, then she rested her head on her pillow. Suddenly she jerked with pain, got up, and raced to the bathroom. I followed her because I knew what had happened.

When I reached the door, Keira began to scream, "shut up, before Edward and Charlie hear you and come in to make a big scene." I growled from the doorway. She stopped screeching and looked at me.

"How did you know where I was?" she asked.

I followed the yellow brick road. "Please, I knew what was up the minute you ran away. You're lucky Edward and Charlie don't pay as much attention to their surroundings as I do." Because if I didn't, I'd be dead by now, I thought but didn't say.

"What is this?" she asked, referring to the cross-like gashes in her hands and feet.

"Oh, you mean like this?" I asked, showing her the same gashes in *my* hands and feet. (but with one big difference, mine had a pentagram in the center, that I received when I 'helped' to resurrect my dad).

"Stigmata." I said when I noticed her expression.

"Stigmata?"

"I take it you've heard about it before?" I said, when I watched the confusion in her eyes be swallowed by understanding.

"Yes, but it was only in a dream."

After I helped her bandage the cuts, she asked, "so, are we the only ones?"

"Yes." I answered.

"Why are yours different from mine?" She asked. Well Keira, that's because *you're* the reincarnation of a holy woman, destined for good. And *I'm* a half demon, who helped to bring back her evil father, destined for hell.

"Don't worry about it." I said.

"Ok. Thanks for putting up with me, I know I'm such a pain to bear sometimes." she said, softly.

"Don't mention it. Um, ever, I *do* have a reputation to maintain." I grinned. (Although I kind of trashed my rep, when I quit being evil).

Hey, I'm being nice, that wasn't so hard!

"How am I supposed to cover these bandages? Edward's going to find out and he's been cranky lately." She said.

"Wear gloves?" I suggested.

"Great…" she moaned.

We went back into her room , and Keira mouthed the word, "Ow." as she walked.

"Hey, what's on your pants!?" Edward exclaimed when he saw her. He sounded genuinely concerned. We both looked down to see that Keira still had blood remaining on her pajama pants.

C'mon Keira, say something! I thought. Finally, I stepped in,

"She's having some, womanly problems." I said, and Charlie and Edward exchanged glances.

"Ok." They said. Keira was glaring at me so I mouthed,

'What, it worked.'

"Did you have to tell them that?!" She exclaimed later.

I shrugged, "like I said before, it worked. Besides, you had a blank stare and I had to say *something*."

"But *that*!"

"Get over it."

She groaned, "why did you-." She began, but I held up my hand to silence her.

"Did you hear that?" I asked. It was really more of a rhetorical question because I knew that she hadn't.

"What was it?" Keira asked.

"I don't know," though I had a pretty good guess, "Charlie did you-?" I began, but he stopped me.

"I heard it, Edward?" he asked.

"Yeah, how far is she." Edward asked, he must've thought it was Violante, also.

"Don't know, two, maybe three, miles." I guessed.

"Oh shit, she's after me again." Keira exclaimed.

"Shhh! She wants me this time," I said bitterly. That wasn't all she wanted.

"And me." Charlie confirmed my suspicions, (why did I care!?)

"You smell that?" Edward asked, sniffing the air, "Hatred, Reilly, cool it."

"That's not me." I said, and we all turned to Charlie.

"What?" he asked as his face turned red.

"Keira, you have to get out of here." Edward said.

"Oh, you don't care do you?" I asked sarcastically, he was a **really** bad liar. (which isn't good considering he is a demon!) "Besides," I added, "you're all leaving, she wants me and that's all she'll get." I turned to go but Charlie stopped me,

"Wait," He hesitated. "Be careful." he finished.

I grinned, "I will." Then I leaped out of the window.

✯ ✯ ✯

I didn't have to go far, Violante was waiting for me.

"Hello." she said, smiling.

"S'up?" I asked, not acknowledging her much.

"Ya know, I'm going to kill you." she said, (and there's that threat again, I'm beginning to wish she'd just do it and quit playing around. Actually, I don't want to die, not yet, so forget that last statement). she continued, seeming not to notice my annoyance, "and your daddy's going to help." (well I didn't see that one coming). Then, as if those were the key words in a play, my dad stepped out of the shadows.

"Great..." I said, "you know, you seem to show up at the worst of times." I noted.

"It's a gift," he snarled. He was already in his full form. (Which, is a lot stronger that mine, so....I'm screwed).

"Can't defeat me on your own so you had to ask my father for help, huh. That's pathetic." I said to Violante.

"Oh, believe me, it will mainly just be you and I, he's just here to give me the upper hand. 'Cause I'm evil like that." she laughed.

"Well, I'm going to kill you both. 'Cause I'm good like that." I said, my eyes flashing with anger.

"We'll see." she said. Then she, too, went into full form.

"Fine, well, I can't hardly be left out now can I?" I asked, then I began to change. (Just so you know, there was a lot of screaming involved. When you haven't used your powers for a long time, it's quite painful to start using them all at once again). The fire surrounded me and my wings and fangs came out. My pupils became slits and my irises turned blood red.

"You're going to loose." Violante taunted, as she gouged out a *huge* part of my side. (this is going to be just so *fun* for me, I can tell! (I hate my life!)

"Probably." I admitted through the blood and pain, "but if I'm going to hell, I'm taking you two with me!" I shrieked, as I clawed her across the face.

"Now's a good time to step in, Lieam." She screamed, using my father's first name.

"You've barely even begun. What? Is my flesh and blood too strong for you?" he asked. He was mocking us both.

"Shut up!" We shouted, then we exchanged glares.

"When I kill you, then I'll have Charlie. I'll kill Edward and the Apostles, and my life will be perfect." she said, smiling.

"Not if I end it!" I screamed.

"You won't have a chance!" my dad shouted, then a hard hit to my chest knocked my breath away.

"Nobody asked you!" I screamed. As I sent flames toward him, he laughed,

"You won't defeat *me* that easily. I'm not weak like your step-parents were." he hissed.

I was losing badly and I'd be no help to *anyone* dead, so I headed back to Keira's, reverting to weak form. (If I haven't already explained it, weak form is our usual form. What we always look like,) as I ran. (Do you know how hard it is to see through blood? Pretty damn hard, trust me. I actually almost hit *three* trees!) I reached the window and collapsed inside.

"Reilly!" Charlie exclaimed as he caught me.

"I'm fine," I said, dizzily. I was extremely pissed off though. They gasped and I'd guessed they'd seen my fangs, (they don't go away all that fast).

"What the hell," Edward exclaimed, "I mean, I have fangs but no one notices mine and they don't stick out!"

"Edward!" Keira hissed.

"No, he's right," (Well that was something I'll never get to say again,) "they'll go away in a minute." I weakly assured them. Charlie was looking at me funny.

"You didn't?!" he exclaimed.

"I had to!" I said, trying to explain the situation without actually saying anything.

"What's going on that I don't know!?" Keira (who else?) asked.

Edward said something about Kara's skills, (which don't actually exist,) but Charlie was whispering to me. "Why?" he asked.

"My dad was there." I whispered.

"What were you thinking!" Keira screeched, which was fine. It helped me ignore the horrified look that Charlie was giving me.

"Look, I don't see *you* fighting so shut up!" I shouted. Before Keira could reply, Violante came floating through the window.

"If it isn't the Apostle, half demon, half demon," here she glared at me, "and devil. Cute devil I might add." here she smiled at Charlie and I.

"HEY! I'M NOT A half demon!" Edward shouted as I got up.

"Dude, you're a half demon, deal with it, and move on." I snapped.

"No distractions this time!" Violante hissed.

"Oh God, not again…" Keira moaned.

"Look who I picked up on my way here." Violante smirked, reveling an unconscious Charity.

"How'd you get Charity?!" Keira exclaimed. She asked the wizard for a heart, and got ripped off?

"Like I said, I 'picked her up.' In other words, I stole her from the Lucien Order when I attacked it." she said, so proud of herself.

"You bitch! I knew you were after me, I knew it, I knew it!" Keira shrieked.

"For the last freakin' time Keira, she's after Reilly, *then* you!" Edward explained. (thanks for clearing that up, Edward. Thanks a lot!)

"For a pathetic half demon, he's right." Violante noted.

"WHAT? YOU CALLED ME A-"

"Cool it, Edward." I said, as I met Violante's gaze.

"How can you tell me to cool it when she called me a half demon?!!"

"EDWARD! SHUT UP!" I yelled, still not looking away from Violante.

I heard Keira whimper, and, unfortunately, glanced in her direction. I looked back in time to see the point of Violante's sword coming right at me. I dodged it and she said, "you think you're so good."

"No," I replied, "*you* just suck!"

"Arg! Why you little-" she shrieked, I got my claws out and prepared for a battle.

"Wait," Keira stepped in between us! What the hell was she doing!?

"Keira, are you an idiot?" Edward asked.

"Shut up, Mr. I-don't-want-to-be-called-a-half demon!" she shouted.

"Hey! Do you *want* to die!?" Violante howled at Keira, as I stepped in front of her.

"All I'm saying is, can we move this fight to a different location?" Keira explained. And that justifies stepping in front of an angry, charging, demon how?

Violante and I exchanged glances, then shrugged and there was s change of scenery. We were on top of a church with a large hole in the roof, (brilliant choice, Violante(?).

Keira looked nervous, probably remembering not to fall off.

Violante jumped toward me. Once again, I dodged her attack, and she fell past me to the ground. "You won't get away with that a second time!" she snarled, then she lunged again, this time her attack connected. She took us both to the ground, and I rolled backwards.

And, right on cue, that's when the storm started. (If I haven't already told you, and you haven't already guessed, Violante controls the weather elements, like I control fire and dark energy).

Violante smiled, and went into full form, AGAIN! And *again* she attacked me. I wasn't fast enough this time, however, because she tackled me and stabbed her claws into my stomach. I screamed involuntarily. Violante smiled. So I gave Charlie a desperate look, "Don't" he exclaimed when he realized what I planned to do.

"I have to, she has Charity." I called.

"It will kill you!" he warned, but I would only die if I *didn't* do it.

"No it won't!" I grinned, it might kill Violante though. Then I went into full form, *again*. (Is this beginning to get old? I'm beginning to think so). It did feel good to use my wings again, though.

"Reilly?" I heard Keira ask meekly. I tuned and looked at her, hoping she'd figure out that I needed her to be quiet.

"Welcome back." Violante greeted.

"Bitch!" I hissed. "Give me Charity!"

"Why don't you come and get her?" Violante asked mockingly, then she added, "Oh yeah, you might kill her! 'Cause you can't control yourself!" Damn it! She was right! (notice that word, remind you of anyone?) Then I felt cold, wet, liquid on my hands and feet.

"Oh, my God!?" Violante gasped as she took notice of my stigmata, they were now gushing blood.

"What, you weren't expecting this?" I inquired, it was a sign that my powers were re-awakening fully. (because I hadn't used them in a while, they were, I guess you could say, 'dormant.' But, now that I was suddenly using them almost all the time, they were beginning to come 'alive' again).

Then I heard whispers. "Charlie, just how bad is Reilly in full form." that was Keira.

"She's worse than Edward." That was Charlie. And I am not! Am I?

"Oh God, she's that bad!?" Keira, again.

"I *can* hear you, you know!" I shouted as Violante made another attempt to fatally injure me, she came uncomfortably close, too.

"We weren't taking about *you*, we were...uh, talking about Edward!" Keira shouted, but I wished she wouldn't have because Violante saw her chance.

"Ugh! Quit talking *to* me! It's distracting!" I shouted as Violante scratched across my eye. I heard a quiet scream, and turned to see Keira disappearing into the hole in the roof. I rolled my eyes, I swear, she's going to get herself killed someday because of that klutziness.

"You know, I think you should join us, you were always Jezaba's favorite." Violante mocked.

"That's because the only other choice he had was you!" I taunted back.

"Why I'll--oh wait, who stayed loyal and who now worships **God?**" she spat the name as if just by saying it, she was somehow being loyal to him.

"Look who's now a sad, lonely, cat lady and who's not!" I remarked. Then my mind became even more alert and my whole body felt like it was on fire. (Which, if I didn't calm down, would be exactly right. Then there would be an explosion and I'd be the only one left standing).

Just then, the rain stopped, the sky turned black, and Jezaba was standing next to Violante, who was seriously injured. (I was quite proud of myself for that, by the way).

"Ah, my dear Reilly, I see you're back." he noted.

"Go to Hell." I snarled.

"I was just there, actually, but don't worry, you'll be joining me soon enough." he said.

"Who'd want to join you?" Keira shouted.

"Well, if it isn't the pretty Apostle, Keira May."

"Stay away from me!!" Keira shouted, no longer brave.

"What's wrong?" Oh God, don't say it. "Didn't you like me kissing you?" He said it, did he want to see my lunch again?

"No! No! No!" Keira shouted, then she continued, "you never answered my question." she noted, did she have to bring *that* up, again?!

"Oh, but Reilly belongs there, didn't she tell you?" he smiled at Keira, then turned back to me. "You'd like to come back wouldn't you? Or would you like for me to tell them what happened, first?" Here I rolled my eyes.

"What happened?" Keira shouted, (this makes me remember my comment earlier, about her not being able to comprehend more than a rock. Well, I'd like to change that to dirt, she's dumber than dirt).

"Don't worry about it." Charlie said. Jezaba laughed,

"Why not Charlie? Don't you think your friends deserve to know about Reilly's **dark** past?" he asked, moving next to me. It's not *that* dark, more like a light gray.

"I'll tell them later," I said, then I kicked him so hard he flew backwards. "After I make you wish you'd stayed dead!"

"Don't worry, you'll come around. But right now, I came here for something more important." He turned his attention to Keira.

"N- not again." She said, backing up.

"Stop! Don't do that!" Edward shouted.

"What the hell am I supposed to do?!" she shouted back, why can't she just listen?

"Aw, isn't that sweet, the half demon trying to protect his girlfriend, the Apostle." Jezaba laughed.

"WE DON'T LIKE EACH OTHER!" They shouted.

"I rest my case." He commented.

I noticed Edward's eyes were glowing. Keira must've noticed too because she said, "Edward, calm down."

"Yeah, you're right." he agreed.

"Violante!" Jezaba shouted, "did you get what you came for?"

"Part of it." she said, with a nasty glare in my direction. I stuck out my tongue at her, (I know, 'real mature,' right? But even demons have their moments). Just then, Charity appeared, she was bound and gagged.

That was all I needed to see. Within seconds I was close enough to Charity to grab her, so I did, knocking Violante out of the way. Then I reappeared next to Charlie. "Watch her." I commanded, as I handed Charity over, then I went back to where I started.

"Ah, well played." Jezaba commented, amused.

"What!? I'm so sorry master!" Violante said, but Jezaba silenced her.

"This round goes to you. But be warned, I'll be back." Jezaba nodded his approval, then they were gone.

I turned around, but I must have looked horrifying because Keira's eyes got huge.

"Reilly?" Edward asked, Keira whispered something to him, and he nodded in agreement. So I went back to weak form. I must have had a really big smile, because I could feel it.

"Reilly, you're ok!" Charity squealed. Oh no, I know what comes next.

"No hugs, please, don't!' I cried, but my pleas went unheard and she gave me a *huge* hug!

"Ouch, ok, can't breathe!" I said, because she really was cutting off my circulation.

"Look on the bright side, Reilly," (what bright side?) "you've got a knew fan." Charlie said, laughing.

I *was* going to laugh too, but a sharp pain in my wrist stopped me as I inhaled a sharp breath. My stigmata were still bleeding.

"Why didn't you tell me that you had stigmata?" Charlie demanded.

I glared at him, "why do you want to know?"

"Because."

"Because, what?"

"Because I care!" Wait, rewind. What did he just say? For the first time, I was speechless.

Chapter 12
Did I hear that right?!

I must have looked stunned, because that's the way I felt.

"You what?" I must not have heard him right, maybe he said 'I like your hair'? (What? It's a possibility!)

"I care." He repeated. Nope, I heard him right.

"No one cares about me." I said, repeating my father's words.

"What? That's bull shit and you know it!" he said. (Ok, so I guess I can't really be in denial any more).

"I- I care about you too." I said, and I felt tears run down my face. I *never* cry, so why was I now?

"You're bleeding!" Edward shouted. Shit, Keira.

"I am?" she said, maybe she wasn't so dumb after all.

"Yes, you are." he lifted up her bangs, "Stigmata?" he asked.

"No! I hurt my head when I fell!" Hey, that could actually work!

"You would've been bleeding then." **Never** leave the excuse to an angel, they *suck* at lying!

"I'm a late bleeder." Shit.

"I recognize stigmata when I see it." Edward said, suspiciously.

"You probably are bad at detecting it." Keira said, oh God.

"No, I know it! You have it!" Edward yelled.

"Oh shit." I mumbled, he heard me.

"You knew!?" Edward screamed, turning on me. After what just happened, (Charlie and I,) I could handle anything, well almost.

"What are you going to do if I did?" I challenged, meeting his glare with one of my own. He backed off.

"Why are you exactly like her!? Why!?" he shouted at Keira.

"Edward, calm down." I said.

"You stay out of this!" he snapped.

"Hey! They aren't the only ones who knew, I did too. We didn't tell you because we knew you'd do exactly as you are now!" Charlie said, stepping in between Edward and I before I could rip his head off.

"Yeah, I guess you're right. Sorry." he said, to all of us. (How come he only listens to Charlie?! Well *that* was a stupid question, wasn't it? Carry on).

"I'm sorry. I was afraid to tell you." Keira said calmly stepping toward him.

"It's fine," wow, he's being nice. "but you still should've told me!" Never mind.

"You are something else!" Keira sighed. So Charlie and I have admitted our feelings, when will they?

Chapter 13
They're fighting... Again!

The next day at school, things were really annoying. First of all, Keira and Edward were constantly yelling at each other, if I wasn't in love with him, I'd kill Charlie for sticking me with them.

I didn't hear the shouting until I got closer to my homeroom.

"Edward, this is all *your* fault!" Keira was shouting.

"What!? It's not *my* fault that you're a hag!?" Edward shouted back.

I walked through the crowd, clapping, "wow guys, that was quite a show, next time maybe Keira should just wear a glowing, neon, sign that says, 'get your Apostle here!" I exclaimed.

"Reilly! Edward insulted that special time of the month!" Wait, did she just say that out loud?

"Oh, how could you!?" I asked, dramatically.

"Hey, this is serious!" she screamed.

"No, what's serious is the fact that everyone's still staring." I said, indicating the crowd forming around us.

"No!!"

"Stop screaming!" Charlie said, pulling her away. When he let her go, she smacked him. He rolled his eyes, "have fun you two." then he and I walked past the few kids remaining.

"Well, that was fun." I muttered, then Charlie slipped his hand into mine and grinned, I smiled back.

"Maybe you should go back and make sure Keira doesn't kill Edward." He suggested.

"Why?" I asked.

"Please." he said, why did he have to do that?

"Fine." I gave in.

"I knew you'd come around, Edward's not *that* bad." he said, then laughed at my look of disgust.

"You owe me for this." I sighed, as I turned and headed back to Keira and Edward.

"See ya." he said.

"Bye."

✫ ✫ ✫

I could hear the screaming from all the way by the steps. I followed the sounds to a door at the **other end** of the hall.

"Miss May! Mr. Dens! Quiet down!" The teacher was yelling, I had to laugh.

"Reilly!? When did you get here?!"

"Well, Charlie couldn't trust you. At first I thought I wouldn't be able to find you but…I could hear you screaming from all the way down the hall!" I said with a smile.

"Miss Scara! Kindly would you SIT DOWN!" the teacher, whom I absolutely despise, screamed.

"Sure." I said sweetly, but as soon as she turned around, I immediately flipped her off.

"Reilly, you can't do that, she's the teacher." Keira whispered.

"And I'm a demon, what's your point?" I asked, amused.

"REILLY!" Keira shouted.

"Miss May! PLEASE BE QUIET, THIS IS YOUR LAST WARNING!" the teacher screamed.

"Yes, ma'am." Keira mumbled.

First period took forever, but finally it was over.

"So, how'd it go?" Charlie asked when we met him in the hall. I rolled my eyes. Was he serious?!

"Huh, I think the only way that they could attract *more* attention, would be if Edward went full demon and Keira turned Apostle." I said, extremely annoyed.

"Oh shit, it's *that* bad?!" he exclaimed, tell me he saw this coming!

"Hell yeah, maybe I should take over." I said, glaring at Edward and Keira.

"Let's just see how the rest of today goes." he suggested.

"Well, let me predict, we bury Keira at noon. Then I kill Edward at two o'clock, sound good?" I said, (what, it could happen).

"Reilly!" Charlie said.

"Oh, so you're planning on killing us?" Keira interrupted.

"Well, no. Jezaba will get to you during **one** of your fights with Edward, then I'll kill Edward for not doing his job." I explained.

"Reilly!" Charlie protested.

"Ok, fine...wait! Do you--" I started, but stopped when Charlie and Edward shook their heads.

"Where is she now?" Keira asked. (Hey, she was getting better. Let's change it back to a rock, she's only dumber than a rock, not dirt).

"Never mind, let's just wait until she shows up." Edward suggested lazily. Maybe I should kill him.

"What!?" I said, giving him an angry look.

"Yeah, I agree with Edward." Charlie said, nervously.

"Oh, now I **know** I must be out of my mind, fine." I agreed reluctantly.

We could tell Keira wasn't listening, so Edward asked, "what is it?"

"Nothing, oh we're going to be late!" she said, we looked around to realize that the hall was deserted.

"Bye." Charlie called as we walked away, but he called me back to him.

"What?" I asked.

"Why are you so jumpy lately? And you have to tell me." he said.

"I'm not jumpy, I'm alert, there's a difference." I protested, but he didn't believe me.

"Yeah, and I'm the king of England."

"Your majesty." I said, making a mock bow.

"Ha, ha."

"What, you said it." I said.

"Are you going to tell me?" he asked, seriously.

"Long story." I said, truthfully.

"We do have time."

"Fine, ok so you remember the night I blew up my house? Well..." and I told him all about everything that happened.

"Whoa." was all he said.

"That's it?" I said.

"Uh...yeah."

Then we heard a gunshot. "Maybe she shot him!?" I exclaimed, Charlie just looked at me. "Fine, let's go check it out." I sighed.

"Hurry."

"I think they're…..great." I said, when we stopped in the hall. We looked up to see a gigantic *hole* in the ceiling.

"Oh God!" Charlie exclaimed.

"Damn it! Charlie, she didn't shoot him!" I said when we approached them in the *vent*!!

"Edward! Do you get the meaning of laying low?! Keira, why do you have a gun with you still!!!?" Charlie yelled. (Has he yelled at *all* in this story?)

"S-sorry." Keira stuttered.

"Violante left." Charlie said, calm again.

"Great…" Edward sighed.

"EDWARD! YOU TOOK ME UP HERE FOR NOTHING?!" Keira thundered.

"HEY, VIOLANTE *WAS* HERE!" Edward screamed back.

"I'M GOING TO GET INTO TROUBLE FOR NOTHING?!" Keira yelled. (Yeah, 'cause that's *so* much worse than an evil maniac who wants to kill you).

"I SAID I'D TAKE THE BLAME, RIGHT?" Aw, how cute.

"Does skipping school mean anything to you?" Keira said quietly.

"Uh…no?" dumb ass.

"Exactly." she said, jumping back down.

"W-wait! Where are you going?!" Edward called, "Keira, wait!" he looked helplessly at Charlie and I.

"Run! Edward, run, go get her!" I said, he nodded and went after her.

Chapter 14
Keira's Boyfriend, Edward's Jealousy.

Lunch time arrived with a whole new surprise.

"Guess what!?" Keira shouted as she ran toward where we were sitting.

"What?" I asked, more to get her to shut up.

"I have a boyfriend!" Wow, so do I. Speaking of which, Edward just spit soda all over him.

"That…was disgusting." Charlie said.

Edward stood up, "who is it?"

"Down boy, you mean, it's not Edward?" I asked, I figured she'd say, 'hell no,' but she didn't.

"Who is he?" Charlie asked, with a glare at Edward.

"Al-"

"I'm going to kill him!" Edward interrupted, his claws were dug deep into the table.

"Oh really? I thought you didn't care about me?" Keira chuckled.

"I-I don't." he stuttered. Yeah, right.

"Edward, if you **don't** care, then why are you trying to dissect the table?" I inquired, he was now holding a large chunk of it in his hands.

"Hi guys!" came a cheerful voice. "Reilly, Charlie, and…Eduardo." ok, not only did he just call Edward, 'Eduardo', but how the hell did he know my name? Every 'danger alarm' in my head went off.

"It's Edward." he said, and the table collapsed to pieces.

"That was my lunch." Charlie groaned.

I was still trying to figure out how 'Al' knew my name.

"Dude, how do you know my name?" I finally asked.

"I…uh…know who you are!" Sure you do.

"Can I talk to you?" Edward asked Keira, "ALONE."

"Oh God." I sighed.

Edward dragged Keira to the corner.

"So... how's school?" Al asked.

"It's school." I said.

"Very true. How is your family situation?" he asked suddenly.

"What!?" Charlie stepped in. Thank God, I was beginning to get very angry.

"I just meant...well, never mind."

"Yeah." Charlie said, eying him suspiciously.

The rest of the day, I couldn't help but think that Keira being with Al wasn't good.

"Edward, would you stop glaring at him?" Charlie was saying, when I met him and Edward after school.

"Why?"

"Because then he'll-"

"He'll know we know he's evil." I finished, awarding me two **very** surprised looks.

"You actually think I'm right?" Edward exclaimed. (Have I **never** agreed with him...Wow I guess not!)

"No, I know you're right. Nothing he said adds up, and how the hell did he know us? Keira sure as hell wouldn't have talked to him about Charlie and I, only you." I said, he glared at me, but nodded in agreement.

"So, what do we do?" Charlie asked, they both looked at me.

"What makes you think I have a plan?" I asked.

"Well, I can't talk to her, I tried, she just thinks I'm jealous." Edward groaned.

"But you are." Charlie noted.

"Well I-I..."

"We don't have time for this! Keira could be dead by now!" I yelled. (What? She could be).

"How do we know where to look for her?" Edward asked.

Charlie and I just looked at him. "Her house," we said.

Chapter 15
The Ship

We arrived at Keira's house in record time, (we were dumb enough to let Edward drive).

"She's not here!?" Edward screamed after we'd checked the house.

"No duh, Sherlock. Tell me, when exactly did you figure that one out, when we saw the mess in her room, or when she didn't answer your call?" I asked, incredibly annoyed.

"So what do we do now?" Edward asked, ignoring my comment.

"We go to Lerajie's ship." Charlie said.

"And that is, where?" I asked.

"Well, if we follow Keira's scent, then I think we should find it."

"What are we, bloodhounds?" I asked.

"Can we go now?!" Edward said, before he ran out of the door.

"I think he's caught her scent, follow that dog!" Charlie yelled, I glared at him and we ran after Edward.

When we got outside, Edward was gone.

"Great, now what do we do?" I asked, more to my self.

"We could try to find Edward?" he suggested, then laughed at my expression. "He's not *that* bad."

"OK."

"He's not."

"Fine. We'd better go save his ass. You know he's going to go into the ship pissed off, then get beat up," I said. Charlie nodded and we headed in the direction that we thought the ship, and Keira and Charity, were.

It turns out that we were right. We found Edward standing on the ground, below Lerajie's ship.

"Can't get in, can you?" I said, when he saw us.

"I haven't actually tried yet." he admitted.

"Why not?" Charlie asked.

"I don't know, something about the ship. Don't you think it's weird how it's just…sitting there?" he said. He had a point. (Hey, Edward had a good point, that'll never happen again).

"Well, why don't we find out what's wrong?" Charlie said. Something on the ground caught my eye.

They headed toward the ship, "wait! I wouldn't do that if I were you." I called. They stopped and looked at me.

"Why not?" Edward asked.

I pointed to the shiny piece of metal I had noticed, it was a barrier. (which is a sort of force field that keeps out demons and devils and every other 'evil' thing. So now I'm wondering how the hell *he* got one, but he probably just stole it like my dad did). "It's motion activated. If it sees you, you'll be fried within seconds." I explained.

"How'd you know that?" Charlie asked.

"You forget who I'm related to. My dad brought tons of these home everyday." I said. "This one's on high, trust me, you don't want to be it's target." I finished. (I speak from experience, even on low they made you feel like your skin was being ripped off).

"Ok, so we're clearly not walking through the front door." Charlie noted.

"No, but I'm pretty sure the barrier doesn't go all the way to the top. It probably cuts off about half way." I said.

"So what do we do?" Edward asked. Then he gulped, "wait, did you say 'pretty sure?" he stuttered. I laughed as I walked over to check on the activator.

"Ok, it definitely doesn't go all the way up. Better?" I asked.

"Not really." he said, still looking nervously at the barrier. "So, what do we do?"

"We…uh…" I looked around, then I noticed a tall hill, "we go up there."

"Ok." They agreed.

We got to the top and looked out over the ship.

"We-we're kind of high, aren't we?" Edward whimpered. (technically, *you're* high in more ways then just elevation, but I'll let it go).

"Are you afraid of heights?" Charlie asked.

"N-no, of course n-not!" he shouted, his voice cracking. I rolled my eyes.

I paced back and forth, judging how far it was to the ship. Too far, I decided, to jump. At least, without risking getting barbecued. But was there another way?

Then I saw the tree. It was dying, and if it fell, it appeared to be able to fall through the barrier.

"Look over there." I said, pointing it out.

"So, it's a dead tree."

"Very good, Edward. Now, look at which way it's leaning, dumb ass."

"Oh, I get it!" he said. Again, I rolled my eyes.

"So how do we knock it over without getting vaporized?" Charlie asked, "If we get even with in ten foot of that thing we're toast."

"Well, I'm going to try doing just that." I said. "If I'm right, it should knock down the barrier, so be ready to run. It won't last long."

"And if you're wrong?" Charlie asked seriously.

"Then it was nice knowing you." I said.

"What do we do?" Edward asked while Charlie was glaring at me.

"You stay out of my way, and hope I'm right." I said.

"Fine with me," Edward agreed. Charlie glared at him too.

"Ok, so I'm going to go try not to get killed," I said, making my way near the tree.

I could see that it was rotting through the bottom, but in the wrong way. If I just pushed, it would fall in the wrong direction, (because **that** would be too easy).

"Ok..." I mumbled. I really wasn't sure how to do this. Suddenly I had an idea, if I burned the bottom of the tree, and **then** pushed, it should fall the way I wanted it to. I tried it, and was successful.

"See, and you were worried." I called shakily.

We entered the barrier just in time. Right after Edward got across, the tree burst into flame. "Cool!" he muttered. "So now what do we do?" (does it seem like he asks that a lot, imagine how annoying it is if you're actually there).

Then I had another idea, (wow, I'm full of those lately). I grinned.

"She's smiling." Edward said.

"That's never a good thing." Charlie noted. (Man, you destroy one city and suddenly every time you smile, every one runs for cover. (Ok, so maybe it was a **little** more that just **one**).

"Hey, *she* is still standing here." I said.

"What?" Edward growled. "any more bright ideas?"

"Well, this thing's got to have a weak spot." I said.

"Yeah…"

"So, if we find it, then we're in."

"Ok…"

"Dude, that's all I got, so far."

"Hey, what about the roof?" Charlie asked, that was a good idea.

"How do we get up there?" Edward asked, honestly he disgraces the whole demonic race!

"We jump." Charlie and I said together.

We jumped up to the top and heard a thunderous crash. "That idiot," I growled.

"What?" Charlie asked.

"He just hit the wall, I guess he found another way in." I shrugged.

"I didn't say he was smart. So, why are we up here again?"

I smiled. "Oh lord," he sighed.

"First, we have to find them, but I'm pretty sure they took her to the center of the ship."

"Where's that?" he asked. (Ok, clearly he's been spending too much time with Edward).

"Tell me you're joking, please!" I begged.

"Sure."

"The center would be in the middle, smart one."

We got to the **MIDDLE** of the ship and could hear screams coming from inside.

"Edward, behind you!" Keira shouted, then there were sounds of fighting.

"So, what's your brilliant plan for getting in?" Charlie asked.

"This." I answered simply. Then I did a full back flip, giving me enough force to crash through the roof. Charlie must've followed my lead because there was another crash shortly afterward.

"That was cool!" I yelled.

"Reilly…?" Charlie said.

"Yes…?" I asked.

"Why are you so…hyper?" he asked. I hadn't noticed.

"Because I always get hyper before I kill someone." Though I hadn't noticed before, that was true. I glared at Lerajie.

"You'll never kill me, I got at least **half** of my power back!" he yelled.

"Which still only equals about a quarter of mine!" I laughed. God he was dumb.

"Shut up, you inferior brat! You're only a miserable half demon and so is the one over there." He said. Oh boy. (why do they always assume I'm miserable? I'm not miserable…now).

"What did you call me?!" Edward asked, then Al hit him over the head. Which, of course, made Charlie and I laugh.

"Dude, you're a dumb ass!" I laughed.

Lerajie was not amused, he sprung at me, but I was so hyper that my speed must have been enhanced, because I easily dodged his attack and hit him with one of my own.

"Hey, hasn't anyone remembered to untie me!? You know, take the chains off because they **really** hurt!" Keira shouted.

I rolled my eyes and shot fire out of my hands, wounding Lerajie, sort of. He was back up quickly and again tried to kill me. It definitely failed.

"Reilly!" I heard Charlie call. I dodged another of Lerajie's attacks.

"Yes…" I answered calmly.

"I can't get these chains undone!" he said, I let out a sigh.

"Would you like to switch?" I asked, still calm though Lerajie was getting on my nerves.

"OK." he said, then he ran in between us to take my place.

"Hey Keira, what's up?" I asked.

"Oh, not much, you?" she said, I had one lock undone already.

"I'm good." Click, the other one dropped to the floor, along with the chains.

"Wow, you're a lot better at that!" she commented.

"Hey!" Charlie yelled.

"But at least you tried."

Suddenly, Al's voice broke through our conversation, "YOU'RE REALLY STARTING TO PISS ME OFF!"

"Really, cool." That was Edward, (duh).

Keira rolled her eyes, I did too, he pissed **everybody** off.

"That Edward, a royal pain just as always." Keira muttered. "Is it just me, or am I forgetting something?" I wasn't sure of the answer to that, but I was getting bored.

"What about me!?" Lerajie screamed. I looked to see that Charlie had returned to my side, which meant that no one was fighting Lerajie.

Everyone looked at me. "Fine," I said, then went over to Lerajie, "do you have a death wish?"

"No, do you?" he asked.

"You're such an asshole, you know that?!" I asked.

"Yes, I try hard. By the way, I know someone who's been looking for you." he mentioned.

"Oh yeah, tell me, is his name Lieam Scara?" I asked. I figured as much, but Lerajie shook his head.

"No, your dad has yet to pay a visit." he shook his head, he seemed disappointed, though for the life of me I didn't know why. Did he really believe that a visit from him would be an honor?! Was there something special about my dad that I didn't know? Then Lerajie looked up and smiled, "However on a lighter note, your uncle has been here many times." He grinned, I must have looked confused, which wasn't surprising, considering, you know, I was.

"Huh?!" I know, I know, I sound like Keira. But I was completely lost.

"Yes, uncle Mathew has paid me a couple of visits. But, you know that. What you don't know, is why. Well that's ok, you'll find out soon enough." he laughed.

"Ok, that's it!!" I screamed, he was really pissing me off. What wasn't he telling me?!!?

"Oh, are you getting angry? He said you would if I didn't tell you everything. But your anger will be your downfall." he said, then he began to charge toward me. But I really wasn't worried.

"No," I said, as he got closer, "it will be yours." I finished. Then, instead of leaping out of the way, I jumped toward him, claws out stretched. They sliced through his neck, then his body fell lifelessly to the ground. (Yeah, I know what you're thinking, and it *was* kind of disgusting. But it was also kind of cool, and at least I got to get rid of him, because you've got to admit that he was annoying!)

"Great." I sighed, his blood was all over my claws and hands.

"Not again." Keira groaned, turning away from Edward and Al. Then she saw me… "There goes my lunch." she said as she took in the sight. Then she spun back around to reveal Edward, "someone get me a paper bag."

"It's not *that* bad." I said.

"Come on Keira, suck it up. It's only going to get more gruesome." Charlie said. Maybe he should leave that whole reassuring thing to Charity….. CHARITY!

"Yeah, 'cause that's gonna help." I said, while trying to find Charity.

"How are we going to revert Edward?" Keira asked. (In case I didn't mention it, Edward went into full form to defeat Al).

"Maybe we should leave him that way?" I suggested.

"Reilly!" Charlie shouted.

"What? It was only a suggestion!" I said defensively.

"Uh, guys, we have other problems." Keira yelled, we both looked in her direction to find that the engine was on fire!

"Oh great!" Charlie and I said together. Then we looked at Edward. He didn't look like he was going to be much help, (not that he *ever* was).

"What should we do about Edward!?" Keira screamed, she sounded worried.

I thought for a while and when no one said anything, I did. "Well, we could leave him-"

"Reilly!"

"**OR**, Keira, you could pull him out of it." I finished.

"How?" she asked anxiously.

"Well…" I trailed off as her eyes widened.

"Oh no! No way!"

"Do you want to die here?" I yelled.

"No."

"Do you *want* to leave Edward?"

"No!!" she answered, loudly.

"Then you have to, unless you have a better idea?" I asked, Keira thought hard.

"Wait, yes I do!" she grabbed a steel pipe, "Hey Edward!"

"Oh lord." I moaned.

Then she hit him in the head with the pipe, knocking him to the ground. He got up quickly and was normal, (well, as normal as *he* gets anyway). "WHAT THE HELL WAS THAT FOR!?" he yelled.

"You're welcome." Keira mumbled, he turned toward me.

"Don't look at me, that was all *your* girlfriend's idea!" I said.

"WE DON'T LIKE EACH OTHER!!" they screamed.

"Right, whatever. Where's Charity, we have to get out of here." I said, looking around.

Suddenly the entire freaking ship exploded! Edward, Charlie, and I landed safely on the ground, but when we looked up, Keira was still free falling.

"Why doesn't she just go Apostle?" Edward demanded.

"I don't know, but apparently Charity went Apostle." Charlie said, pointing to a winged figure flying toward Keira.

Charity caught her and they landed safely beside us. "About time." Edward smirked.

"Hey, I'm not like you three, I don't have the same kind of strength as you!"

"Well, if you were as smart as Kara," must he bring that up!? "you would have went Apostle."

"Really? You're still mean to me even after I saved you?!"

"You hit me with a pipe!" Yeah, that was cool.

"It worked didn't it?! Besides, it's not my fault you're so retarded." can't argue with her there!

"I uh…um…well you are…uh…" Oh, good comeback.

"Idiot." Keira finished.

Chapter 16
Humanity Sucks

"WE'VE BEEN STUCK HERE FOR THREE DAYS!! I'M MISSING SCHOOL!!" Keira shouted at Edward. They'd been fighting the *entire* time! (Now, who the hell would actually *miss school?!*)

Edward had his ears covered, "damn it, (there's that word again). could you scream any louder? Wait, don't do that!"

"I'm hungry, tired, and cranky!" well, she had that last one right!

"Guys, couldn't we all just get along for just one second?!" Charity yelled.

Keira screamed something, but I was concentrating on some strange noise I heard. I didn't know what it was, but it was bugging the hell out of me. It sounded kind of like whispering, but I couldn't tell what was being said. "What the hell?" I muttered.

I followed the sounds but it stopped when I approached the direction that I thought it was coming from. I knew that I would have to find out eventually what it was, otherwise it would annoy me all day.

"SHUT UP!!" Keira screamed, then she tried to *kill* Edward. Charity, unfortunately, held her back.

"Clearly, someone needs to have anger management!" Edward shouted.

"I'll show you anger management!" Keira screamed, then pulled away from Charity's grasp. She tackled Edward to the ground and Charlie had to pull her off of him.

"Why won't you let me kill him!!" she shrieked.

"Believe me, I've been asking that question for a long time." I remarked.

"When did *you* get here?" Edward asked. (I wasn't gone *that* long. Maybe Edward's the one as dumb as a rock). then his expression turned to panic, "what time is it!?" he asked.

"Almost sun down, why?" Keira answered. I had almost forgotten, panic flooded through me.

"I gotta go!!" Edward muttered.

"Uh…me too!" I said, rushing in the opposite direction as Edward.

I finally reached a clearing, and prepared for the pain. "Oh shit, I hate this." I complained, as I watched the sun sink over the hills. Then it began, my hands felt like fire as my claws vanished, my eyes also burned and my whole body felt like I was exploding from the inside out. In case you haven't figured it out, I'm changing human. It happens to all demons and half demons every once in a while. For me, it's every quarter of a century, and it hurts like hell, because we are loosing not only our powers and weapons, but also our extra senses as well.

"This sucks!!" I screamed, when it was over, at no one in particular, "I am so screwed!"

"Why?" came Charlie's voice from the direction I had come.

"When did you get here?" (God, I sound like….like…Edward!! Now I'm really screwed!) "How much exactly *did* you hear?" I asked.

"Enough. What's happening?"

Well, no point in lying now, "I'm human." I admitted.

"Yeah right! What's *really* going on?" he asked, laughing.

I just looked at him, begging him not to make me say it again. "You're actually serious?" he asked. I nodded. "Well, how long does that last?"

"Until morning."

"Guess I finally get a chance to protect you." he said, (yeah, but I wouldn't need protecting if my stupid dad would have stayed stupid dead like he was stupid supposed to! Ok, now that I've gotten that out of my system, continue).

I glared at him, but let him give me a hug anyway. If he *really* wanted to protect me, I had no choice at the moment but to let him.

We headed back toward the others, and I heard the whispers again. This time I could understand the names; Reilly, Charlie, Keira, Edward, and Charity. I also heard the words; dad, Lieam, and Jezaba. I stopped dead, "did you hear that?" I asked, panicked.

"Hear what?" he said, looking at me. They started again.

"That."

"Uh…oh, yeah, I do. What is it?"

"I don't know, it sounds like whispering. Should we go check it out?" I asked.

"Maybe you should stay here." he suggested, but thought better of it after he saw the look I gave him. "Maybe not." he said.

"Yeah."

We walked toward the voices, and they stopped again.

"We're **never** going to find it!" he said. I was beginning to agree with him, when a loud screech filled my ears.

"Ouch! What the hell **was** that!?"

"What was what?"

"That, you didn't hear that?"

"No, hear WHAT!?"

"Great, now not only am I human, but I'm crazy. This is just so helpful to my self-esteem." I groaned.

"Tell me what you heard." he said, as he finished, I heard it again.

"Ow! Ok, that hurt." I said.

"WHAT IS IT!!"

"Ok, ok, uh…I'm not sure." I admitted.

He sighed angrily, then looked at me, "what does it sound like?" he asked.

"Like nails on a chalk board." I said, "times ten." I added.

"Ok, who do we know besides you that has claws?"

"Edward, Violante, and…uh-oh."

"What?"

"Well, it's not Edward."

"How do you know?"

"Well, not only does he know that I can kick his ass even human, but he's human too, so it can't be him." Yeah, Edward turns human every month!

"What about–"

"Violante? Could be, but I doubt it."

"Why?"

"Because she doesn't know, and she wouldn't come back that quickly."

"Know what?"

"That I'm human! Keep up!"
"Ok, so who else?"
"Well, that leaves...Uh-oh."
"Who!?"
"Just follow me." I said, leading him *away* from the screech.
"Why are we going this way?" (Ok, he is not allowed to see Edward *anymore!*)
"Because I'm human and you'd get beat up." I said.
"Oh---hey! I think I can handle-"
"My dad?"
"What!? Yes, of course, where is he?" he said, looking around.
"Just follow me." I said, dragging him with me. "No you aren't going to try to kill my dad. Got it!?" I asked, he hesitated. "Charlie!"
"Fine, but if he comes any where near you, he's dead."
"Whatever."
After a short while, Charlie stopped. "What?" I whispered.
"He's close." My stomach did a summersault, but I kept calm. (I hate being human, I feel so...lost).
"I hate this, I can't sense *anything*." I hissed. He continued to walk.
"I think he's gone. He must not realize how weak---I mean, helple----I mean...uh..."
"Yeah, yeah, I get it. I'm an innocent *human* girl."
"Innocent?"
"Shut up. How far until we get back to the others?"
"Reilly?" came a shaky voice.
"Charity?! Where are Keira and Edward!?"
"I-I d-don't know. She went after him and they left me here."
"ALONE!?" I asked.
"Uh...yeah."
"But they shouldn't do that with my-" I began, but Charlie cut me off.
"Which way did they go?"
"I think they're right over there." she nodded in the direction she meant, then her eyes widened, "Reilly, why do you look so...normal!?"
"Well, I am...uh."
"It's hard to explain." Charlie said.
"Try me." (Aw man, now what?)

"I'm human." I said without thinking. (that'll work).

"Yeah, right!" Why do I always get that reaction!?

"Yes...that's right." I said, she stopped laughing. Apparently, I don't have to be a demon to shut people up.

"Would someone please explain to me *exactly* what is going on!?" Charity yelled.

I opened my mouth to say something when I caught a glimpse of movement. I turned to see Violante standing off to my left.

"Where the hell did *you* come from?!" I exclaimed, she smirked.

"Not expecting me this time?"

"Nope, I have more important things to worry about." I declared, (yeah, how *not* to lose my sanity. And the ever popular, *not* getting myself and my friends killed by my dad!)

"Really? Well, what a disappointment."

"Yeah, whatever. Look, can we postpone this to a later time? In case you haven't noticed, I'm a little, well, how do I put this?"

"Weak, defenseless, annoying?"

"No, I could still kick your ass, but I thought I'd save you the embarrassment of getting beaten by a human."

"Enough of this shit!" Great, just what I need. She ran toward me, but I was actually fast enough to dodge her attack.

"Well that was odd." I muttered.

"Ok, this time you won't be that lucky!"

"Uh...I think there was a little more to that than luck. What's wrong with *you*, Violante. I mean, Reilly has an excuse for being weak," here, Charlie looked apologetically at me, I nodded, "but what's yours?" he finished.

"I...uh..."

Suddenly, everything made sense. And I couldn't help but laugh. "You're a moron!" I said, while trying to control my laughter.

"I...wait, what?!"

"Did you really think I wouldn't figure it out?!" I said.

"Uh...figure what out?" She played dumb, (which wasn't hard for her).

"You're no more of a demon that I am right now!" I accused.

"Ok, fine, but I *can* still beat you!" she yelled.

"Dude, you couldn't beat me as a demon, what makes you think that you have a better chance now?" I asked.

"Well, the fact that you're human too."

"Yeah, ok, you just keep telling yourself that."

"Why don't we just settle this!"

"Whatever, so exactly how do you plan on beating me anyway?" I asked.

"Like this." she came running toward me and, (you're gonna *love* this!) tried to scratch me! I caught her hand in mid air and snarled,

"Don't *do* that!!"

The rest of the 'battle' (if you want to call it that, mostly it was just Violante making a lame attempt at a fist fight,) went like this:

Violante kept trying to literally 'claw my eyes out' and I kept kicking her ass, (which was especially easy considering our circumstances).

Finally, she gave up, "we will soon finish this!" she said, breathing hard.

"Yeah, ok, but maybe we should wait until tomorrow. You know, considering," I said. I was equally tired, but better at hiding it I guess.

"Maybe, but be ready, because--"

"I'm sorry, did you just warn me!?!" I asked, pretending to be taken aback.

"Well I...ugh!!" she screamed, then she ran into the trees.

"That...was really strange." I commented. Then I breathed a sigh of relief, I was *so* tired.

When I got back over to where Charlie and Charity were waiting, Charity was giving me the strangest look. "What?" I asked.

"You mean, you're actually...well you know." she said shakily.

"Yes."

"But how will you protect me?"

"Hey, what am I?!" Charlie asked.

"Right now, annoying." I commented.

"At least I didn't get into a fist fight with Violante."

"Maybe, but you know, you could've stepped in at any time." I said, he made a face and said,

"No way!! She freaks me out!"

"Then quit being...well, Edward." I said. He glared at me but then smiled when I glared back.

"S-so she's going to wait for her *full power!*" Charity broke in.

"Probably." Charlie answered, she looked worriedly at me.

"And you'll have yours back by then, too. Right?"

"Yes, I should."

"Should?"

"Fine, I will."

"So, is Violante the only worry I should have?" (now why in hell would she bring that up? She couldn't just nod her head and say 'ok, Reilly' and leave it at that?! What, it's only a suggestion, and it would be so much easier). At this, Charlie and I exchanged glances, he could tell that I was debating on telling her the truth, so he shook his head, 'no'.

"You don't have to worry about anything." I stated.

"Because I'll protect you *and* Reilly." Charlie added, as he moved to put his arm around my shoulders.

"Fine." I said in defeat. It was easier than arguing.

Suddenly Keira's loud shriek broke the quiet, "SHUT UP EDWARD!!" she screamed.

"Let's go." Charity said. We walked a short ways until we saw Keira and Edward. "Hi guys!" Charity called.

Keira looked around, then noticed where Charity's voice had come from. I must have looked really mad, or else just 'normal' (as Charity put it). because she looked nervous when she saw me.

Keira muttered something, (I hate not being a demon, I can't hear a thing!) and Edward said *something* in reply. (Ugh!!)

"Here they go again." Charlie sighed.

"What!?" Keira shouted, "it's *you're* fault! Go ahead Edward, tell everyone why we're in this mess in the first place."

"Do I have to?" Edward whined.

"Yes, right now!" Keira continued.

"I didn't tell Keira that I turn human every month!" he explained.

"EVERY MONTH!? YOU DIND'T TELL ME **THAT** PART EITHER!" Keira screamed again, (does it seem like she does that a lot to you? You're right, she does).

"What else happens when you're like this?" Keira asked with a glare.

"Well, let's see, my sword won't do shit 'cause I can't wield it," (ya know, like you could *ever* wield it!) "Um...I have no claws, so pretty much, I'm as helpless as you and Charity." He finished.

"I knew it, we're screwed."

"Wait, there's more!" Charity said, Keira turned to her and seemed to notice me for the first time.

"Oh no, don't tell me. You're human too!?" she yelled.

"Yep, me too." I agreed.

"Could this get any worse!?" she exclaimed. (every time she says that, it does).

"Don't say that, it could. But there is good news, Violante is human too." I said.

"How do you know?" Keira asked, Charlie suppressed a laugh but I ignored him.

"Trust me." I said.

"God, why don't you just kill me now!!?" Keira asked. (be careful what you wish for!)

"You can't die!" Edward shouted. He is so in love with her! "Uh...I mean, go ahead, I don't care if you die." and bad at hiding it.

Keira grabbed Edward's sword and said, "shut up, or I'll hit you with it!"

"Ok you two, stop arguing." Charlie said, taking away the sword.

"I can't help it if she's in psycho bitch mode!" Edward remarked, which only pissed Keira off more.

"Psycho bitch, uh?" she asked. She was about to kill Edward but Charlie held her back.

"Keira calm down!" he mumbled which earned him a glare from Keira.

"How can I calm down when he called me a--"

"I know, I know, but you can't hurt him." Charlie said.

"Why not?!" she screamed.

"Uh...well..."

"Hey! You're not helping!" Edward screamed, Charlie couldn't think of anything because there wasn't a reason, but we won't get into that.

"Idiots." I said, rolling my eyes.

Chapter 17
Voices

We walked for about an hour and a half. The whole time, Keira and Edward were arguing.

"Guys, shut up!!" I yelled, they stopped and looked at me, "what time is it?" I asked.

"It's almost dawn." Keira said.

"FINALLY!!" Edward shouted, "how long!?"

"Ten minutes."

"No!!!" he screamed, "why can't it be one second left!?"

Keira glared at him, "shut up and stop complaining."

"How about you two stop fighting?!" I shouted, "can't you two get along for a few minutes?!"

"Sorry." Keira mumbled, Edward kept his mouth shut, (smartest thing he's done all day).

"Keira," a soft voice moaned, "Keira." she froze.

"I must be hearing things." she tried to convince herself.

"Reilly." a *very* familiar voice called, too familiar. I froze, too.

"No…it can't be." I gasped, suddenly short of breath.

"Keira." the other voice called again, impatiently. I knew that one too, but it didn't concern me.

"Reilly? Are you hearing voices too?" Keira asked.

"Yeah." I sighed.

She turned to the rest of them, (Charity, Charlie, and Edward,) "are you hearing them too?"

"Yeah." Charlie said worriedly. He knew who was calling my name, too.

"At least we know we're not crazy." Keira said.

"I'd rather be crazy." I mumbled, (remember that whole, 'could this get any worse?' thing earlier? Well, I believe it just did).

"Keira!!" the voice hissed, then out stepped Jezaba from the shadows.

"Hello, Reilly." said a figure from the shadows.

"Why don't you come out of the shadows?" I asked. He laughed.

"Alas, it isn't time for that yet." my dad said.

"Yeah, and when will that time be?" I inquired, anxious and nervous at the same time.

"Soon enough."

"Uh, hello. Trying to make an entrance here!" Jezaba howled.

"Whatever." I rolled my eyes.

"Don't push your luck." My dad said, the shadowed figure moved slightly. So did Charlie, he was now right behind me.

"Be careful." he whispered.

"Aren't I always?" I whispered back.

"Seriously, don't make him come out here." he warned.

"You talk as if that's what I want." I said. In a way, I did want that, but not with them, (my friends) here.

"I can't guarantee there won't be a fight if he steps into the open where I can see him." Charlie said angrily. I was about to reply, but my dad interrupted,

"He can't save you." he taunted.

"Doesn't mean I won't try." Charlie growled.

"Calm down." I said, taking his hand in mine.

"Hey!! I was talking first!!" Jezaba screamed, as he glared back at where my dad stood, he didn't say any more.

"The sun isn't moving! Why isn't it moving? It stopped! Reilly, did you freeze time!" Edward panicked.

"Dude…duh!" I said.

"Oh yeah." dumb ass.

"So, Edward, why are you concerned about the sunrise?" Jezaba questioned.

"I…uh…am afraid of the dark."

"What?" Keira asked, probably realizing how dumb that sounded.

I looked over at her and noticed Violante for the first time. She had a black eye and a bloody lip. "Hello, all." she said, "what's going on?"

"Uh…Violante? Are you aware that you have a-" Jezaba started.

"Yes, I know!"

"How'd that happen?"

"Ask…her…" she said, pointing a shaking finger at me.

"Oh yeah, stand back. Reilly could kill you because you're helpless right now!"

"Well…Reilly's helpless too!!" she whined.

Jezaba busted out laughing, "Reilly is helpless too! This is very interesting!" he managed.

"I might be human, but I am *far* from helpless!" I said, fiercely. Charlie squeezed my hand as a warning.

"Anyways, moving on. You guys already know what I'm here for. The Apostles!" Jezaba shouted.

"Get the hell away from me!" Keira said, backing away.

"Aw come on, I only did it so I could make Edward mad because he-" Jezaba began.

"Shut up!" Edward growled.

"Ok, ok, yeah we get it," my dad shouted. "Edward likes Keira, and Keira likes Edward."

"Hey!" Jezaba snarled at him, "shut up! *I'm* the Alpha and the Omega, and not you! So stuff it!"

"Why don't *you* stuff it?!" My dad growled back.

"No you!"

"You!"

"You!" Jezaba screamed.

"You!" My dad growled back.

"The sun! It's risen! YES!!" Edward shouted.

Violante looked at me and I glared back. "Thanks for the warning." she snarled at Edward.

"Uh-oh…oops."

"Yeah, oops." I growled.

Violante smiled evilly, "Reilly, I think we've waited long enough."

"Says you." I groaned.

"C'mon Reilly." my dad snarled.

"Hey, no body asked you!" I snapped.

"Be kind to your elders, Reilly. Isn't that one of those… commandments?!" Violante taunted.

"Maybe." I mumbled. Then the light appeared. The sun was up!

"Uh-oh." Edward, Violante, and I groaned in unison. Then a stinging pain made me inhale sharply. (the transformation takes a little less then three minutes, but it hurts like hell. That is only because our powers are returning all at once. There's another catch as well, but you'll find out about that in a minute). I clutched my head in both hands and hoped it would end soon, when it did, I looked up in time to see Violante coming straight at me.

"Aw C'mon!!" I screamed, as I jumped out of the way. I was flying! "Great…" I sighed, I was in full form. (see what I mean?)

"This ought to be good." Jezaba said, (it's like he's going to the movies and not a demonic battle!) "You know, I missed their last battle." he finished.

"I didn't." my dad said, wait, WHAT!!?

"What!?" I said, then I got tackled to the ground. "Ok, ow!"

"Stay focused, Reilly! This is no fun if you don't put up a fight!" Violante laughed.

"Fine, but remember, you suggested it!" I said, pushing her off of me, she had landed on top of me, pinning me to the ground.

"Can I kill her!?" she shouted to Jezaba.

"No!" he and my dad shouted together. I looked at them, confused.

"Not that I'm complaining, but huh?" I said. They laughed,

"All in good time." my dad said, earning him an angry glare from Jezaba.

"I wanted to say it!!" he whined.

"Hey! Kind of busy here!" Violante hissed at them, as she *tried* to once again tackle me. I kicked her, hard, and she backed off. When she came at me *again* she was truly enraged.

"I wish I could kill you!" she shrieked.

"Aw, well isn't that just too damn bad." I said.

"Reilly! Be careful!" Charlie shouted.

"Ya know, you'd think he'd get tired of always having to warn you." Violante noted. He doesn't *always* have to warn me, only sometimes.

"I'd rather have to warn her than have to see her die!" he shouted back.

"Too bad." Violante said. Then it began to rain.

"Must you *always* do that?!" I asked, incredibly annoyed.

"Yes, I must." she said. Then the lightning started. I rolled my eyes, as a bolt of lightning came straight at me. I held up my arms, letting it strike me, then I re-directed it's energy, and hit Violante with a line of fire. It knocked her away from me, but she's way dumber then she looks, because she tried it *again*!

"You'd think *you'd* get tired of getting your ass kicked, but apparently not." I said, as I deflected yet another lightning bolt.

"I never get tired of it! Wait, hey!!"

I laughed, "you know, you're incredibly stupid."

"I am not!" she shrieked.

"Yeah, ok, whatever." I said, skeptically.

"You know what?! I don't have to take this abuse, I'm leaving!" Violante screeched.

"Thank God!" I screamed, she rolled her eyes then shimmered away.

"Yeah, me too." Jezaba said, then he, too, left. I went into weak form, and joined the others on the ground.

"So now where do-" Edward began, but I stopped him.

"We're still not alone." I warned. My dad laughed.

"Very good, Reilly, you're learning." he said, Charlie moved closer to me and my dad laughed again. Then I didn't sense him anymore, I glanced up at Charlie and he was looking at me.

"Gone?" he whispered.

"I think so." I whispered back.

"Is he gone?" Charity asked in a meek voice.

"Yeah." I sighed.

✧ ✧ ✧

I heard the rumbling *long* before I saw the helicopter. But when we did see it, Keira started waving her arms.

"What are you doing!?" I yelled. "You're acting as stupid as Edward!"

"Hey, I'm not *that* stupid!" Edward shouted, does he hear himself when he talks?!

"By the order of…well, Order. Hand over the Apostles!" someone on board the helicopter yelled.

"I knew it, we're saved!" Keira screamed.

"You mean Charity and you." Charlie corrected her.

I looked up and saw that the helicopter was descending…over us! (Charlie, Edward, and I, that is). we leapt out from under it just in time. But some monks were escorting Charity and Keira into the chopper. A few others were pointing puny, human, weapons at us. Easily dealt with, but then Sister What's-her-name, came over and told them to lower their weapons (?).

"The really small one over there asked if you could come along. Just so you know, I *still* hates demons and devils." she glared at Edward, "especially ones who wreck my offices."

"That's ok, I *still* hate nuns and monks." I said, glancing around for Mathew.

"Yes, and *you* have nothing to worry about here. Mathew's soul has gone astray." she said, how'd *she* know about that. Did Mathew tell *everyone* who I am?!

"You mean, he went to the dark side!?" Edward asked, (I'm sorry, what did he say?!)

"May the force be with him." I shrugged.

"That's not what I meant!" Edward snapped, I rolled my eyes.

"Do you think this is a good idea?" Charlie asked on our way to the helicopter.

"Nope." I said.

"Ok…"

"But we can't let them take Charity and Keira without us, and we sure as hell can't let Edward go along without us, so we have no choice." I explained, he nodded in agreement.

"You ok?" he asked.

"Nope." I said, matter-of-factly. "I'm terrified, but if I let that stop me, he'll kill us both."

"He'll *try* to kill us both."

"Yeah, remember when we had this discussion earlier?" I asked. "do me a favor, please, don't get in his way." I said, focusing on the ground in front of me.

"I'm not going to let him kill you."

"You have to. Or he'll kill you too. And I'm not going to let *that* happen." I said, then I got into the chopper before he could protest. He sat next to me and gave me a look that said, ' I don't care what you say, he won't kill you.'

Chapter 18
The Past. My Past!

We flew over town and Keira began to jump up and down singing something about home. I rolled my eyes, "stop before you fall out of the chopper." I said.

"I'm not going to fall out of the-" she tumbled over the edge but Edward caught her.

"Idiot," I said, "told you." Edward didn't let go right away.

"Edward, you can pull me up now."

"Oh, uh yeah…sorry."

"What's wrong with him?" Keira asked Charlie.

"Don't know." he replied.

We arrived at the order and they took us over toward the weapons building. "where are we going?" Edward asked.

"To our weapons expert, AKA: the craziest old loon in the world, Mark." Great…

He knocked on the door, and it opened automatically. "Mark, are you in here!?" the monks shouted.

"Why are we here?" Edward asked.

"He's the last one to speak to Mathew." Damn it! Why can't' we just forget about him!?

"What does that have to do with us?"

"It could have something to do with Jezaba."

"Great." I moaned, "just what I need."

The lights came on and an old man, Mark I guessed, came out, "yes?" he asked, then he spotted me, "you're her, the one he spoke about, Reilly."

"I am? I hadn't noticed." I said, sarcastically. But I had a bad feeling about this. You know, like when you *know* something bad is about to happen but you don't know what. It made me nervous.

Keira glanced over and noticed a huge gun. Oh lord.

"Can I have it!? Can I have it!?" she shrieked, jumping up and down.

"No!" Edward shouted, dragging her away.

"No, Edward I want it!" she yelled and started kicking and screaming like a kid.

"No and that's final." Nice going, genius, now she'll yell louder.

"But we wants it!!" Keira screamed, (ok, now that was just creepy!)

"No! Shut up or I'll…uh…I don't know!"

"Anyways," Mark interrupted, "so you're Mathew's niece. You all might as well sit down, I've got **A LOT** of explaining to do." he sighed.

"Ok, start explaining." Edward said, impatiently.

"Well, for starters, Mathew now has my most powerful weapon."

"WHAT!? I'm so screwed." I said.

"Calm down." Charlie said.

"How can I calm down when my uncle is trying to **kill** me!?"

"Reilly, it could get a whole lot-"

"Shut up!" I screamed, "when your whole family tries to **murder** you, then talk to me."

"Hey, do you want me to explain or not?" Mark called.

"Explain! Tell us!" Edward yelled, I glared at him.

I heard whimpering and turned to see Charity in tears, "I c-can't believe your uncle wants to k-k-kill you."

"Oh God." I said, holding my head in my hand.

"I'm not done!" Mark interrupted.

"Yes, you are! If they want to know, then tell them. But I don't want to know anymore." I said, then turned and walked outside.

"WAIT!!" Charlie yelled, I rolled my eyes.

"Don't you want to hear my life's story?" I asked.

"Not if you don't want me to." he replied.

"I don't care," I sighed, "do you want to hear why he wants to kill me?"

"Kind of."

"Fine, ok so…where to start?" I mumbled, "when I was…when my dad was alive, I mean before this time. He was always very…embarrassed of me. I guess because of the fact that I was only *half* of who he was. He used to test his powers on me, you know, target practice. My mom didn't like that, so he...got rid of her..." I trailed off, as I remembered that night.

"So, that's when Mathew came into the picture?" Charlie asked, when he realized that I wasn't going on.

"Uh...yeah, pretty much. He is my dad's brother, and my dad wanted help to 'take care of me.' so Mathew moved in and they **tried** many different ways to end my life. None of which, had any effect. When I met Jezaba and Violante, Jezaba promised that if I helped him, he'd help me. So I listened. But when we got back to my house, Mathew was gone, and my dad was dead." I said, "I still don't know what happened." I finished, looking up at him.

"I'm sorry..."

"Don't be. Besides," I grinned, "I get to prove that I *can* win against them, I *can* kill them both." I said, my voice shaking with anger and hatred.

"But that still doesn't answer my question."

"A while back, Mathew became a monk, in hopes that he could somehow 'absolve' himself of his sins." I explained, "well, that day that Keira got taken to the order, before we saved Charity, Mathew wanted me to stay with him there, he said he could save me from my dad. He got mad at me because I refused. Guess he decided just to kill me instead of arguing." I shrugged.

"You wanted to stay with me?" he asked.

"You're surprised?"

"No, not really." he said, I elbowed him in the side.

"Ow!!"

"Don't be so arrogant." I warned.

"Ok, ok, I'm glad you chose me." he said.

"Yeah, me too." I agreed with a smile, he smiled back. Then we heard a crash.

"You think she shot him?" I asked hopefully.

"Why do you *always* assume that?"

"Because, one day, she will."

"We should probably go check it out." he said, I shook my head.

"You go ahead, I'm gonna stay out here for a while." I said, he nodded and ran toward the weapons building.

I walked around for a few minutes before heading back. I was about to turn around when I sensed something that stopped me. "How the hell?" I muttered.

"Well, you know, I have my ways." Mathew laughed, I turned around to see him not too far away.

"Why are you here?" stupid question, but I was in denial!

"Honestly Reilly, haven't you figured it out yet?!" well yeah, but I'm not going to say anything, the longer you explain, the longer I, or you, will live.

"Maybe." I groaned.

"You know, your dad will probably kill me for this. But I don't care, at least *I* got to do what he never could. *I* got to kill you!" he said, I heard a gasp and turned to see a nun, who looked like Sister what's-her-face, standing, open mouthed, staring at us.

"What are you waiting for, RUN!!" I yelled.

"Uh…yeah…" she stuttered, then she ran toward the weapons building.

Mathew laughed, "how sweet, Reilly, let her escape."

"You weren't going to kill *her* anyway."

"True, but still." he is so annoying! I can't wait to kill him, and yes, I do plan on killing him.

"C'mon Mathew, you didn't come here to criticize my saving Sister Elizabeth." I remarked.

"How right you are." he pulled out a gun bigger than the one Keira wanted.

"Mark is an idiot!" I growled.

"Oh, so you've met. Remind me to thank him, oh wait, you can't, you'll be dead!!" he laughed hysterically as I rolled my eyes.

"Yes, Mathew, that was hilarious. It was so stupid it was actually… no, it was just retarded." I said.

"So calm in the face of death." he remarked.

"You forget, I've faced death before and always seem to win." I said, he glared at me.

Suddenly, an arrow came flying at me, I moved backward to avoid getting hit, then I glared at the source, it was Keira!!

"Hey! I want to kill her!!" Mathew shouted, "do you want to die too?!"

"N-no." Keira muttered.

"Then *I* get to kill her!!" Mathew yelled, then his expression changed to hatred, "Kara!?"

"Huh?" Keira said.

"I thought you were dead!"

"It's her reincarnation!" Edward pointed out.

"Oh, 'cause that's *so* much better!" Mathew hissed.

"Reilly, I see how you're related." Edward remarked, I glowered at him for a second before turning back to Mathew.

"Enough! I'll deal with Kara in a minute. Now for what I came here for!" Mathew screamed.

"Whatever." I sighed as he pointed the gun back toward me. (he had it aimed at Keira when he realized who she was).

"Ok, Reilly, now you can die!" it's like he's granting me permission, did you notice that?!

"Yeah, sure."

He took aim and…pulled the trigger!

I didn't even know that the bullet had hit me, but I did see Mathew's surprised expression when the smoke cleared, and I noticed what he was looking at. I was glowing!

"Wh-what?"

I grinned, "bye." I snarled, then I released the energy. It hit Mathew all at once, his expression turned to panic, then he exploded!!

"Uh-oh." I mumbled, before the shock waves knocked me backwards and threw the wall of the main building behind me.

For a couple of minutes, all I did was lay there. I went through the wall, and then the whole building crumbled on top of me. I was laying beneath about a foot of rubble, but I couldn't manage to get up, (mostly because I had hit my back really hard on the wall and the ground).

"Reilly!? Are you ok!?" Charlie called from the direction I had come.

"Ow." I managed to say. Then I felt the rubble lift and I could see the light above. "that wasn't what I had in mind." I remarked, he laughed as he helped me stand up.

"REILLY SCARA!" Sister Elizabeth's angry voice came blaring from the 'clearing.' (it was actually all a clearing now, seeing as how I destroyed the weapons building *and* the main building).

"What?" I groaned.

"Oh, good, you're alive. Now I can kill you for what you've done to my beautiful buildings!!" she shrieked.

"Ok…"

"We're going to have a talk in that building, oh wait, you destroyed it. Ok, my office then. Nope, it's gone too!" she growled, I rolled my eyes.

"Next time I'll let the big, angry, demon kill you all then." I said.

"Well, I…"

"Yeah, that's what I thought. What exactly happened?" I asked.

"Uh…well…" Charlie said, then I saw it. A bloody pile of what looked to be flesh and bone, (though most of it was disintegrated from the blast,) was laying not to far away.

"No way, did I really…?" I began, but they both nodded, yes. "Oh God." I sat down, suddenly sick to my stomach.

"Are you sure you're ok?" Charlie asked.

"I'm fine, just…surprised." I said, still looking at the ground.

"Reilly! Are you ok!?" Charity screamed.

"Yeah---ow!" I said as she gave me a hug. "Ok, you can let me go now. Seriously, Charity, let go!"

"Sorry."

"Charity…"

"Ok."

Sister Elizabeth had been standing beside us quietly the whole time. Now, she moved toward Edward and Keira. "YOU TWO COME WITH ME!!" she shrieked.

"But we didn't do anything!" Edward shouted, she glared back at Charlie and I.

"You two, also!"

"Great…" I groaned. I had a really bad headache and I had a feeling that she wasn't going to help it any.

Elizabeth led us back to where her office *was*. She sat at the desk and wiped the dust from her outfit. "Anyway, the reason I called you here was to say I got something from Jezaba." (Huh?)

"WHAT!!?" Edward yelled.

"Sit down!" she exclaimed, "It's still in here." she pulled out a folder and handed it to Edward. (Yes, she actually gave something of great importance to Edward. God nuns are stupid.)

"Stand back!" he growled at Keira when she tried to look at the folder. He opened it to reveal what appeared to be a map of the U.S. It had a huge circle around Washington.

"He wants us to go to another state?" Edward asked. (Well no shit Sherlock, what was your first clue?)

"Well obviously he wants us to go there, but why?" Keira asked.

"Ok, now I'm confused. He wants us to go to a dormant volcano? Why?" Charlie asked when Keira flipped the map over to reveal a large circle around Mt. St. Helens.

"Do we look like Jezaba to you? I don't know about you, but I'm going home!" Keira said, then she left.

"Aren't you going to go after her?" Sister Elizabeth asked Edward, he glared at her but left anyway.

"And as for *you*." she said, pointing at me.

"Yeah?" I asked.

"You have some explaining to do."

"Oh, yeah, and what am I supposed to explain?"

"Why did Mathew target you?" she asked.

"Who says he did?"

"Do you think I'm stupid-?"

"Do you want me to answer that?" I asked, cutting her off. She glared at me and continued.

"If he wasn't here for you then he would've killed me before." she said. (Damn, she had a good point.)

"I...uh..." (I couldn't think of a lie, WHAT IS HAPPENING TO ME!!?)

"He was here for the Apostles." Charlie said, glancing at me. I nodded.

"Right." Sister Elizabeth said skeptically.

"He was."

"Fine, I'll talk to you later." she said, then she motioned for us to leave.

"That was close." Charlie said when we were away from the Order.

"Thanks for that." I said, still trying to come up with a lie.

"Not a problem." he said. I could here the smile in his voice. I rolled my eyes. "Let's go check on Keira to see if Edward's still breathing." he suggested.

"Why? You think she killed him?" I asked, not unhopefully.

"It's a possibility."

Chapter 19
Jezaba's Plan

We entered Keira's room, (through the window,) and noticed that she was waving her hands around the wall.

"Keira, why are you frantically touching the wall?" Charlie asked as we entered the room.

"Nothing, never mind." she mumbled. "So did you ever find anything else?", she changed the subject. (real smooth, Keira.)

"No."

"Ok, what if he-?" Keira began, but stopped when Charlie, Edward, and I looked at her. I was suddenly overcome with a sense of despair. Which, I guessed, was exactly what Jezaba had intended.

"Maybe he's-" Charity started, but we gave her the same stare and she was also silent.

"Why are you three so dreary all of a sudden?" Keira asked.

"Because, unlike you, we can sense every little imbalance in the world. And Jezaba has seen to it that there are a lot of those lately." Edward said.

"I think I know what he's planning." I said, suddenly coming to a reasonable conclusion.

"Oh yeah? What's that?" Edward shouted, but got quiet after a look from Charlie, (actually, it was more like a glare.)

"You know how I can sense things that have to do with the Earth's core, because of all the fire in it?" I continued. (It has something to do with my power over fire, I still haven't quite figured it out completely, but I know enough to understand what was happening.)

"Yeah, go on." Charlie said encouragingly.

"Well, there has been a huge raise in the pressure surrounding all of the openings." I stated, my voice barely a whisper. I knew all too well what that could mean.

"Volcanoes?" Keira asked.

"Yes."

Suddenly, the ground began to shake.

"We don't have earthquakes in Missouri!!" Charity shouted as we all crowded under the doorway. (Yeah, so you're telling me that all the brick and rock will fall, but this little, wooden doorway will survive. Fine, but when I die, stay away from my funeral!)

"We do we do now!" Edward said meekly.

"Are you…crying?" I asked.

"No! I got dust in my eye!" he shouted back.

"My room is *not* dusty!!" Keira screeched.

"Guys, we have more pressing problems." Charlie yelled, but the earthquake seemed to be over.

"You felt it too that time, didn't you." it wasn't a question, I could tell by their faces that Edward and Charlie had felt the psychic jolt of energy.

"Yeah." they replied anyway.

Then their eyes widened. I'm sure my face mirrored theirs if I looked the way I felt. Why hadn't we seen it before? It all made sense.

"What!?" Keira exclaimed as we all looked at each other and nodded to confirm that we thought the same thing.

"He wouldn't dare!" Edward shouted.

"He's a maniac!" Charlie exclaimed.

"Did you expect anything less?" I inquired.

"What the hell are you three talking about!?"

"Charity?!" Keira exclaimed.

"Uh…that was weird." Charlie said.

"Never mind. Jezaba's going to start over." Edward said. ('cause that explains everything.)

"What?!" Keira shouted.

"He apparently doesn't like our world because he's going to start again, make his own." Edward explained.

"He's going to need a lot of fire power to do that." Keira said, (She's learning.)

A sudden dread over came me. There was a moment of silence, then I realized they were all looking at me. "Yeah, like *I* would ever help Jezaba.

But I know someone who would." I said shakily. Still overcome with the shock of my realization.

"Who do you think-"

"My dad." I said, before Edward could finish.

"But he's dead."

"Uh, about that." Charlie said.

"What!?"

So Charlie explained the whole thing, starting all the way back to daddy dearest's resurrection, (Yeah, you remember it.)

"Oh my G-"

"Don't say it." I said, Charity was about to say the G-word. (After all, I haven't seen *him* lift an all powerful finger to help save our asses.)

"So what do we do?" Keira asked.

"**You** do nothing, he still needs you two." I said, "**We'll** go after Jezaba."

"But, Keira seems to get into trouble no matter where she is and, I need to be with her to protect her so, maybe they should come." Edward suggested.

"What?! I think Reilly's right on this one." Charlie said.

"That's only because-"

"Guys! If it will shut Edward up then they can come. We don't have much time." I yelled.

"Right." Edward said, but Charlie still looked worried.

"How are we going to get to Washington?" Keira asked.

"Uh…well, I hadn't thought of that." Edward said.

"Neither did I." Charlie admitted.

"Hello. Are there not airplanes, trains, cars!?" I exclaimed, "pick one."

"Well, I've never been in an airplane before." Charity admitted, "Well, not a legal one, anyway."

"Wow, neither have I. Guess we're flying then." I stated.

"Yeah, I guess so." Keira agreed.

Chapter 20
Plane Ride from Hell

Upon arriving at the airport, I began to get *very* nervous. Considering, I was pretty sure my dad would be waiting for me, not to mention Violante, (Not that *she* worried me much) I think I had a right to be a little shaken.

I was in the middle of coming up with ways to go home when Charity's piercing scream snapped me out of my trance. (And probably scared the shit out of half the business people in front of us.)

"Charity! Shut the hell up!" Keira thundered as she tried unsuccessfully to detach the now shaking Charity from her arm.

"Please don't make me go! I don't want to go!"

"Charity, we *have* to get to Washington." Edward explained.

"Reilly! Please don't make me go!" Charity whined, turning to me.

"You're going." I said firmly, then I smiled, "unless you'd like to stay here by yourself."

"Never mind."

We got through the security checks and were soon on the plane. I immediately went to the very back, and the rest followed. Charlie took the seat next to me with Keira in front of us. Charity was still glued to her arm, and Edward sat in front of them.

"Charity! Let go! Go cling on Edward!" Keira hissed as she *tried* to place Charity's suitcase in the overhead compartment. "Damn it! What the hell are you carrying in here?!"

"Some clothes, and my stuffed animals!"

"What!? Your twelve years old, not four!"

Charity looked down, "I know but…"

"Just sit down." Keira commanded quietly, slumping down in her chair.

"Keira, just leave her alone." I muttered, not looking away from the window. I was still almost terrified of what we were about to do and their screaming was giving me a massive headache.

"Edward, do you have your sword?" Keira asked, after several minutes of angered silence.

"Why?" he asked, confused. (And how the hell did he get it past security. I'd be *very* worried if I were you.)

"I'm going to kill myself with it." she replied, Edward gasped.

"No way!"

"Why? There would be one less Apostle to worry about, until I somehow get reincarnated."

"No!" Edward shouted.

"Fine, then I'll jump out the window."

"Keira, stop being stupid." Edward said.

"And suicidal." I added, not looking away from the clouds. Something was about to happen. I didn't know what, or when, but it was definitely coming, and it wasn't going to be good.

I heard a strange noise and looked up to see that Charity was hyperventilating!

"Charity, are you hyperventilating?" Duh, Keira!

"N-no...I'm n-not..." Charity choked out.

"Charity you are the worst liar in the world." Keira said.

"Keira, stop it. She must've gotten traumatized by Lerajie's ship exploding." Charlie said.

I grinned at the memory, "Yeah, that was cool." I laughed. Charity looked horrified but my good mood must've been contagious because with in seconds she was also smiling, (which is odd, because I didn't feel anything like what I was acting like I did.)

Then a mechanical voice came over the speaker, "Please fasten your seat belts ladies and gentlemen. Sorry about the wait, but we are now ready for take off." it said. Charity's hyperventilating re-started, and I sighed.

"You look tired." Charlie noted, pushing my hair away from my face.

"I *am* tired." I said.

"Then go to sleep."

"I'm tired, not sleepy. Besides, I'm too…" I paused, debating on whether or not to tell him that I was nervous, "excited to sleep." I decided against it.

"Yeah…sure" he said skeptically. Then he pulled me over to where I was leaning on him, "just try."

"Ugh, fine." I sighed in defeat. Then I closed my eyes, but the pictures that flashed through my mind would've given anyone else nightmares. I knew them as memories, so I sank into a troubled sleep.

It seemed like seconds later when I was jarred awake. The plane was shaking.

"What's happening?" I asked, drowsily.

"We don't know, the plane just started going out of control." Charlie replied. It was dark, probably night, and there didn't seem to be any electricity. I could feel the seatbelt around me, but it was highly uncomfortable, so I unbuckled it and stood up.

"Where are you going?" Keira asked from in front of me.

"To see the pilot." I replied.

"How are you gonna get there?" she asked.

"I'm a demon, I can see in the dark." I whispered.

I made my way up front and through a curtain to where I hoped I'd find the pilot. But I found….absolutely no one.

"Ok…" I muttered, looking around. (Well that would explain why the plane was crashing, no one was driving!) then I saw him, an old man slumped in the corner, the pilot, I guessed. His head was at an awkward angle. Then I heard footsteps.

"Sir. We're experiencing some difficulties out here." came a flight attendants voice just outside. But the scent that arose all around almost made me gag.

"Ok, the plane is out of control and I'm standing in the control room with the murdered pilot. That might look a little suspicious." I whispered to myself, then I set the pilot up to where he looked…well, alive.

"Sir?" the flight attendant asked. Then she walked in and revealed her true identity. Violante. She looked around with a smile, "Excellent."

"You know, I fail to see what's so excellent about a murder scene." I said, stepping away from the wall.

"Even more excellent." she grinned.

"What?"

"You're here. You'll die too." she said, then we heard a crash. "It has begun." she said as the sound of shredding metal filled the air.

"What?!" I demanded.

"You'll see." she laughed, then she was gone.

I rushed out into the main area only to see that there was a big hole just before the last section. "Great…" I looked around to find that no one had moved. They were all perfectly content to just stand there. "Hello, you're all going to die if you don't move!" I yelled, trying to push one passenger out of the way. I was surprised to find that it burned my hand to do so.

"Even more excellent." I mocked Violante as I kicked the human puppet out of my way. Then I noticed that I was surrounded. "Oh, shit." I said, leaping out of their grasp. I was now right next to the opening. I could see the others in the back. "Well, here goes nothing." I muttered. Then I took a step back, and jumped.

I landed on the other side safely, (unless you count the fact that most of my internal organs were still somewhere on the other side of the plane.)

"She did what?" Charlie was saying.

"Relax." I said, walking to his side. We heard another explosion and saw that the front of the plane was no longer in one piece.

"Damn it." Edward said as the shock waves knocked us against the back wall. I could feel the whole thing plummeting downward at an accelerating rate.

"We have to get out of here!" Keira said.

"Well no shit Sherlock!" I yelled over the roar of the explosions that followed.

"What did you have in mind?" Edward asked me.

I kicked the handle at my feet and the baggage compartment opened up behind me. "follow me." I said as I fell in. Once we were all in, I clawed a hole in the wall and jumped, motioning for the others to follow.

We were soon outside, but the rest of the plane exploded over us, sending a shower of sparks and debris flying our way.

I landed on the edge of a very large hole in the ground. I swayed a little but managed to steady myself just in time. "Well that was close," I murmured. Then I heard Keira,

"Whoa!!" she yelled as she ran into me, knocking us both over the edge.

"Keira, what the hell?!" I yelled just before we hit the bottom.

"Ow," I moaned, "Keira?"

"What?"

"Get off!!" I yelled, she had landed on top of me.

"Ow…" Keira muttered after I pushed her off.

"Reilly? Keira, are you ok?" Charlie called from the top.

"Yes." I answered.

"I'm fine." Keira yelled. (Yeah, that's because you landed on me!!)

There was a noise that sounded like rocks falling, and then Edward, Charlie, and Charity were also in the cavernous space.

"What happened?" Edward asked, suppressing a chuckle.

"Why don't you ask your girlfriend?" I asked, he glared at me, then turned to Keira.

"Well…"

"I kind of…fell." Keira stuttered.

"No, you tackled me!" I accused.

"Not on purpose."

"Whatever. We have to get out of here." I said, looking around.

"So soon?" came an evil question.

"Jezaba." Edward growled.

"I am the Alpha and the Omega. Yes! The beginning and the end, the start to finish. The one who is, the one who was, and the one who is…uh…what was it?" Jezaba asked.

"Coming." Violante said.

"What?"

"Coming!"

"What?" he so needs hearing aids.

"COMING!" Violante shouted.

"Oh yeah, coming. The one who is coming! The almighty, Jezaba!" Oh, lord.

"You are truly a stupid idiot." Violante remarked.

"You just figured that out?" I asked.

"No! I've worked with him longer than you did!" did she **have** to bring that up?!

"You worked with him?" Keira asked. I was about to reply, but Charlie did for me.

"Long time ago." he snapped.

"Charlie did, too!" Jezaba said, gleefully.

"You too?" Keira asked Edward.

"No! I've *always* hated this guy."

"You hate me and yet we have so much in common…Kara…"

"I want to know what the hell is up with this Kara lady!!" Keira said, (No you don't.)

"Are you sure you want to know?" Jezaba asked.

"Yes!" No.

"Another time." Jezaba said.

"What?!"

"Lieam, you can come out now." Aw come on! (This just gets better and better.)

"Who is Lieam?" Charity asked, I cringed.

"No one." Charlie and I said at the same time.

"Oh, come now, Reilly. I'm not *that* bad, am I?" my dad asked.

"Yes." I mumbled.

"Ok, ok. That's enough Lieam! This was *my* evil plan, not yours." Jezaba interrupted.

"But I-"

"No!" Jezaba cut him off. Only to get an angry glare from my dad.

"Anyways, what should we do now? We got the last three Apostles."

"Nuh-uh! You don't have the hidden virtue!" Edward piped up.

"We do now! *You've* brought her to us." Jezaba laughed.

"Oh, ha, that." Edward laughed nervously.

"What?!" I yelled, "don't you look at me like that!!"

"Edward?! Is there something we should know?" Charlie growled.

"Oh God." I moaned.

"That's right, Reilly." Jezaba said.

"EDWARD! You knew didn't you!?" I yelled at him.

"Well I, thought you were evil."

"Oh, you better hope I'm *not* evil Edward, because I'm coming after *you*!" Edward gulped.

"What's going on?!" Keira yelled.

"Reilly is the hidden virtue." Jezaba announced what everyone else already knew. "The final Apostle: Justice."

"Reilly's the same as Keira and I." Charity said.

"Oh God." I groaned again.

"What's wrong, Reilly?" Charity asked.

I looked at her, my eyes wide with shock and disbelief, "I'm a **demon**, not an angel!" I yelled.

Chapter 21
Oh No!!!

"No! I have a reputation to maintain!" I continued, "This can't be happening."

"Wow, Reilly, you're over reacting over being a-"

"No! I can't be! It's not true!" I glared at Jezaba, "it's not true, right?"

"Yep, you're an Apostle. Deal with it." Jezaba said, (fine, but the way I'll deal with it involves killing you and Edward.) "Ok, the damn door should be appearing right now."

"Well, didn't you ever get the key?" My dad asked, Jezaba looked surprised.

"What key?!"

"There's some stupid key that goes to it with the Apostles! Don't you ever research anything, you clueless idiot."

"I'm not an idiot, you are!"

"No you!" Oh dear God, please tell me I'm adopted! Please!

"You!"

"You!"

"Ok!" Lieam silenced Jezaba, who glared at him. "Let's just carry out the rest of your 'brilliant plan'."

"You're both kind of dumb." Violante muttered.

"Shut up!" they shouted at her.

"Ok, besides the Apostles and the Door to the Darkness, what else did your plan consist of?" my dad asked.

"Well...me ruling the world!"

"Besides that."

"Uh..."

"Fine, let's go with my plan."

"And what's that?"

"What do *you* think?"

"Oh, Oh, I know…" **Charity** began, (was she *trying* to get me killed?!) but Keira and I covered her mouth.

"Oh, how original." Jezaba sighed, my dad laughed.

"It's a good plan, and I get to kill Reilly!"

"And then what?"

"Well…I hadn't really thought past that part."

"We need her for the door, you can't kill her."

"Hey," I asked, "don't *I* get a say in this?" they both glared at me,

"No!" they shouted together.

"Can we carry out my plan, NOW!!?" my dad shouted.

"Ugh, fine! Just make sure she doesn't die!!" Jezaba snapped, (well, don't *I* feel loved,) and then he put up his *pink* barrier and departed. (I would say 'real men wear pink,' but I don't think it really applies here.) "See you all in hell."

"Oh. My. God." I said, emphasizing each word as we watched him leave.

"Well, now that *he's* gone." Violante said, exchanging a look with my father, who said,

"Give the others something to do." she nodded and then waved her hands around. Suddenly, we were surrounded by other demons of all levels.

"Demons!" Charity cried, clinging on to Keira, "Somebody save us!!" a few of the upper level demons laughed at her panic.

"Charity, get the hell off me!" Keira screamed. (Dude, it's like they've never seen demons before, *hello!*)

"Keira, Charity, go hide over there." I heard Edward yell, pointing to a large rock.

"Come on!" Keira shouted, dragging Charity with her as she ran to the boulder.

"Keira, don't pull so hard!" Charity whined. I stopped listening, Edward had begun to fight the demons, Charlie and my father were glaring at each other, but I couldn't find Violante.

"Looking for me?" came a shrill laugh from behind me.

"Not anymore." I said, turning to face her.

"Well, this is it." she said, more to herself.

"Oh, you know you'll miss me." I taunted.

"No, I'll kill you!" she said, taking out her sword.

"How about you all just leave me alone!!" I yelled, finally frustrated.

"How about not, send me a postcard from hell."

"Didn't you hear? Angels go to Heaven." I grinned. I knew I'd picked the right words. She came toward me and *tried* to throw me off the cliff that we were standing on. But at the last second, I tripped her. She fell over the edge, instead of me.

"That was way to ea-" I was about to say 'easy,' but something hit me in the back and I fell to the ground. I could tell that my back was bleeding because I could see it soaking through my shirt and pooling on the ground. But I couldn't feel anything because my back was numb.

"Come now Reilly, get up." my dad laughed. I realized I had my eyes closed. I opened them to see him standing over me, smiling. He kicked me in the ribs, forcing my body to roll over so that I was laying on my side.

I stood up shakily, just inches away from him. Something registered in the back of my mind, I realized that the last time I'd seen him, he was fighting Charlie. I looked around and finally, to my relief, noticed that he was helping Edward.

"Oh yes, he's fine. I saw my chance to fight you and he went to help the other pathetic demon you keep company with." my dad laughed, I re-focused on him.

"He's a half-demon." I muttered, still in shock from my wound.

"So are you. And not only that but you're an Apostle too, you just don't belong anywhere, do you?" he was right in front of me now. "You soul is *mine*." he hissed.

I saw his hand move forward, claws outstretched. I heard the sickening crunch as they connected with the bones of my rib cage. But I didn't feel anything until he stood back and grinned. "A-asshole." I hissed. "I ha-ate y-you." I said, my voice getting fainter as I lost blood and oxygen.

"I know. I love your hatred. I feed off of it." he grinned. Then I felt someone's arm curl around my throat. I was being pulled off the cliff backwards. I lost my balance and tumbled over.

I grabbed a ledge just in time but I felt Violante's claws dig into my foot.

"Ow." I mumbled weakly.

"Shut up. Pull us up!" she screamed.
"I can't." I cried.
"Why not!?"
"*You're* too fat!"
"I'm not fat, just big boned!!"
"Well, your big bones are going to get us **both** killed!!" I screamed.
Suddenly, the rocks I had a hold of began to crumble.
"We are so dead!!" I groaned. Violante laughed.
"But at least I finally get to kill you."
"Not if I let go." I warned.
"Don't you dare." Charlie growled, he was standing on the ledge above us.
"When did you get here?" Violante hissed.
"Shut up." I said.
"Can't you just…let go?" Charlie asked Violante.
"That wasn't funny."
"I'm serious."
"NO!!" She shrieked. She was moving around so much that my grip loosened.
"Quit moving!!"
"Why?"
"Just don't do it--whoa!" she jerked again and my hand slid down the side of the cliff.
"Stop it!!" Charlie said, panicking.
"Aw, but why?"
"Violante, if we live through this, I'm gonna murder you!"
"That's a big 'if'!"
"Try to reach my hand!" Charlie called. So I tried, but I couldn't, (at least, not with fatty holding on.)
"I can't!" I said, then my hand slid again.
"Try again!"
"I-stop moving!!"
"Why?"
"Because, if we fall, you'll die too."
"Good point."
"Try again." Charlie begged. So I let go of the rocks with one hand, and they fell!

"We're gonna fall!"

"No! You are *not* going to fa-" Someone pulled Charlie away from the edge. Whoever it was, and I had a pretty good guess, was now fighting him. (And there's more good news,) the rocks were now falling, and so were we!!

"This is all *your* fault." Violante shrieked.

"Excuse me?! You were the one who wouldn't just *die*!!" I shouted back.

Then we plunged into the lava.

Chapter 22
The End...I Think

At first, all I felt was intense heat all around me. But that slowly went away. 'I'm dying.' I thought. But I could still hear the battle, 'Great, I really am in Hell. Where's Violante?'

I heard Charlie's voice, it was right next to the edge. "I will **kill** you for that." he hissed. Then I heard the sound of pure evil, my father's laughter.

"Oh, you truly are stupid if you envisioned any other end for you two than this." my dad said. Charlie screamed in frustration and his voice was closer.

"Even if **I** don't kill you, Edward will for what you said about Kara." he said. What?

"I don't care, Reilly's dead, and that's all I wanted to do. Killing you is just a bonus." then I realized what was happening, Charlie was being forced off the cliff! That was definitely **not** going to happen. Not him too, not this way!

I didn't care if I was dead, alive, or even an angel. I was going to save Charlie. I went into full form, (It's much easier now,) and flew to the top. The lava followed me and I reached the edge with a ton of fire power behind me.

I leapt in between my dad and Charlie and glared at my father, "Next time you kill someone," I hissed, (But I was pretty sure I was alive,) "you might want to make sure they're dead before you kill the one they love." (Did I just say the L-word? I **must** be part angel.)

"Amazing, the Apostle of Justice awak-"

"Is gonna kick your ass." I finished for him. (Though I was sure he was going to say 'awakens' but where's the fun in that?)

"I thought you were dead." My dad hissed, losing his good humor. I still had mine.

"I know, but falling off a cliff into a pit of magma has *so* been done before." I said.

"Ugh!!" my dad screamed in frustration. Clearly this was *not* what he had envisioned.

He tried to attack me, but my powers were way stronger now. (Maybe this whole Apostle thing wasn't so bad.) I moved and dug my claws into his back. He stopped and flinched away from me.

"You…are going to pay for that." he said through the blood.

"When?" I asked, he didn't have an answer, so I laughed.

"I'm as strong as you, Reilly."

"Yes."

"And as fast."

"Yeah…but are you as pissed off as I am, and don't say 'yes' because I highly doubt it!" I growled, my voice shaking with fury as I moved toward him. When I attacked, so did he, and the resulting explosion was equal to a nuclear warhead. The impact knocked us both backward, but didn't' knock us out of the air.

My dad was the first to recover from the shock. He came toward me and I remembered something he'd said before. *'I know, I love your hatred. I feed off of it.'* I grinned and tried a different approach.

"Daddy?" I asked meekly. He stopped so I continued, tears filling my eyes, (mixed with blood from my multiple injuries.) "Please don't hurt me." I cried, my voice breaking. It was barely a whisper, but my dad looked, almost sorry.

"What?!" he asked. Stunned, he began backing away.

"No! daddy, don't leave me." I screamed, panic flooding my voice. I realized I was no longer faking it, I went with that feeling.

"Shut up!" My dad thundered, springing toward me. He smacked my face with his claws out. Fresh blood filled my mouth but I continued, saying the words that would, surely, destroy him,

"Daddy, I love you." I said. He screamed and shimmered away.

I looked around and found Charlie. Seeing that he was safe I smiled. Then…everything went black.

Chapter 23
Nightmares

I was almost positive that I was still unconscious. Considering A.) I was completely unharmed, and B.) I was looking at my mother.

"Mom?" I asked, still shocked. She nodded, and held out her hand, beckoning me to come to her.

I stood up and ran toward her. But then her expression changed, and I stopped dead. It went from kind and loving, to horrified in an instant. But she wasn't looking at me, she seemed to be looking *passed* me at something.

I turned around to see what she saw, and there they were. Violante and my dad were just a few yards away, behind them was a whole *army* of demons. None of them were legion, they were all *way* stronger than that.

My dad shimmered away and I heard my mom scream. I whirled around to see that he was killing her all over again. And I was forced to watch it happen, again. I tried to scream, but nothing came out. I tried to run to her, but I couldn't move.

I closed my eyes and heard the screaming stop abruptly. I knew it was over then. I turned back to Violante, and my dad was back in his place next to her.

"Where are your friends now, Reilly?" Violante mocked.

"It's not real, just a nightmare." I told myself. They all laughed.

"Oh, it's very real." my dad noted.

"This isn't happening, only a nightmare." I said again. But I only half believed it was true this time. Then I felt all of my injuries returning to me with more force than before. I screamed and sank to the ground in pain.

"They left you here." Violante said, I could hear the laughter in her voice, but didn't look up.

"They wouldn't leave me, well Edward would, but Charlie-"

"Ran for his life. If he really cared about you at all, he would've taken you with him. But he didn't, he saved *his* life because he doesn't care whether or not *you* survive." my dad said.

"He *does* care." I said. I meant to sound strong, but the words came out in a whisper and my voice shook with understanding.

"You know you don't believe that." Violante said. Then her laughter echoed through the cavern.

"I-I do be-lieve it." I said quietly.

"You're not dreaming Reilly. you're completely awake. And now I'm going to make sure I kill you," My dad said. I looked up and realized that he was now only a few *feet* in front of me. He closed the space with about two steps forward and lifted me up by the arm. Which hurt like hell because it was the same side that he'd clawed down my back on earlier.

"This will be fun." he smiled, (yeah, for *you* maybe, but something tells me that *I'm* not going to enjoy it at all.) He moved his other hand so that his fingers were enclosed tightly around my neck. I could no longer breath.

"Just do it." Violante begged. Clearly she wasn't happy that she couldn't help.

"Just killing her is *not* fun." my dad said, throwing me back to the ground. "She needs to suffer first."

"What!?" Violante shouted.

"Get up!" my dad screamed, I didn't move. "I said, GET UP!!" he grabbed me by the throat once more and lifted me off the ground.

Then he flung me backwards effortlessly. I landed on my feet, but was unable to save myself from slamming into the rock wall behind me. My back hit the wall with so much force that it knocked me forward again and I fell, face first, to the ground.

I didn't move, "Get up, now!" my dad shouted. He couldn't have been too far away.

"Why?" I asked.

"Because I'm going to *fight* you. Then, after you're dead, I'm going to kill Keira, Edward, Charity," I looked up, waiting, "and Charlie." his face twisted into a hideous grin. Then he tried to put his foot on my back, pinning me to the ground. But I rolled out of the way and escaped behind a rock. "Oh, Reilly, don't tell me you're *running away*! Come back out here and face me, I want to **watch** the life leaving your eyes!" I gritted my teeth, if he wanted a fight, he had one.

"As you wish." I growled, coming out into the open, my hands clenched into fists. With a growl, (yes, he actually **growled** at me,) my dad went into full form. I did too, (minus the growl.)

"I hope you like hell because you're going to be spending the rest of your pathetic existence there." I snarled. Then I tackled him to the ground, pinning his arms with my hands.

"You'll be coming with me." he howled, then he rolled over, sending me flying into the air and sliding a few feet when I landed.

Suddenly, I felt as if my head was being ripped off and my body shredded. Which is what I thought was happening, until I saw that neither my dad and Violante, nor the army of demons, had moved.

Then they all disappeared, and I was in a hospital bed surrounded by doctors and nurses and hooked up to all sorts of machines. I screamed as loud as I could and the pain continued. Then I got up and ripped all of the needles out of my skin.

A doctor looked at me, grinned, and then his face twisted into my father's. He came toward me, arms outstretched in my direction. "No!!" I screamed, sending a blast of dark energy toward him. It knocked him out of the windows, along with shattering all of the glass, (including the windows,) and blasted the door into the hall.

I glanced over to the hall and saw, standing in the doorway, Edward (who was rubbing his head,) Keira, Charity, and Charlie, all looking horrified.

I was trying to be thankful that I **had** been dreaming before, but more doctors or images of my dad, (at that point I wasn't sure which they were anymore,) were coming toward me. I turned on them, trying to remember if these were doctors or demons. Then one glared at me as if I'd tried to kill him, (which I hadn't, yet.) I decided on demons and leapt toward them.

Chapter 24
Goodbyes

"Reilly, don't!" I heard Charity scream. I grabbed one's collar but something stopped me from clawing his heart out. I heard a strange, angelic, sound. I heard *singing*. I hesitated, then blocked it out and went with my original, gruesome, plan.

"NO! Reilly, stop!" Charlie shouted. I couldn't tell where his voice was coming from, but something was holding me back from killing a doctor or demon.

"I have to make him go away!" I shrieked.

"Who?" Charlie asked, spinning me around to face him.

"My dad! He's here, he's *everywhere*, and he won't leave me alone!!" I said, I started to cry both out of frustration and desperation.

"No, he's not here, Reilly, these are doctors. they're trying to *help* you, not kill you." he assured me, I shook my head.

"No they're not."

He turned to the others, "It's not working, she doesn't believe me." he shouted, helplessly.

"Try something else!" Edward cried, his eyes wide with horror. I broke free of Charlie's grasp and went back to the demon or doctor, or *whatever* it was, but Charlie caught me around the waist.

"No, Reilly, please listen to me." he begged.

"You're lying!" I screamed, "You're only trying to protect him!" my voice sounded betrayed. He looked hurt, he let go of my waist and held my face in his hands.

"Reilly, I love you, I would *never* try to hurt you." he promised, then he moved his face closer to mine.

"But you---he said that you…left me, back at the volcano." I said, my voice barely a whisper.

"He lied, I couldn't have left you because I never would've tried." he was whispering now, too.

"I…" I couldn't think of anything to say, then the pain started again, the horrible pain that made me feel like I was being forced into a paper shredder. I screamed and sank to the ground. Charlie knelt down with me, his face helpless. "Help me, please." I begged. Everything was blurring, and I felt dizzy. He must've thought I was going to pass out, (And, to be honest, so did I,) because he caught my arms, pulling me closer to him. He looked into my eyes, and then, we kissed. For the first time in my life I felt safe, not like at any moment my life would end. But whole, completed.

It didn't last long, and when it was over a new wave of tears flooded down my face. He just sat there with me and held me close as I cried. That's when I realized what had just taken place. I pulled away and stood up.

"I'm sorry." I whispered.

"For what?" he asked. I looked up at him and noticed that everyone else had gathered around us.

"Everything, especially this." I said, then I backed away.

"Please, no." he begged, but I kept retreating.

"What's happening?" Keira asked.

"Reilly's l-leaving." Charity said.

"Why?" Keira screamed.

"Because if I stay here, I could kill you all." I answered her, not looking away from Charlie.

"Reilly, don't." he said. Coming toward me, he grabbed my hand and pulled me into a hug. I hugged him back.

"Goodbye," I whispered, "I love you."

It was the first time I'd ever said the words. And we both realized it. Then, I pulled away from him, and shimmered away. Away from my life, my friends, and the only person I'd ever loved, **never** to return again. At least, that's what I thought, but I've been wrong before.

The End

Angel of Darkness
By: Amanda Boyer with Ellen Ritchie

Angel of Darkness

'Gliding among the living,
   with unseeing eyes.
Feeling like a mere shadow,
   ever since my soul died.
Humans remain unknowing,
   my kind flee with fear.
Even the strongest of us,
   now cower when I come near.
Damnation is a curse,
   no one has but me.
My prison was locked long ago,
   and destiny threw away the key.'

-Amanda Boyer

Contents

Secrets	129
Sedrick	133
Spy	137
Chase and Capture	141
Imprisoned	142
Sedrick's Story (part of it, anyway)	146
Sign 2	150
Friend or Foe?	153
Goodbyes *Never* Last	157
Promise	162
Return	166
My Demented Brother	171
Broken Vow	175
Strange Demons	177
Cross Barrier	180
Keira's Rescue	184
Evil Plan	187
Tragedy	190
Guilt	195
The Key	198
Mind Trick	206
The Hall of Scrolls	209
Secret Password	211
More Secrets	221
A Miracle?	225
Kara's Final Words and The Real Evil Villain	228
Taste of Darkness	231
Captive	237
The Apostles' Purpose	241
Free At Last	251
Enter into Hell	257

Chapter 1
Secrets

I was utterly confused now. I had been so busy trying to get away from Charlie, (who had been following me since I left, two weeks ago,) that I hadn't been paying attention to where I was going.

Now, though I wasn't sure, I guessed I was somewhere in the far southern corner of the Underworld. But I had to get to the far North.

"This is just great." I sighed. Not only was I *way* far away from where I needed to go, but I was in a place that I had spent my entire life trying to escape.

"Hey! What are you-? Oh my Lucifer!" a demon exclaimed when he saw me. "Your majesty."

"What!?" I said, looking around for Jezaba, if I haven't told you, *he* is the ruler of the Underworld.

"Get King Lieam down here fast, I've found the princess!" he called into a small cell phone. Wait, did he just say, 'princess!?'

Lieam is my father, and he has been trying to kill me, (long story). That's why I left Keira, Edward, and Charity behind. (I tried to leave Charlie behind, but as I said before, he followed me).

"Reilly!" Charlie called, (well, speak of the devil, quite literally actually). snapping me out of my thoughts. I looked around to see him standing off to my left. But he wasn't the only person who had appeared. My dad, flanked by six other demons and devils, was now in front of me.

"Reilly, what are *you* doing here?" my dad asked.

"I'm looking for Sedrick, have you seen him?" I inquired. Now I *know* you don't know who *that* is. Sedrick is sort of like my brother, we're not actually related, but he acted like my older brother, (he's older by about a year,) and he helped me escape here. My dad's been trying to find and kill him ever since. But Sedrick's almost as sneaky as me, so needless to say, my dad's had little luck.

"No, I have yet to see your brother, do you know where he is?"

"Why would I be **looking** for him, if I **knew** where he was?!" I yelled.

"Just making sure. Oh and Charlie's here as well. I should've known that you'd follow her." he laughed, I noticed that Charlie was now right beside me. "Any way," my dad continued, "Reilly, you have to come with us." the soldiers closed in tighter in their circle around us. (Now when did *they* get here?)

"Do I? Why is that?" I asked.

"Because, we can't have the heir to the throne of the whole demonic empire running around with two Apostles of God, a pitiful half-demon and, " he glared at Charlie, "a pathetic excuse for a devil."

Normally I would've tried to rip his throat out for those kinds of comments, but something he said confused me, "heir to the **what**, now?"

"Oh, that's right, no one's told her!" my father laughed, he was no longer speaking to me, but to the many demonic soldiers surrounding he, Charlie, and I. They joined in his laughter. Then he stopped laughing and made a motion to cut everyone else off as well, "You are the heir to the demonic throne, princess of the Underworld.

"What? How!?" I demanded.

"Because, dear daughter, I am the king." he said simply.

"Jezaba is the king." Charlie growled.

"No, I let that charade go on simply because it works in my favor. You see, if everyone thinks that Jezaba rules, then when there comes time for a power struggle, they'll kill him. Then I am free to take his place."

"What happens when there's **another** power struggle?" I asked.

"Then they'll kill *you*." he shrugged.

I let out a short laugh, "not if I don't go with you."

"You seem to be under the mistaken impression that I'm giving you a choice." he laughed, then made a signal to the many, waiting demons. All he did was move one finger, but neither Charlie nor I missed it.

"I think we should leave." Charlie suggested, as the soldiers got ready to attack.

"Uh…yeah." I said, I grabbed his hand and shimmered, taking him with me.

"Where are we?" Charlie asked, when we reappeared seconds later in front of a cave.

"Uh…somewhere in the northern part of the Underworld…I think." I answered, he looked at me,

"You *think?!* I-"

"Don't *have* to stay here, you have powers and can return to the others any time you like. Besides, I'd rather you *did* go back to Keira, Charity, and Edward. My dad will eventually kill me and I don't want him to kill you too," I said, fiercely.

"I'm not leaving you! Especially after what happened two weeks ago!" he said. Two weeks ago I was in the hospital in a coma. When I woke up, I kind of tried to kill everyone inside the room. But I had a feeling he was referring to what happened *after* that. You see, after I tried to kill half the hospital staff, Charlie and I kissed for the first time. And I told him that I loved him, also for the first time. We both knew it, of coarse, but it was the first time I'd actually *said* the words.

"Have it your way then." I said. Deciding that this was the cavern I needed, I walked through the opening.

"Where are you going!?" Charlie demanded, keeping close by my side.

"Just trust me, I'm going to call Sedrick." I explained.

"Who *is* this guy?!"

"He's my brother, sort of. I mean, he's not actually related to me, but he helped me escape here and he always acted like my brother." I said, then I added, "besides you, he's my best friend."

"Are you sure we can trust him?" he asked, I glared at him.

"Yes, I'm positive. Were you listening to *anything* I said just now?" I asked.

"Fine, how are we supposed to call him?" notice how he didn't answer my question?

"I use my powers, and you wait."

"Fine." he sighed. We got away from the mouth of the cave and I sat down in the middle of an open area. "What are you doing?" Charlie asked.

"Shhhh." I hissed. I closed my eyes, and concentrated. Letting the darkness help me send Sedrick a signal.

I don't know how long I sat there, but it must have been a while because I felt Charlie's hand on my shoulder, "Reilly? Are you ok?" he asked.

I jumped, "what?" but then recovered quickly, "yeah, I think he got it."

"Ok, I need to talk to you." he said, he looked worried.

"What is it?" I asked.

"Before you left the hospital, do you remember what you said?" he asked, I nodded,

"Yes."

"Did you really mean it?" he asked, I answered without hesitation,

"Yes." I said.

"Really? Or are you just saying that?"

"Really. I meant exactly what I said, I do love you." I sighed, "even when you don't listen to me and you follow me to the Underworld anyway."

He grinned, "good, because I have to tell you something."

"Oh yeah, what's that?" I asked.

"Reilly, I love you." he said, I rolled my eyes.

"You already said that." I said.

"Yes, but I haven't said it when you **weren't** trying to kill me yet."

"I wasn't trying to kill *you*." I noted, he put his arm around me.

"Close enough, you said that I was protecting your dad."

"I was delirious." And on too much pain medication apparently, because I definitely don't remember that part.

"I know," he sighed, "that's why I thought-"

"You didn't let me finish. I was delirious until *after* we kissed, I don't remember what I said *before*."

"Sure you don't." he said, rolling his eyes.

"Really, I don't."

"Reilly?" came a familiar voice from the mouth of the cave. I looked up to see someone walking inside.

Chapter 2
Sedrick

"It took you long enough." I said, pretending to be angry. "Well I would've been here sooner, but the message I got was *very* hard to understand!" he laughed, I rolled my eyes.

"Whatever." I sighed.

"Who's he?" Sedrick asked, indicating Charlie.

"This is Charlie." I said.

"Hi, I'm Sedrick."

"I think he figured that out, stupid." I said, Sedrick ignored me.

"Why are you here?" he asked.

"Because I followed Reilly here." Charlie said.

"Why? What's wrong, Reilly?" Sedrick asked, turning to me. I began to explain what had occurred with my dad, but Charlie answered for me,

"I followed her because I love her, and what's wrong is that her dad is trying to take her back to the castle." he explained.

"Oh."

"Sedrick, did you know about this?" I asked, glaring at him.

"You mean that whole princess thing? Kind of. But I didn't think he would actually *want* you to take his place."

"Sedrick, I need your help." I said.

"With?" he asked.

"Control over my powers, my choices were either you or dad." I said.

"Ah, I see." he sighed.

"So do I!" said another voice, Sedrick and I froze. Charlie moved next to me.

"Lieam!" Sedrick hissed.

"Sedrick, please, call me father."

"Ok, *father*, what do you want?" Sedrick asked. Then he, too, moved closer to me.

"Judging by the way that you and the devil are standing next to Reilly, I'd have guessed that you already knew!!" my dad laughed again before appearing a few yards away from us.

"Why do you need Reilly?" Sedrick asked.

"I think you know."

"No."

My dad sighed, "because, Sedrick, Reilly has to come to the castle with me.

"I don't think *that* will happen." Charlie growled.

"Then I'll get *you* out of my way." my dad hissed, then there was a flash of light. When it was gone, Charlie and Sedrick were unconscious and my dad had me pinned against the wall. "Reilly, that was too easy. You shouldn't keep company with such weak people." he said.

"They aren't weak." I said, struggling to get free.

"Oh yes, I'd forgotten how much you 'care' for Charlie. Well, don't worry, he and Sedrick will wake up soon. Though it will be too late to save you."

"I don't need saving." I growled, putting as much acid into my voice as I could manage.

"Don't you? Look around, Reilly, your brother and boyfriend lay unconscious and it's just you and me." he said.

"And I'm sure you remember what happened the last time it was just you and me." I snarled. He seemed to remember something, then he smiled,

"I seem to remember watching you fall backwards off a cliff." he laughed.

"And I seem to remember coming back and kicking your ass."

"You cheated." he said.

"I'm a demon, we tend to do that occasionally." I said, the words made his smile widen,

"Half-demon, let's not forget what else you are." he said. This time, it was my turn to smile,

"Yes, I seem to recall using that 'other half' of my power to send you shimmering back to the Underworld." I said, my grin widening. I could tell that he was weakening.

"You won't have a chance to-" he began, but I didn't give him a chance to finish, my entire body erupted into flames, and I slid out of his grasp. Once I was behind him, I used my dark energy to pin him to the wall in my place. This only made him laugh, "very good, Reilly, you're getting the hang of this little game."

"Game over, dad." I snarled.

"No, my dear, this was just round one." he smiled again, and then was gone.

"Damn it." I hissed, then I turned back to Sedrick and Charlie, only to see that they were awake and giving me very surprised looks. "What?" I asked.

"Are you sure you need my help?" Sedrick asked.

"Trust me on this one." I sighed, walking toward them. Then everything faded to reveal many pictures passing through my mind. The first was of Kara, the second Keira, then Edward came into view. After that was one of Kara and Keira fighting, then I saw Edward help **Kara** and not Keira. Then they disappeared to reveal two *very* concerned faces looking at me.

I realized that I had, at some point, fallen. I also realized that Charlie had, apparently, caught me because I was in his arms.

"What happened?" he asked.

"Keira, and Kara, and Edward." I gasped.

"Kara?" he asked, I nodded and sat up so that I was sitting in his lap. "What about them?" he asked, putting his arms around me and leaning me against his chest.

"Not sure." I managed, "not good."

"Do you want to go check it out?" Sedrick asked from somewhere beside us.

"Not if I have to leave her." Charlie replied.

"I'll be fine." I said, but it didn't sound as convincing as I would have liked.

"I'll look after her, besides, I have to teach her to control her powers." Sedrick said. Charlie looked at me,

"Is that ok?" he asked.

"No, but you can go anyway. After all, I would **hate** for something bad to happen to Edward." I grinned. He rolled his eyes, gave me a hug, and then left.

I was surprised when I felt tears run down my face because I wasn't sure why I was crying. "he'll be fine. And the sooner we get started, the sooner you can join him." Sedrick said reassuringly.

"Ok." I whispered, still short of breath.

Chapter 3
Spy

"Reilly, you have to control your anger." Sedrick was saying for about the millionth time.

"Don't you think I know that? It's a lot easier said than done." I complained.

"Reilly, you're not listening."

"Sedrick, you're getting on my nerves." we had been 'training' for over a week and I was tired of hearing the words, 'control' and 'anger' in the same sentence.

"Do you want to see Charlie again or not?!" he asked, he's such a cheater!

"Fine." I sighed angrily in defeat. I took a deep breath and Sedrick began to make me very angry by taunting me. (he said it was the only way to 'test' me, but I think he just wanted to piss me off. We may not be blood but he is **definitely** my brother).

I could feel my self getting mad so I took another deep breath, then I could no longer hear anything. "Sedrick?" I asked, alarmed at the sudden silence. I couldn't sense anything either, which both freaked me out and pissed me off. "Sedrick?" I asked, I sensed him shimmer behind me and I whirled around to face him. "What the hell was that about?" I asked.

"You started glowing, so I left." He shrugged.

"Glowing, how?" I asked suspiciously, I was recalling a time a while back when I had also been glowing. That was right before I sent a wave of energy straight at my uncle, Mathew. He had tried to kill me so I defended myself and my friends, but I wasn't aware that I had **that** much power. He kind of…exploded.

"Well, you were surrounded by orange and black light. Your fire and dark energy, I guess." he explained, in answer to my question. I snapped out of my thoughts and listened. "it was like you were directing all of your power to focus on the thing that was making you mad. Since that was me, I bailed." he finished.

I grinned, "so does this mean that I have control?!" I asked, excited.

"It means that you have *some* control, yes. But you have to be in complete control in order to have the kind of power you're going to need." Sedrick explained, I frowned.

"the kind of power I'm going to need for what?" I asked, confused.

"Reilly, now that Dad has decided to take you to the castle, you're going to have to kill him in order to stay." he said, seriously. I glared at the ground in front of me,

"Fine with me." I said, icily.

"Let's do that again. But this time, try to hold back, don't attack. We can't have you killing everyone who makes you a little pissed off, now can we?" he asked, smiling.

"Ok. And I don't see why I can't kill everyone who pisses me off. I mean, it would give me a *great* excuse to get rid of Edward." I said, Sedrick rolled his eyes.

☆ ☆ ☆

That's pretty much how the rest of the day went. I kept trying to attack and to hold back. And Sedrick kept telling me what I was doing right and wrong. But by that night, I was anxious to leave.

"What if something happened?" I asked Sedrick, while pacing back and forth.

"Nothing happened, he's fine." he assured me, as he had been for the past hour.

"But what if Dad followed him and he-" I couldn't say it, but we both knew what I meant.

"Reilly, please, you need to quit worrying about Charlie's safety and start worrying about your own. You know that dad's after *you*." Sedrick said, standing in front of me to stop my pacing.

"Sedrick, move." I snarled.

"Reilly, calm down." he hissed, with just as much venom.

"Ugh! This is so *frustrating!*" I screamed at myself.

"I know, but you have to realize that Charlie isn't the one in danger, you are." Sedrick said soothingly.

"Yeah but that doesn't mean that I can't worry about him. Dad knows that if he kills Charlie, he destroys me." I said.

"But he also knows that if he kills Charlie, you won't go anywhere near the castle." Sedrick pointed out.

"When can I leave?" I asked.

"Why are you in such a hurry?" he asked with a grin. I glared at him,

"You are so not amusing." I said.

"I haven't seen you since you escaped when you were *five* and now you want to leave with in the month you got here. I missed you, little sister." he said.

"I missed you too but-"I trailed off. It was the smallest of sounds, but Sedrick and I both heard it.

"Play along." Sedrick whispered, then more loudly he asked, "so, what should we try next?"

"Uh...I don't know. Don't I need to work on more, *'control'*?" I asked, Sedrick motioned for me to continue, "I don't think I will be able to kill Dad...yet." I said.

Suddenly, Sedrick jumped into a shadowed area of the cave, when he reappeared, he was dragging what looked like an over grown frog.

"Ashelin!?!?" I screamed, recognizing Violante's servant from before.

"Ahhhh! Don't hurt me!! I swear, I didn't know what she wanted me to do, she just said to wait here for her." Ashelin screeched, hiding behind Sedrick.

"Friend of yours?" he asked, raising his eyebrows.

"Hardly." I said, dragging Ashelin out into the open. "is Violante coming here?!" I growled.

"I think so." she said, I sighed angrily and she added, "please don't hurt me."

"How much did you hear? How long have you been here?" I snarled.

"Uh...since before the other guy left. All I heard was stuff about a throne, and a castle." she said.

"What else?" I hissed. My words made her flinch as if I'd smacked her, (which I was seriously considering).

"That's it! Oh, except something about a King Lieam and a Princess Reilly. And about Kara, is she really back? Oh I mean...

oops." she said. She knew the minute she'd said it that she'd revealed too much.

"Don't you *dare* tell Violante *anything* you heard." I growled.

"But she'll kill me!" she shrieked.

"That's ten times better than anything I'll do to you if she *does* find out." I threatened, she nodded frantically in agreement. "Go, and if I find out that you told her, and I will, I'll hunt you down." I snarled, she shook her head, 'yes' and then left.

"Who is that?" Sedrick asked.

"Ashelin, she's one of Violante's helpers." I explained.

"We need to leave." Sedrick said, suddenly freezing as he listened for a sound that I hadn't heard yet.

"What, why-whoa!" I exclaimed as he suddenly grabbed my arm and shimmered, dragging me with him. "what's going on!?" I screamed when we reappeared in a place that I wasn't familiar with.

"Lieam is following us, he's after you and this time he doesn't plan on asking politely." Sedrick said before shimmering again.

Chapter 4
Chase and Capture

"Sedrick, where the hell are we?" I asked the next morning. We had shimmered around all night trying to escape my father.

"Uh…"

"Tell me you know," I begged, "please!"

"Well…I wasn't really paying attention to where I was going, I was just trying to get away from Lieam." doesn't *that* sound familiar.

"Well, you're not very good at it." came a harsh voice from behind us, "I had no trouble tracking you." my dad continued, as Sedrick and I turned around and Sedrick got in between Lieam and I.

"How sweet of you, Sedrick, to protect your baby sister. But you know it will do you no good. I effortlessly flung you aside last time and I won't hesitate to do so again." Lieam cackled, appearing just a few feet in front of us.

"I'll be ready for you this time, I'll protect her."

"Like you did when she was a baby?"

"I was younger then too, you know."

"What are you talking about?!" I demanded, getting the feeling that I'd missed something.

"Sedrick, would *you* like to explain?" my dad asked.

"No." he mumbled, looking apologetically at me.

"Then I will later, after I bring her to the castle!" my dad said, he talks as if 'her' isn't standing right there.

"I'm not going to the-" I began, but this time I was the one who didn't finish my sentence. He moved so quickly that I didn't have time to. He was behind me in seconds. Though I couldn't see his face, it was easy to hear in his voice that he was smirking at Sedrick as he said,

"Goodbye, Sedrick. It was nice to see you again." then, everything went black.

Chapter 5
Imprisoned

I woke up to see a very large wall. (I know, I know, very anti-climactic, right? But, hey, it's what I saw). "So you're finally awake." Ashelin's shrill laugh rang from behind me.

"Ashelin!? You were the one who led my father to me!?" I yelled.

"Yes. You only said that I couldn't tell Violante where you were. So I didn't." she laughed again and it echoed throughout the small, metal room.

"I'm going to-" I started, but as soon as I moved toward her, there was a sharp pain in my head, forcing me to the ground.

"Going to what? You're surrounded by a barrier, if you so much as think about moving, then you'll get electrocuted." she laughed as she pulled a small control panel out of her pocket, "and only *I* can control that force field." I wasn't sure, but I assumed that if that control was destroyed, that the force field would be also.

"Where's my dad?" I asked, more out of annoyance of her than anxiety to see my father.

"He'll be back, he had to go talk to Jezaba." the little toad laughed.

"Why?" I asked, hoping she wouldn't notice that there was now a whirl of dark energy circling just above her head.

"Well, he's going to have Jezaba give a false message to Charlie." she said, oblivious to the danger she was in.

"What message?" I asked, now mixing fire with the darkness. Just a little more time, and I'd be free.

"Jezaba is going to tell Charlie that you're dead." she clapped gleefully, "that way, he won't come looking for you!"

"What happens when Sedrick tells him what really happened?" I inquired, waiting for her to be distracted again.

"That's the beauty of it all, Sedrick has gone into hiding again. No one knows where your brother is!" she laughed. I'd heard enough, I directed the energy straight at her.

"Do you know how stupid you are!?" I asked, standing up, "you really are as dumb as you look!" I said, answering my own question.

"What?" she asked, suddenly terrified.

"Ashelin, I'm a demon and you're a toad. Did you really think that you could keep me here!?" I said, I let out a laugh.

"N-no, I d-didn't th-think I c-could." she gasped, "he said that you wouldn't wake up until he got back."

"He lied, he does that a lot." I growled, as I released the energy. Because I was in a hurry to leave, I didn't aim. The attack missed Ashelin, hitting around her. It left her alive, but knocked out, on the ground, the control in pieces next to her. That wasn't all it did, however, my power was aimed well enough to blow up the walls surrounding me to reveal what I had feared all along. I was in the castle, trapped with in my childhood home.

"This is not good." I groaned.

"Princess Reilly, you must stay here!" a soft voice said. I whirled around to see three demons looking at me from where the door had been. Guards, I guessed, and they were armed.

"If you call me Princess one more time, I'm going to royally kick your ass." I said, they looked stubbornly at each other, and I saw my chance. I leapt passed them, (hoping I could move now without getting shocked,) and sprinted down the hall.

"Wait! Pr---your majesty! Wait!" I heard one of them call, but I didn't even slow down.

I knew from when I was little that the entire castle was protected from shimmering. Everywhere except one room, but it would be damn near impossible to get into.

I heard shouts of protest as I pushed past a group of soldiers on my way to the throne room, but I kept running. I really wasn't sure what I was going to do when I arrived at my destination, considering that there would probably be a whole butt load of soldiers waiting at the entrances. Not to mention, **King** Lieam.

"King, my ass, he's more like the court jester. And he's not even very funny, so I guess he's just worthless to the whole empire." I said to myself.

Though I didn't think so, I was still in shock from the past month's experiences.

I burst through the throne room doors and, sure enough, there was everyone I'd expected. "Reilly!?" my dad thundered, more angry than surprised.

"Yes?" I asked.

"You blew up my dungeon! You've destroyed that whole building!"

"Yeah, I'm good at that." I sighed,

"Stop her!" my dad shouted, several guards moved toward me but I was way faster. I shimmered before they came within a foot of me. There was one more thing I needed to find out, and I knew *exactly* where to get my answers.

✫ ✫ ✫

"Jezaba!!" Violante was screaming. I was hiding behind a pillar in his castle, and had been for what felt like an hour. Though I was sure I'd just arrived.

"What?!" they had been arguing since I got there, (which I wasn't sure how long that was anymore). At one point, I'd actually thought she was going to kill him.

"Kara can't return without more herbs! Keira's soul is stubborn!" (Why does that not surprise me?!) Violante shrieked for about the millionth time.

"Fine! Then get them, you know where they are!" Jezaba howled. Violante sighed angrily, and then shimmered out of the room. "Finally, she's gone." Jezaba sighed.

"Tell me about it." I laughed, stepping away from my hiding place.

"B-but h-he said that y-you were dead!" Jezaba stuttered.

"Do I look dead to you!?" I yelled, advancing forward with my claws outstretched.

"N-no, I guess n-not." he said, backing away.

"Jezaba, what *exactly* did you tell Charlie!?" I asked through clenched teeth.

"Uh…just that you were dead. And I might have mentioned the fact that if it hadn't been for me, your dad would *never* have been resurrected. But that was strictly for gloating purposes only!" he said,

then he grinned, "it did seem to make Charlie *really* mad, though."

"What happened!? What did you do!?" I snarled, his grin widened.

"Well, that's for me to know and you to never find out. You're not leaving here alive so you-"

"Ugh! I don't have time for your stupid, pointless speeches, Jezaba! I'm being *followed,* so either you tell me now, or I seriously *injure* you! Got it?!" I shrieked, frustrated.

"I'm in big trouble, aren't I?" he asked, but the grin didn't fade.

"Yes, you are." I said. I leapt at him, tackling him. We both flew over the throne, (actually it's an ugly chair that Jezaba sits on to feel important,) and landed, hard, on the ground.

I ducked my head, rolling to my feet. But Jezaba landed with a thud. "Ouch! Mean!!" he accused, I shrugged,

"Runs in the family." I sighed, (half of it anyway).

"Go away!!" he shouted, tripping me so that I fell not too far from him.

"Tell me what you did to him!" I hissed, getting back up. Jezaba, too, was rising to his feet.

"Never. You will find out if you live long enough. But, I assure you, you'll wish you never knew. Charlie was always weak, Reilly, unlike you and I. Now, however, he's not only weak, but pathetic as well."

"If one more person tells me how pathetic Charlie is, I'm going to rip their throat out!!" I snarled, once again lunging toward Jezaba. He caught my arm and twisted it behind my back, I heard a snap, and my arm filled with staggering pain.

I heard a shrill scream and was surprised to find out that it was me. "Jezaba!" I shrieked, twisting around to face him, his face was pale and he jumped back from me. I looked down to see that my hands were glowing and my stigmata were bleeding, but that wasn't the strangest part, where my blood had touched Jezaba's hand, it had eaten through his skin. "Great, acid blood. As if being an Apostle, *and* the Princess of the Underworld, wasn't enough." I growled, more to myself but I'd guessed that Jezaba had heard it.

"Help me..." he said, weakly. At first I thought he was speaking to me, but then I turned around to see that my dad and a few soldiers had appeared.

"Shit!" I mumbled, shimmering away. The last thing I heard was what *really* freaked me out,

"She burned me!" Jezaba whined.

"Good, it's beginning." my dad said triumphantly, now what the *hell* did he mean by that?

Chapter 6
Sedrick's Story (part of it, anyway)

I stumbled into the cavern about twenty minutes later. "Sedrick?" I called, not really expecting an answer.

"Yes?" well, that was odd.

"What are you doing here!? Do you have any idea how much danger you're in!?" I yelled, as Sedrick came over to me and looked at my shattered wrist.

"Yes, I'm well aware of that fact. What happened?" he asked, taking that hand in his to get a closer look.

"I got in a fight with Jezaba." I muttered.

"What?!" he asked, jerking my hand and sending waves of pain up my arm.

"Ouch!! Don't do that!" I said, in hailing a sharp breath with pain.

"Sorry, you got in a fight with Jezaba!?" he said, letting me go. I cradled my arm against my chest.

"Ow."

"Tell me!"

"He did something to Charlie, and he wouldn't tell me what. So I kicked his ass." I said, then I hesitated. Not sure if I should tell him **how** I beat Jezaba.

"And..."

"Well, I burned him."

"What's so bad about that?"

"I burned him with my blood." I said, his eyes widened.

"This is not good." he said.

"What? What does it mean?" I asked, panicking at the fear in his voice.

"Uh…nothing, don't worry about it." he said, as he bandaged my hand. But immediately following this, the bandage burst into flames and disintegrated into ash.

"What the hell?!" I shouted, jumping back from the pile of dust. "Why did it do that?"

"What are *you* worried about, Reilly?" Sedrick asked, also backing away, "it won't hurt *you*."

"What does it mean?!" I asked, he shook his head, "tell me!!"

"It will only scare you." he said, I glared at him.

"Sedrick, I'm terrified. Tell me!!" I snarled.

"It's the first sign, but I didn't think it would appear that quickly."

"First sign of what?" I hissed, he was beginning to be as vague as Edward.

"Dad told you what you are, correct?" he asked.

"You mean that whole, 'princess' thing? Yeah, why?" I asked, suspiciously.

"Well, the ruler of the Underworld can't be a half-demon, nor can they be good. The first sign is when your demon blood begins the change to be strong enough to take over." he explained, at first I was only stuck on the whole 'blood getting strong enough to basically ruin my life thing. But then the first part of what he'd said sunk in, my eyes widened and my breath came in gasps.

"I-I'm turning e-evil?" I asked, weakly. I couldn't help but think of what Edward would've said, "Aw sweet Jesus!" I groaned.

"Well, it's going to take a while. Especially with the whole Apostle thing." Sedrick said encouragingly.

"You're not helping." I groaned, "is that all?" I asked, afraid of the answer.

"No."

"What else?" I sighed.

"Uh…well…"

"Sedrick, tell me." I snarled.

"But it's not as easy to go through as the first sign." he said, "it's more painful."

"Sweet Jesus, Sedrick, just say it!!" I yelled.

"Well, the second sign involves your stigmata." he explained, "they'll re-open and spread across your entire body, covering you with markings that are a warning. Any demon or devil who sees you will know what's happening to you." I gulped.

"All of them?" I asked.

"Yes, Reilly, I'm afraid so."

"Great…"

"Reilly, if he loves you then he'll understand."

"When does it start?" I sighed.

"Should start soon."

"Any more 'signs' after that?" I asked.

"One."

"What is it?" I sighed again. I was beginning to get extremely annoyed.

"I'm not positive."

"What!!?"

"Well, I never knew that one! Dad didn't tell me!"

"Why did he tell you the first two? And that reminds me, what the hell were you two talking about before?!" I asked, Sedrick winced.

"I don't want to talk about it."

"Oh yes you do!" I said.

"No, I really don't."

"Sedrick…"

"Reilly…" this is so unfair!

I began to reply but my vision was once again blocked with scenes from something else. This time, however, the pictures were moving, as if they were happening at that exact moment. I saw Kara pointing several arrows at me and releasing them. They pinned me to the wall and one went through my hand, which I felt, surprisingly.

Then the vision fast forwarded to where I glanced over to see arrows lying not to far away. "give me those." a harsh voice commanded and I realized that *I* was the one speaking, but the voice belonged to Keira.

"Why? You can't hold-" a familiar voice said from somewhere beside me.

"Give me the God damn arrows!" I, or rather Keira, shouted. Then the vision skipped ahead ***again***, (which was giving me a major headache,) to reveal Keira, or me, ***throwing*** the arrow like a spear. It landed about two feet in front of us.

"That landed pretty far." Charlie laughed.

"Shut up! Just because some ancient Greek barbarian can do it, doesn't mean I can!!" Keira shouted, I laughed, (I don't think the Greeks *were* barbarians).

"You're so stupid, Keira." I remarked. Then the vision ended, bringing me back to reality with staggering speed.

"Whoa." I said, before I felt the stinging pain in my hands. Sedrick looked at me with horror.

Chapter 7
Sign 2

"Reilly, don't panic." Sedrick said calmly, though his face was pale white.

"Don't panic!? Sedrick, my freaking *hands* are on fire!!" I yelled, my voice shook with fear.

"It's not my fault she stumbled off the cliff!" I heard Keira's voice. But I didn't see anyone. (great, not again!)

"Reilly, are you ok?" Sedrick asked.

"H-hold o-on, I-I'm listening to an-other conversation." I said.

"Huh?" he asked, but it was faint, because Charlie's voice was louder.

"You're the one who shot the arrow." he said.

"Damn it Charlie!" I heard Keira say, I stepped in.

"Leave him alone." I growled, Keira started screaming about 'voices' and I rolled my eyes. Then she was talking about how mad I was, "I'm not mad, I'm in pain." I began, referring to the cuts covering my hands. Again, more yelling.

"Keira, listen to me." I began, "you're all in serious danger, I'm changing. And I don't know how long it will take. Don't come near me, and I will probably not come *anywhere* near you all. Bye, Keira." I said.

"What are you doing?" Sedrick asked.

"Warning Keira, hold on." I replied, Keira didn't understand, I could tell.

"Aw, sweet Jesus." I sighed, then I began to channel my voice through Keira. (which means that I speak through her).

"Ow!" she screeched when she felt my pain.

"Sorry about that Keira." I said.

"Reilly? Keira?" Charlie asked.

"Charlie, listen. I'm changing, turning evil, into a full demon. I'm not coming back, Charlie." I said, "I'm sorry. I love you." I finished.

"What? Reilly?" he asked.

"Goodbye." I said, this time I was pretty sure it was permanent and the thought depressed me entirely, but I knew it was for their own good. I came back to reality in a fog, like I wasn't really there. Sedrick noticed this and stepped in,

"Reilly, it's for their own good. But don't worry, I'm going to find a way to stop this, I promise." Sedrick said.

"Don't make promises you can't keep." I sighed, looking at him.

"I didn't." he said.

"You owe me an explanation." I said, changing the subject. I was regaining some of my alertness.

"What am I supposed to explain?" he asked,

"Tell me what you and dad were talking about!" I said, he sighed.

"You are extremely annoying when you're about to turn evil. Did you know that?!" he grinned.

"Yes, that I was aware of. Tell me!" I yelled.

"Fine. He was trying to piss me off."

"Yeah, I got that. I'm turning evil, not stupid." I hissed.

"Well, he figured that a good way to do that would be to remind me of how I always tried, but somehow could never manage, to save you from him." he looked down at the ground, "I can't even keep track of how many times I tried to smuggle you out of the castle without him noticing."

"You tried to save me?" I asked, not sure if I'd heard correctly.

"Of coarse I did. You *are* my sister, after all." he said.

"Not technically." I said.

"Well you might as well be, considering you annoy the hell out of me most of the time." he said, I grinned.

"Hey, that goes both ways." I said.

"Yeah, whatever."

"Are you *really* going to try to stop this?" I asked, referring to the cuts that were now halfway to my elbows and knees.

"Yes, I am." he said.

"Even if I turn evil and kick your ass?" I asked.

"Don't flatter yourself, you couldn't beat me if I had both arms broken."

"That can be arranged." I challenged.

"Try it." he grinned.

"My arms hurt." I said, looking at them. (normally, I probably would've accepted his challenge, but I really was in a lot of pain, not to mention the whole 'acid blood' thing).

"Aw, are you a wittle afwaid?" he asked, in a baby voice.

"Of you? Hell no." I said, "but they really do hurt." I added, as if to prove me right, they started to sting. "Ow."

"Anything I can do?" Sedrick asked.

"Yeah, answer one more question." I replied.

"Oh lord, what now?" he sighed.

"Do you really not know what the third sign is?" I asked, looking him in the eye.

"Don't you believe me?" he asked, innocently.

"Not when you say it like that." I replied, seriously.

"Well…fine, but don't freak out, ok?" he said, I nodded. "the third sign involves all of your powers." he explained.

"And…"

"They all kind of, strengthen, at once. You'll go into full form and possibly kill anyone close to you." he said.

"I should leave here." I said, shakily rising to my feet.

"Sit down." he commanded, but I stayed standing. "Reilly, you're not going anywhere until I figure out how to save you."

"But you don't know how long this will take, " I said. "For all we know, I could wake up tomorrow and try to kill you."

"*Try* being the key word. Trust me, you won't hurt me."

"If I wasn't so tired, I'd be insulted by that." I yawned.

"Go to sleep." he laughed.

Chapter 8
Friend or Foe?

I woke up the next morning to a stabbing pain in my side. I snapped my eyes open and sat up. The stigmata had progressed yet again, it had now covered my stomach. "Great..." I sighed.

"Well, **that's** not good." Sedrick said from the entrance. Tell me about it, I was about to say, but then I realized that he was looking *outside* the cave.

"What?" I whispered.

"A group of soldiers. Actually, it's more like an army." he looked at me, "they're searching for someone."

"I'll give you three guesses who *that* is." I sighed.

"There looking for me." he shrugged, "they think that **you** are back with your friends by now."

"How do you know?" I asked.

"Because, I heard them talking. They said that their orders were to find me, and then force me to tell them where you are."

"Maybe you should go somewhere else. They'll never find you if you leave now." I suggested, he just looked at me. "ok, scratch that plan. What do we do?"

"We wait. They might not even look over here. They didn't sound too enthusiastic about the search, they probably won't try very hard." Sedrick said.

"And they might try like hell for fear for their lives." I said, glaring at him.

"Possibly. But I doubt it, relax." he said.

"How am I supposed to relax when I-" I stopped, there was the sound of talking outside.

"We're **never** going to find him! King Lieam, **himself**, couldn't find him!" one voice said.

"If we go back now, the army will turn us in, and the king will kill us. Do you want that to happen!?" another yelled at the first.

"No."

"Then quit complaining. If he *was* around here, he isn't now." the second voice said. She sounded agitated. I heard Sedrick chuckle.

"What do we do?"

"We leave, and check somewhere else."

"Hey, wait! What about over here? We haven't checked this cave yet." the first voice called, he sounded a lot closer.

"How do you know? They all look the same to me." the second shouted back, her voice sounded farther away, though it was moving toward us.

"We haven't even been over here yet."

"Ok, then let's check it out." Oh shit. What now, Sedrick!?

"What now?" I whispered.

"We wait."

"Why?!" I hissed, fighting the urge to strangle him.

"Because, if we shimmer then they'll sense us, and if we run, they'll see us."

"So what you're trying to say is that we're screwed." I said.

"well, sort of. But not exactly. I don't think that they'll find us. In case you haven't noticed, they aren't the brightest guards dad has." he grinned, but I didn't find our situation funny.

"It doesn't take that many brain cells to find two demons in a deserted cave." I said.

"Well, it takes more then they have, and who said this cave is deserted?" Sedrick asked. I looked over at him, completely confused.

"What?"

"Follow me." he said, leading me deeper into the cave.

✸ ✸ ✸

We had been walking for about twenty minutes and I had still only seen rocks, dirt, and a lot of mold. But no other people had made themselves seen or heard.

"Sedrick, are you positive that there are others in here?" I finally asked.

"Almost."

"What? What do you mean, 'almost'!?" I asked, almost forgetting to lower my voice.

"I mean, they were supposed to wait for me here. But with dad capturing *you*, and *me* having to leave for a while, I'm not sure that they listened. You see, I also gave them orders to protect themselves and flee should I not return."

"Very brave, Sedrick. But that doesn't exactly help us now." I said.

"I think they're here, do you hear that?" he asked. He stopped walking and motioned for me to do the same. As soon as the echoes died down, I heard what he was talking about. It sounded like music.

"Yeah." I replied. Sedrick whispered something, and I heard a reply come from somewhere over to our left.

"Sedrick?" a voice asked.

"Max!" Sedrick said, walking toward a shadowed figure.

"So you did make it. I knew you would, they wanted to leave, but I talked them out of it." Max said, walking into the light. He looked to be about Sedrick's age.

"Of coarse I made it. Do you really think that old fool can capture me!?" Sedrick laughed. And as he stepped aside, Max seemed to notice me for the first time.

"Is that her?" he whispered to Sedrick, who nodded. "Is she-?" he didn't have to finish the sentence for both Sedrick and I to grasp his meaning. Sedrick opened his mouth to reply, but I answered for him.

"No she isn't, not yet. And I'd appreciate it if you'd call 'her', Reilly, from now on, got it?" I asked.

"Uh…sure." he looked embarrassed and Sedrick laughed.

"I tried to warn you." he said.

"About what?" I inquired.

"Uh…nothing…" Sedrick and Max said.

"Right…"

"Let's move on, shall we?" Sedrick said after a few seconds of awkward silence.

"Yes." Max said, glancing nervously in my direction. I rolled my eyes and followed them reluctantly. I had a very bad feeling about Max. It was something I was sensing from him, something was wrong, but it could have just been someone he was around recently. I was positive, however, that I *had* to find out who, soon.

✯ ✯ ✯

We walked a little ways and Sedrick stopped at the entrance of another, large, cavern. He glanced back at Max, who nodded.

"This is it." Max said, taking the lead. I glanced around and noticed several people, peeking out from behind rocks. (Hey, maybe they're related to Charity?!)

"This is the army of rebels." Sedrick said, noticing my apparent confusion.

"Ok, this is all?" I asked, looking around once more as the men and women all stepped from their hiding places.

"No, this is a small scouting party. The rest are scattered all over."

"Oh." I said, they were all giving me distrustful looks. "why are they staring at me?" I asked.

"Because they don't trust you yet. Though I'm sure that they know who you are…" he hesitated, " because I might've told them about how you sank an entire city by yourself."

"What!!? That was one time! Atlantis wasn't being used anyway and Charlie and Edward helped!" I said angrily, Sedrick backed away and held his hands up, defensively.

"Ok, ok, I'm sorry. I was just trying to get their minds off of the whole 'turning evil before our very eyes,' thing." he said.

"Oh, very brilliant, Sedrick. Tell them about when I *was* evil, so they don't think about me *turning* that way!!" I snarled. I was still fuming when we stopped next to the fire.

Chapter 9
Goodbyes *Never* Last

At some point I must've fallen asleep, because I awoke to voices arguing that sounded several yards away. One of them was Sedrick, another was Max, but I didn't recognize the third. I listened in:

"I've told you, she's not evil yet. And if I have anything to do with it, she won't be." Sedrick was saying angrily. Clearly they had been at this for a while and he was getting no where.

"It's the *'yet'* that concerns us. And that's just it, Sedrick, you don't have anything to do with it. This has been programmed into her since she was born." that was Max, his voice was pleading. Which also supported my theory about how long they had been arguing, he was now **begging** Sedrick to understand. But **what** was he supposed to understand?

"Quit talking about her like she's a computer, she's a human being. Well, ok, not a *human* being but you get it. People change." Sedrick snarled.

"Sedrick, Max is only looking out for you." the third man said, calmly. "For all you know, she could be a spy." A WHAT!? I don't know about you, but I *already* don't like this guy.

"A WHAT!?" (Thank you,) Sedrick hissed, "don't you **dare** accuse her of that."

"Sedrick, he's her *father,* a bond like that is hard to break." Max said.

"They never had a bond. He's a *monster,* and he's always acted like one toward her." Sedrick said. He was right but the short silence that followed could only mean that the others didn't believe him.

Finally, the third man spoke, "we'll give her **one** chance, but the second she shows *any* signs of treachery, she's destroyed."

"WHAT!?" Sedrick and Max(?) exclaimed. That was clearly not what either of them expected.

"Dad you-" Max said. I could imagine him looking apologetically at Sedrick, who would most likely be glaring at them both.

"I'm sorry, Max. But you know what it would mean for us if Lieam found the rebels." the third man continued, "Most of these people are legion, they wouldn't last five seconds with Lieam's army."

"I brought her here to *save* her from him, Abraham, but it turns out she's in more danger here than she was at the castle." Sedrick said. His voice was right next to me. "Maybe we *should* go back there." he finished, my whole body tensed up. And as much as I was trying to relax, I couldn't. So I gave up and opened my eyes.

Sedrick looked apologetically at me, "That wasn't even a little bit funny." I hissed. But my anger faded quickly at the sight of his face. "what's wrong?" I asked, looking away from him. He was worried and what ever it was, it was far worse than a fight with his friends.

"Nothing, we're leaving." he said.

"Why?" I asked, innocently. But my voice was coated heavily with sarcasm.

"Because, we're not *welcome* here." he said, angrily. But something I sensed told me that we weren't going anywhere.

"S-Sedrick, w-we're in t-trouble." I gasped.

"What do you mean?" he asked, kneeling beside me. Max and Abraham (check out *that* name, talk about a mouth full). came over next to me, but still kept a safe distance from Sedrick, who was seething at the sight of them.

"Remember those two scouts from the army?" I asked, glancing at the other two.

"It's ok, they know." Sedrick said.

"Well, they have friends, *a lot* of friends." I finished, looking nervously at the entrance. Knowing that at any minute the army would blast through it put me on edge.

"Where are they?" Sedrick asked.

"Uh...well..." I began, then the entrance filled with people. Soldiers.

"Damn it." Sedrick hissed, (doesn't *that* bring back memories!?)

"Princess you-"

"What did I tell you about that?!" I snarled, the general's expression turned from calm to hatred and fear. "Don't remember? Well, then I'll just have to remind you, won't I?"

"Just come with us, and none of your friends will get hurt." the general said, calm once again.

"The only ones that will get hurt will be you and your army." Sedrick growled, then he remembered something and added, "how did you know she was here?"

"We have our ways," the leader smiled, then to his army he commanded, "attack, leave *her* alive, kill any who get in your way. Take no prisoners unless necessary!"

They listened well for a bunch of brainless idiots. They charged toward us, but the rebels blocked their path. The two armies fought each other brutally, both sides losing equal amounts of lives.

Sedrick, Max, and I helped the rebels, but Abraham fled. Soon the army general had to call for reinforcements. "Shit!" Sedrick hissed as a new wave of soldiers forced their way inside and pushed the rebels back.

"We're screwed." Max sighed, I glared at them both.

"We are *not* screwed! I *refuse* to go back there. More importantly, I *refuse* to let you all die." I snarled, "there has to be another way out of here! Abraham ran, didn't he?"

Max nodded, "there's another opening about a mile away, but I don't think-"

"Then let *me* think for you." I hissed, cutting him off. "get as many as you can out of here, if *I* run, they'll just follow you. So I'll stay here."

"Not by yourself, you're not. I promised you that I'd keep you safe and I don't intend to lie!" Sedrick yelled.

"This time, I'll forgive you, just go!" I shouted back.

"No!"

"I can take the survivors alone, Sedrick can stay here." Max said, I glared at him. I figured he was only trying to make up for his father's threat, but he was pissing me off.

"Please, Reilly, you can't stay here alone." Sedrick said.

"Ugh! Fine! Just go!" I shouted in frustration, then ripped the soldier about to tackle me to shreds.

"Uh…I'm just going to leave, now." Max said nervously, running toward the exit. He shouted orders for the others to follow him, and soon it was Sedrick and I against the entire army.

"This could get interesting." I said.

"Very interesting." Sedrick sighed.

"Spread out." I said, moving away. He did the same until we were on separate sides of the cave.

"That was a bad idea, Reilly." the general laughed, making a signal to half of his army to go to Sedrick. Then he and the remaining *five hundred* men surrounded me.

"Why?" I asked.

"because, now no one can save you."

"Who am I, Cinderella?!" I hissed, "I can save myself." I jumped over the general and into the crowd of soldiers.

"Ok, Reilly, we'll do this *your* way. But you could make this so much easier for yourself." the general said.

"How, by going with you?! If I do that, I'm screwed." I said.

"You're screwed either way. But surrendering will make everything go so much quicker for you." at this, I'd heard enough. My claws sprang out, and fire surrounded me and my half of the army, then I let the flames collapse inwards, disintegrating everything in their path. When it was over, only a few of the soldiers around me, and the general, remained. "Very well played, Reilly, but when I said it would be easier for *you*, I meant for you, *and* your friends." the general grinned, and the circle forming around us, made a pathway for a band of soldiers carrying Sedrick, Max, Abraham, and a few others, into the opening.

"Son of a Bitch." I mumbled.

"Reilly, run." Sedrick muttered.

"I don't run…" I hesitated, looking around at the five hundred and something soldiers that now made up the circle, "I fall back." I finished, shimmering out of the cave.

✧ ✧ ✧

I arrived *somewhere* else in a matter of nano-seconds. I **really** hoped that Sedrick would forgive me for leaving, but I'd be no help to any of them if I'd gotten captured too. At least, that's what I was telling myself to keep calm. Then the vision started. (these 'visions' are really starting to annoy me, I have enough problems in *my* life without trying to live parts of someone else's).

It began very blurrily. But as it cleared up, I could make out the people in it. I could see Kara, and Edward, but no Keira. Then I was actually *in* the vision, which meant that I must *be* Keira.

"Edward!!" I, or rather, Keira shouted. ('cause I wouldn't *care* what happened to him).

"Edward!!" Kara said with hatred. (Wait, I thought she *loved* him).

"Kara, *you* may hate me, but the feeling isn't mutual! I never stop thinking about you!!" Wait, Edward can think. Wait, WHAT DID HE SAY??? Oh, I could have fun with this.

"What the hell did he say?!" I exclaimed.

"No Edward, listen to me!" Keira shouted.

"Keira, do something why don't you?" I asked Keira, who hadn't moved.

"I-I'm sort of...stuck."

"Aw Sweet Jesus, must I do *everything*!?" I asked angrily. I guessed that Keira was 'held' to a tree. (cause that's all Kara can do,) so I concentrated on trying to free her. I heard her gasp and guessed that the tree had caught fire, as I'd intended it to do.

"Keira, you're not stuck anymore. Go get Edward!" I said.

"Edward!" Keira screamed. Kara glanced over at her and smirked evilly, (if that's even possible when you're a holy woman,) then she leaned forward and KISSED Edward, who looked completely high.

"No! Get your hands off of him, he's MINE!!!" Keira screamed. That, plus the kiss, would haunt me for the rest of my life I was sure. I pulled out of the vision before I saw *anything* else.

I came back to reality and immediately sensed that something wasn't right. I looked around me and there, coming out of the shadows to my left, was my father. That, however hard it is to believe, wasn't my most recent problem, though. I had to get back to the others quickly. I couldn't say what it was exactly, but while I was in the vision, I sensed something coming. Something bad. I turned to face my dad but I was mapping out escape routes as well. All I planned to do was get away, this time. I thought that was all that would happen, but I was dead wrong.

Chapter 10
Promise

"You're a very hard person to track down, do you know that?" my dad asked.

"That's kind of what I was trying for." I hissed, anxious to leave.

"Finally, something you're good at." my dad said, making me wish that I'd chosen to kick his ass, rather than run. But I still couldn't help but feel like something bad was going to happen to the others.

"What do you want now?" I asked, in my signature bored way.

"I see that the second sign has begun." he said, ignoring my question.

"Yes, it has. And you'll be happy to know that it's excruciatingly painful." I said.

"I am, and you'll be happy to know that I haven't killed your brother and his friends…yet." he smiled and I froze. I had forgotten all about Sedrick, (but don't tell him that,) now what was I supposed to do?! (Oh, I know, lie like hell!!)

"Really? Wow, and here I was about to go and save him. But if you haven't killed him yet, I guess he's safe, then!" I said, calculating my chances of getting out of this quickly. They weren't good.

"What was the vision about, Reilly? What did you see?" he asked.

"Now what would make you think that I had a vision?" I asked innocently.

"I've been around for a while-"

"You're telling me." I said, he ignored my comment and went on,

"And I know what was going on. You were having a vision and now you're looking for a way to leave here and go do whatever that vision led you to. Now you need to tell me what you saw and where you're going." my dad moved closer.

"Why? Why do you care?" I asked, almost forgetting to hide my panic.

"Because, as I have stated before, you have to go to the castle." he said.

"Yes, I believe you've established that. But I also believe that I've made it clear that I **don't** have to go to the castle. More importantly, I won't. So I guess you're just SOL, aren't you?" I said, furious that I hadn't left yet.

"Ok," my dad said, I could clearly detect annoyance in his voice, "I'm guessing that you're not going to come willingly."

"No shit! Wow, genius, did you figure that one out all by yourself?!" I asked, completely pissed now.

"Reilly, there's no need to raise our voices. Let's handle this like adults, shall we?" my dad said, though I could tell that he was trying to suppress his own anger. "You know what to do to make this all end."

"Nothing will ever make this end. Nothing except killing you. But you're in luck, I have more important things to do right now." I said, then I tried to get around him. That was…probably not my smartest option. (if any of you tell Edward I admitted to that, I will hunt you down). he grabbed my elbow and flung me back, slamming me into the side of a large rock.

"Because you refuse to come quietly, I'll just have to use force. But you won't be trouble for long, I will make sure of that." now why would he go and say something like that? I got my answer to that question just seconds after I wondered it. He moved forward and I felt a sharp sting in my left shoulder. At first I thought that he'd stabbed me again, as he had a couple of months ago. But when I looked over, I saw no blood, but only a syringe sticking out of my arm.

"What was-" I began, but he put his hand over my mouth, keeping me from finishing.

"You'll figure it out soon enough." he said, then he left.

Now, normally if he'd have said something like that, I would've followed him and **made** him tell me. But I had more important things on my mind, so I dismissed it as another of his tricks. That was mistake number two. (Again, any of you blab to Edward, and I will kill you).

As soon as I was sure that he was gone, I *tried* to shimmer to the others. I say 'tried,' because I couldn't make it all the way. In mid-shimmer, I began to feel dizzy and every muscle in my body began to twitch uncontrollably. I stopped a little ways from my intended destination. But I stopped in mid-air! I barely caught a tree branch before I plummeted about two hundred feet downward. "What the hell?" I stammered, pulling myself onto the branch.

I looked around and gathered that I was *very* high up, but I wasn't too far from the others. Considering I could hear them talking. What the hell had happened?! Why couldn't I shimmer *all* of the way?! I had a feeling that it had something to do with my father's 'cure' that I would find out about 'soon enough.' (It would be so much easier if the bad guys would just tell you what the hell was going on, don't you think?)

"I'm a freaking demon," I groaned, still shaking, "we don't have seizures!" I leaned back, against the trunk of the large oak I had 'landed' on. The seizure ended shortly afterward and I stood back up. Then I heard something coming toward me through the trees. I put my hand up in time to catch an *arrow* about an inch before it hit my face. But it wasn't just any kind of arrow, it was a purifying arrow. (which, in case you don't know, will kill any demon, devil, half-demon, etc., that gets hit with it). "Keira." I growled, "fine, you want to play a game? Let's play catch." I snarled, tossing the arrow aside. Then I formed a fireball in one hand and threw it in the direction that the arrow had come from.

"It's Reilly! It's Reilly! I know it's Reilly 'cause she throws fire!" Charity screeched, I rolled my eyes. At least she's smart.

"No, Charity, it's just a pissed off squirrel that can…throw fire…somehow." Keira said, she's not so smart.

"Oh. My. God. What an idiot." I mumbled. Then I tuned them out. I really wasn't sure what was happening, but whatever I had sensed before, had arrived. Which would explain why Keira was using the arrow in the first place. And unless she planned to shoot Edward or Charlie, with the purifying arrow, it must be demonic. (Shooting Edward was likely, but shooting Charlie better not be). but who would she be shooting at? It couldn't have been Jezaba or Violante because I would've recognized their scent. This one did seem vaguely familiar, though.

"Reilly." Came a faint whisper. Causing me to almost fall off my branch. "Reilly."

"What? Where are you?" I asked the forest around me. No answer. "Hey! Answer me!!" I shouted.

"Reilly." the voice said. Then I recognized it.

"Sedrick? Where are you?" I asked.

"Reilly, listen. I'm still at the castle. We're in the dungeons, I need your help. I need you to come here." He said, something was wrong. He didn't sound like himself.

"But, they'll kill me." I said.

"No, they won't. They need you. Besides, even if they did catch you, they'd have to wait for Dad's orders. And he's not here." Sedrick said, sounding more un-Sedrick like by the second. I had known him for my entire life and I knew that he would *never* want me to put myself in danger to save him. (I seldom if ever listened to this, but that's beside the point).

"But-" I began, but he interrupted.

"Reilly, please. I need you." he said, his voice fading.

"I'll try." I replied. Then there was silence. I didn't know how, or when. But I knew that I *would* save Sedrick. I owed him my life. So, I promised, I would save his.

Chapter 11
Return

"This could be fun." I said sarcastically. Now I had to choose, and if I didn't make the right one, I could wind up loosing someone I loved. "This is so not fair! Why do you hate me so much!?!" I shouted at the heavens. Stupid question considering that I was a demon and He was God, but I figured I deserved at least a thank you. I was, after all, half Apostle. At least, for now.

In the middle of my little breakdown, I heard shouting coming from where the others were. One voice in particular, stood out from the rest and I realized why what I had been sensing was so familiar. It was Daniel.

For those of you who don't know who that is, let me clear that up. Daniel is Edward's half brother. He's a full demon and likes to rub that in Edward's face. Mostly he just wants to kill Edward, but about one hundred years ago, he attacked me. (Hey, I did say he was related to Edward, which means that he's not the brightest). so I killed him, but lately everyone who hates me has been resurrected (My dad and Kara,) so his sudden appearance didn't surprise me.

Anyway, I heard Edward shout, "You can't be dead! I -" I raced to just behind the tree line to see the look on Keira's face when he finished that sentence.

"Let go, Edward! I'm fine!" she said. Stupid, stupid Keira! I thought. Then I spaced out for a while, (Because, if you must know, I was having another seizure, (if any of you know how to stop those, feel free to speak up. And I mean, demonically caused seizures too, just thought I should let you know). When I could once again control my actions, I focused on the others again.

"Charlie..." Edward was saying.

"Yes?" he asked.

"Reilly's going to murder you." Edward finished. Now why would I do that? What did they know that I didn't?

I was so busy trying to figure this out that by the time I started paying attention to them again, Charlie and Daniel were fighting. Both of them were in full form, but there was something different about Charlie. I didn't have time to figure out what, however, because just as Charlie was about to injure Daniel, he lost his powers. When Charlie was again in weak form, Daniel laughed. He sent Charlie flying backwards, then he said, "I win." he raised his sword, but I raced in between them and caught it before it could kill Charlie. Something was very weird about how fast I was however, I realized that I was in full form. Without even meaning to, I'd gone into my full form before I caught the blade.

"That can't be good." I muttered.

"I-I'm alive?" Charlie stuttered, I rolled my eyes.

"Hell yeah, you're alive. Now move, I can't hold the sword forever." I said.

"Reilly!!" Charity screamed.

"God damn it! I'm doomed!!" Edward groaned. I let go of the sword and Daniel backed away. I stood in between him and Charlie.

"So, you've decided to return," Daniel said, "good, now you'll die."

I glared at him, "Daniel, haven't we been through this? I killed you once, I can do it again." I said, surprising myself at how very...*evil* I sounded.

"We'll see-" Daniel began, but then he noticed the stigmata.
"No. you?" he gasped.

"Yeah..." I sighed, temporarily remembering what was to come. Then I calmed down, or at least made myself look calm.

"..." Daniel couldn't think of anything to say. I noticed Keira grabbing for her arrows, but she didn't have any left. She looked over at me and I rolled my eyes.

I held one hand out to the trees where I had come from and the arrow came soaring toward me. I caught it one handed and threw it to Keira. "Looking for this?" I asked.

"Uh..."

"I'm sorry!!!" Charity screeched.

"Charity...shut up. So, pissed off squirrel huh?" I glared at Keira.

"Uh…" (Well I see she hasn't enlarged her vocabulary at all since I've been gone).

"Hello, still here!!!" Daniel shouted. He and Edward are definitely related. It's obvious, they're both incredibly dumb.

"Do you have a death wish, or are you just stupid?" I hissed. Daniel flinched and I was again surprised at how acidic my voice was.

A couple minutes later, something soared passed me, hitting my hair as it flew. I turned and glared at Keira as an arrow hit Daniel. Who glared at both of us. "I'm leaving! But when I come back, I will kill all of you!!"

I sighed and went to weak form. But as I did so, the stigmata progressed. I wonder if anyone noticed…

"Reilly!!!" Charity shouted, "something's growing on your arm!!!" (Oh yeah, they noticed.)

"I knew it!" Edward blurted out, "you're evil! I knew it!"

"Edward, I'm *turning* evil, there's a difference." I growled.

"Oh." he said, what a dumb ass. I guess he wasn't expecting that one.

"You're turning what?" Charlie asked, surprisingly calm.

"Uh…yeah. I'm turning evil. Part of that thing we found out about before. The one that could alter my life forever." I said. He nodded, understanding immediately what I was talking about.

"Who cares!!! I'm so glad that you're back!!" Charity shrieked.

"Uh-Oh." I said, before Charity launched herself into my arms, taking us both to the ground.

"Well it's obvious that *I* didn't miss you." Edward said, still looking nervously at the stigmata.

"I know Edward. But while I was gone, my powers got stronger. I had visions…of Keira's life. Want to guess what I saw?" I challenged, standing up.

"No." Edward said.

"Fine, but Edward, just curious. Exactly how often do you think of Kara? Oh wait, you never stop!!" I said, quoting him from his conversation with Kara. (That I'd unintentionally and unwillingly eavesdropped on).

"Shut up!" Edward shouted.

"I bet you liked it when she kissed you, huh?" I continued.

"Must we go there?" Keira asked.

"Well...I...uh..." Edward stuttered.

Suddenly, some cross between a midget and a sock puppet jumped onto Charity's shoulder. "What, in the name of the sweet Lord Jesus, is **that?!**" I asked.

"I'm Pindel," it said, "I'm a dwelf."

"A what?" I asked.

"A-"

"Never mind." Keira said, glaring at Edward. "So, Edward, answer Reilly's question."

"I...uh..." (Edward's gonna die, Edward's gonna die!!)

Charlie walked over to me, "for the record," he said, taking my hand, "I missed you."

"Good," I said, "Cause I missed you, too."

"Answer the question now!" Keira was shouting at Edward.

"Uh..." Edward said, "I like clouds! They look like giant marshmallows!!" he finished, (That was random).

"Right now, answer the question, you asshole!" Keira screamed.

"You're right Keira, he is an asshole." an unbearably familiar voice said. Keira looked around, but Edward, Charlie, and I were already glaring at where we knew Vincient was.

"Who are you?" Keira asked. For those of you who don't know, Vincient used to work with Charlie and I back when we were loyal to Jezaba. (I don't want to talk about it).

"The name's Vincient. I'm a full demon and a 'friend' of those three." Did I mention that he's also a chronic liar, cause he is.

"Actually, you're the biggest asshole I've ever met." I said. (what, he tried to kill me for Violante).

"You're still as pretty as ever. I always liked you better than Violante." Vincient said.

"Is that why you tried to kill me for her?" I asked sarcastically as Charlie moved in front of me, kind of in between Vincient and I.

"Charlie, you haven't changed a bit. Except for the fact that you've lost your horns." Vincient continued, ignoring my comment. (Wait, what did he just say?!!?) suddenly, everything made sense. I glared at Charlie, who was glaring at Vincient.

"What?" I asked through clenched teeth.

"I was gonna tell you." Charlie said, giving me that unbelievably unfair 'puppy dog face'. "Ass hole." he growled at Vincient.

"Poor you." Vincient taunted. Then he turned back to Edward and Keira. "Dating the reincarnation of Kara, are we?" (I bet you five bucks he denies it!)

"I'm not dating her!!!" (Pay up!) Edward snarled, his eyes almost glowing with hatred.

"Calm down." Keira said.

"You're actually prettier than Kara." Vincient said. (That whole flirting thing he does, is starting to get on my nerves!!)

"I'm just going to go over here." Keira said, backing away.

"Keira, there's no reason to be scared." Vincient lied.

"Oh yes there is!!" Edward growled, yanking Keira behind him.

"Keira, relax. Just stay still." I warned, hoping she'd listen.

"Well, as pretty as you are, Reilly. I can't have you interfering with my plans." Vincient said. He said a spell and a portal appeared beside me.

"What the hell?" I asked, glaring at Vincient. "Where are you sending me?"

"You'll see." he said. (I *hate* it when people say that! I never seem to see until it's too late!) then the stupid wormhole pulled me in! (See, that's *exactly* what I'm talking about!!)

"Well, this sucks." I sighed while falling through darkness.

Chapter 12
My Demented Brother

About twenty minutes later, (at least that's what it felt like,) I landed, hard, on a stone floor.

"Where the hell am I?" I asked to no one in particular.

"At the castle of the Underworld." a familiar voice answered me.

"Max?" I inquired.

"Reilly?" he asked, stepping from the shadows. He was chained to the wall, a prisoner. I looked around and realized that I was in a cell. "What are you doing here?"

"I just thought I'd drop in." I said, rolling my eyes.

"Ha, ha. You shouldn't be here. The king, your father, has almost every soldier out looking for you. He, himself, left about an hour ago." Max continued.

"Then this is probably the safest place for me." I said.

"Point well made." Max said. Then a look of, almost regret, crossed his face. "There's something else you should know." he said.

"What?" I asked. But before he could answer, an alarm went off.

"Oh, no." Max groaned.

"Reilly!!" someone called. I turned around to see Sedrick running toward me.

"Sedrick, we have to get out of here!" I said as he reached our cell. He unlocked the door and came toward me. Then I realized that something was dangerously wrong with my brother.

"You're not going anywhere, Reilly. Not now, not ever." Sedrick said. Before I could protest, or even express my confusion, Sedrick had chained me to a different wall of the cell.

"But, why?" was all I could say.

"Because, he's right. He has always been right. I see that now, and soon, so will you. Whether you like it or not." Sedrick grinned in the exact same evil way that my father had. Then he locked the door as he left.

"Max?" I asked the darkness.

"Yeah?" he said.

"Do you want to help me massacre my family? Meaning Lieam and Sedrick."

"Reilly, he can't help it. Meaning Sedrick. Lieam brainwashed him when we got here." Max said.

"Fine." I sighed angrily, leaning my head back against the stone wall behind me. Then I thought of something else, "do you want to help me kill my father?" I asked.

"Now that, I will do." he said.

"Good."

What felt like ages later, a strange smell filled the cell. "What is that?" I asked.

"Knock out gas." Max replied slowly.

"Why are they," I paused, feeling drowsy. Then I shook it off and continued, "trying to knock us out." I finished.

"I don't...know..." Max sighed sleepily. Then silence.

"Max? hello...Max! Wake up!!!"

"I wasn't..." he yawned, then was out cold.

"Max?" I asked, but I knew he wouldn't answer.

After about ten minutes of trying not to fall asleep, the knock out gas did it's job. I woke up in , (you'll *never* believe this one,) the throne room!! *On* the throne!

"Well this is awkward." I muttered.

"You like it?" a voice inquired from the door.

"No." I said.

"Well you'll get used to it. You'll have no choice." Abraham said with a smile. I thought of where I was and immediately remembered an important detail about that particular room. But when I tried to shimmer, nothing happened. At least nothing that helped, the restraints holding my arms to the chair started to beep and Abraham laughed. "You aren't going anywhere." he said.

"Why? Why would you betray the rebels, us, your son?" I asked.

"He was not supposed to take Max, or even Sedrick, only you." Abraham's eyes narrowed to slits and I could sense the hatred emanating from him. Then I realized why I couldn't sense his presence before.

"You're human." I accused, "but I thought that-"

"That I was where Max got his demon side? No, that was his mother, Satan rest her soul." Abraham bent his head and the hatred subsided. For about two nanoseconds, then it was focused on me once again. Nearly burning my skin with its intensity.

Once again I tried to move, temporarily forgetting that my arms and legs were held to the throne. I sighed, hoping that he understood that I could've killed him many times had I truly been evil.

"Now, now, Reilly. Be nice." my father cackled as he walked into the room. Following him were Sedrick, Max (in chains,) and someone I didn't know.

"Eyla! Watch him!" Sedrick snarled at the woman whom I hadn't known. Then he moved to my father's side and glared at me.

"Who's she?" I asked anyone in the room.

"This is Eyla, she's the new general." my father answered.

"But I didn't kill the other one, did I?" I looked toward the ceiling, pretended to try to remember, "no, I didn't."

"But I did." Sedrick said victoriously. "Because he didn't do his job. He didn't capture you. So now he's been replaced with someone who can."

"That's correct, Sedrick." my father said, smiling down at him. "**You** did exactly what I said." At this, he glared at me, "Why can't you be more like your brother, Reilly?"

"Because *I* haven't been turned into a brainwashed puppet who's only vocabulary consists of phrases like, 'of coarse father,' or 'you are always right." I said. They all glared at me except Max, who suppressed a laugh.

"Reilly, you will soon learn not to be so stupid." my dad said, angrily.

"Well, I get that trait from you, dad." I said.

My father turned to Eyla and whispered something about Max. she nodded and took Max and left. Then he talked to Abraham, who also nodded, and followed the other two.

"Sedrick, go and see if the other prisoners are," he laughed, "comfortable." my father said. Sedrick laughed with him, then left in the opposite direction as the others.

"Where did they take Max?" I asked.

"He and Abraham are being…'taken care of." my dad answered.

"What in the hell does that mean?!" I snarled.

"It means that they have outlived they're usefulness and now they're being executed as we speak." he said, smirking.

"Why?! You got what you wanted, Sedrick is evil and I'm here, soon to follow in his footsteps. Why can't you just let them go?!" I growled, furious now and trying to forget my guilt.

"Because, they know too much." he answered simply but added, " You know, if you'd have just listened to me in the first place, no one else would've been involved." then he turned and left the room, leaving me with more guilt than before.

Chapter 13
Broken Vow

After a short period of time in the throne room, (Most of it being spent hooked up to all kinds of machines to make sure that the stigmata were doing their job, and most of the machines being insanely painful,) I was returned to the cell I had shared with Max. Only now it would just be me.

"I hope you like being alone." the guard laughed as he shut the steel door, leaving me **very** alone.

After what felt like forever of pacing back and forth, I heard the bolt slide back, and then the door opened. Unfortunately, the figure who appeared in the opening, was the person whom I least wanted to see.

"Reilly, I came to tell you that in merely four months, your transformation will be complete." Sedrick said, as he closed the door behind him.

"Oh yea." I said, dully.

"I thought you'd be pleased." Sedrick said, looking confused.

"Sedrick, in four months I'll be evil. What would possibly give you the idea that that would make me happy?" I asked.

"Dad." he said.

"He lied, he lies all the time. You used to know that." I said, temporarily losing the sharp edge in my voice.

"I know, but now…" he trailed off, as if he wasn't sure what he believed any more.

"Sedrick, why are you doing this? Why are you betraying me? Not to mention your friend, Max." I said, at this he looked at me as if I had said something insane.

"What do you mean? Max and his father were returned to their home, dad said so." Sedrick said, I rolled my eyes.

"They're dead, Sedrick. Surprise, surprise, daddy dearest lied again." I said, angrily remembering that it was *my* fault they had died. Then I realized that this whole time, the door had been unlocked! (well, I was a *little* distracted, after all). "I'm such an idiot." I mumbled.

"What was that?" Sedrick asked.

"Nothing." I said, flipping over his head and in between him and the door. I flung it open and turned back to a surprised Sedrick. "Give my regards to Dad, and my sincere apologies for not staying." I rolled my eyes and closed the door, leaving him in my cell alone.

"Reilly!" he shouted through the small opening in the door as I locked it. "Don't you remember what you said to me when I contacted you. You promised that you'd save me!" he shouted, I ignored the fact that not too long ago he'd made the same promise to me.

I turned around angrily, "consider it broken." I snarled. Then I ran to the throne room, and shimmered out of the castle.

Chapter 14
Strange Demons

I'm not sure exactly *where* I shimmered to. But wherever it was, it was dark and cold. Not to mention in the Underworld still.

"I *hate* my family!!" I shouted at the darkness around me. My voice echoed off the walls and came back to me. "Yeah, cause that's not creepy at all."

"Your majesty? What are you doing in the forbidden region of the Underworld?" someone asked, I sensed demons, a lot of them. Someone summoned fire, and I could see that my suspicions were correct. Leading about thirty soldiers, was Eyla, the general. (Does it seem to you that no matter how many of them we kill, there are at least ten ready to replace them? Yeah, me too).

"Eyla, how did you know where I was?" I asked, I had a very bad feeling about what her answer would be.

"The king has requested that we follow you." she said. Yep, that was what I was afraid she'd say.

"And then, let me guess, you're to kill whoever I go to? Am I right?" I asked.

"Yes, that's exactly correct." she said, amused at my angered expression.

"Ok, so you have to follow me, huh? Fine, try to keep up." I challenged, then I shimmered again. Once I reappeared, I shimmered again. This continued until I appeared above ground in a forest. I thought that I'd lost them, but I was wrong. Deciding that they were tracking my shimmer, I ran through the trees. Soon I could see a clearing ahead, (I figured that if it was a road, thirty soldiers wouldn't want to risk exposure by stepping into the open, but it wasn't a road). I ran through the last of the trees and had to stop suddenly before I ran into Charity!

"Reilly! You're back! Where were-" she began.

"Not now Charity. Demons, right behind me. A lot of them, run!" I said quickly. Then the soldiers burst into the clearing. "Uh-Oh. Charity, take Pindel and hide!" I commanded, she nodded and she and Pindel ran behind a very large rock. (I love it when they listen. And I'm not even going to asked how the rock got there).

"Wh-what d-do the-they want?" Edward asked, nervously.

"To kill us." Charlie answered.

"Wh-why?!" Edward shouted hoarsely.

"Because I'm here." I said. Then, because I knew what Edward would say to that, I added, "and my leaving wouldn't help. They already know who you are and they'll kill you anyway. Your only chance is if I stay and help you get rid of them."

"How do you know how to do that?" Charlie asked.

"Because I watched them train. I know what they do. How they fight." I answered.

"How did you watch them-"

"Long story." I interrupted.

"Guys, if you don't mind, I could use a **little** help!" Edward shouted.

"No, Edward, you could use ***a lot*** of help which I can't give you. But I'd be glad to kill those demons for you." I said.

"That's' not what I-" he began, but one of the demons sent him flying backward so he didn't get a chance to finish.

"Idiot." I mumbled as I took his place fighting the demons.

Soon most of the demons were either dead or fatally injured. Those that still could, fled into the woods, as far away from the 'crazy ass demons' as they could. (At least, that's what they were saying as they ran).

"No, you cowards, where are you going!?" Eyla was shouting. "Stay here, burn them if you have to! Burn them all!!"

"Are you on something?" Edward asked her.

"No! I don't think so…I can't remember." she replied.

"That's convincing." I said.

"I have to go lie to the king now. I mean…"

"Just go." the three of us said, she nodded and left.

"That was weird." Edward said when she was gone. "I mean, how she was all mad and then completely calm."

"Yeah, what's wrong with her?" Charlie asked me.

"Uh…I really don't know." I said, then I turned to where Charity and Pindel had run to. "Charity, you can come out now." I called. They walked slowly out from behind the rock and over to us.

"Who was that?" Charity asked. Everyone turned to me.

"That was a good example of insanity. Her name's Eyla, she's the new general." I answered.

"Oh." everyone answered. (Somehow I don't think that they will leave it at that. Well, Charlie and Charity won't anyway. Edward and Pindel don't really care as long as she doesn't come after them).

"Yeah, and she pretty much hates me, so let's get out of here before she brings reinforcements." I said.

Chapter 15
Cross Barrier

"We have to find Keira!!!" Edward shouted.

"Well she wouldn't be in this mess if you hadn't been so preoccupied with finding Kara, now would she?" Charlie said.

"I don't think I want to know what you two are talking about." I commented.

"They're talking about how Vincient distracted Edward by saying he saw Kara. Then he took Keira while Edward wasn't paying attention." Charity explained.

"Charity, when I say, 'I don't want to know,' don't tell me from now on, ok?" I asked, then I turned to Edward. "I hate you. If you could just let it go, we wouldn't be trying to get inside a high security building to save Keira."

"Uh…sorry?"

"I should kill you." I said, sounding *very* demonic. And actually tempting myself to carry out the threat.

"Reilly? Are you ok?" Charlie asked.

"Reilly, your eyes are glowing!!" Charity shouted. I closed my eyes and tightened my hands into fists.

"What's happening to you?" Charlie asked.

"I don't know." I admitted.

"Hey, I found the entrance!!" Edward shouted, forcing me to open my eyes. He was running to the door but common sense told me that we shouldn't get too close. (Well that and the fact that there were about four cross-barriers that I could see).

"Uh…Edward…" I began.

"What?" he snapped.

"You know what, never mind." I said. He continued racing to the door only to run into the barrier, get electrocuted, and then knocked backwards almost back over to us. "I tried to warn you."

"We can't get in!!" Edward shouted.

"Well no shit!" I shot back.

"Are you sure you're ok? Because you look like you're about to kill Edward." Charity said.

"She's always about to kill Edward." Charlie said, but he came over to me and whispered, "Calm down. If something happens and you loose your temper, the stigmata will progress farther."

"How did you know that?" I asked.

"Because that's what happened when you fought Daniel, when you fought those demonic soldiers, **and** when you threatened Edward. Which kind of scared me, by the way." he said.

"Yeah, you and me both." I admitted.

"Just be careful." he warned.

"I'll try." I promised. I looked over at Charity, who was watching Edward repeatedly fling himself into the barrier. "It's finally happened, Edward's lost what little mind he had."

"Be nice." Charlie laughed, then he added, "he wasn't *always* stupid." I looked at him disbelievingly.

"Really? You could never tell."

"Hey, stop talking and get your asses over here!!" Edward shouted. We looked over toward him in time to see him, yet again, run into the barrier.

"Hey stupid!!" I called, he looked over at me, "glad to see you know your name, dumb ass. We're never going to get in that way. Actually, we're never going to get in at all, unless…" I began, but Edward interrupted.

"Unless Charity and Pindel go in first!" he shouted.

"Exactly. They can…" once again, I was interrupted by stupid.

"They can go save Keira!!" he shouted again. (That wasn't what I had in mind). then he turned to Charity and Pindel, "Well, what are you waiting for, GO!!!" he yelled. They hurried off through the barrier and then disappeared into the building.

"Brilliant idea, now they'll get caught!" Charlie said.

"There was no other way." Edward announced.

"Yes there was. They could've just moved the barrier so that we could get in. But instead, *you* sent them off the get themselves killed!!" I said angrily.

"Reilly, I'm sure that they'll be ok. The most Vincient will do will probably be to capture them." Charlie said. (Yeah, but we *still* can't get in!)

"Maybe." I muttered. Then I walked back away from the barrier.

"What happened to you?" Charlie asked from beside me. I hadn't even noticed he'd followed me, so when he spoke I jumped.

"What do you mean?" I inquired.

"First of all, those markings. All you said was that they were part of you being," he glanced over at Edward, who wasn't paying attention, "The princess of the Underworld."

"The ruler can't be a half-demon, or…" I paused, waiting for him to decide to tell me never to see him again. When he was silent, I continued. "Or good. The markings are a warning. Telling anything demonic what's happening. They're changing my demon blood, making it more powerful so that it can overcome my human, or Apostle, side."

"So, you're turning evil, huh? Not if I can help it."

"That's what Sedrick said. And now he's… never mind." I said, heading back toward the building. Charlie caught my wrist and stood in my way.

"That's what's been bothering you, isn't it? Your brother's been captured."

"No, if that were the problem I'd have gone to save him. Sedrick is…" I couldn't say the word. But Charlie could.

"Evil?" he asked.

"How did you-" I began.

"Let's just say that Jezaba revealed a little more of your father's plan than he was supposed to." he said, answering my question before I could finish asking it. But that reminded me.

"Speaking of Jezaba, when were you planning on telling me that he ripped out your horns?" I asked.

"I'm going to *kill* Vincient." Charlie mumbled under his breath. "I was going to tell you when you got back." he said.

"But you didn't." I pointed out.

"Hey wait. How did you know that *Jezaba* was the one who did it!?" he asked.

"Don't change the subject." I said.

"I'm not. I answered your question, now it's your turn."

"I might've went and asked him." I said quickly.

"You what!!?" (Why do I always get that reaction!?) "He could've killed you!!" Charlie said, outraged.

"Yeah, and he could've killed *you* too." I said calmly.

"I was there because-"

"Because why? Because you were trying to get yourself killed!?"

"No, because he had vital information that I needed."

"And what would that be?" I asked, he hesitated.

"It was about…"

"Yes…"

"Uh…"

"Yes…"

"Well…"

"Oh just say it!" I said, frustrated.

"Well it was about-"

"Hey guys, Pindel's back!!!" Edward shouted. (Saved by the idiot).

"We should go see what happened." Charlie said evasively. He started toward the others, dragging me with him.

"No, but, wait-" I shouted. He was no where near off the hook. I was going to find out what he needed Jezaba for, even if I had to ask Jezaba myself. Hey, there's a thought.

Chapter 16
Keira's Rescue

"Charity...got captured...Vincent...still...has Keira...and he's... really...annoying!!!" Pindel gasped, out of breath.

"Did you run all the way here?" Charlie asked.

"As a midget? Well, shorter than usual, anyway." Edward asked. After glaring at Edward, Pindel nodded 'yes.'

"What do I do?" Pindel asked.

"You have to-" Edward began.

"Move the cross-barrier so we can get in." I said before Edward could send him off to get killed.

"Uh...yeah, that's what I was going to say." Edward lied.

"No it wasn't." Charlie said, disbelievingly.

"Hey, who's side are you on, anyway?" Edward whispered to him.

"Hers." Charlie said. Smart man.

"Hem, hem." Pindel said, "You can go in now."

"There, Edward, *now* you can run to the door." I said.

"OK!" he yelled, then he took off at full speed, (**Demonic** full speed). seconds later we saw him smack, face first, into the steel door.

"I said to, not *into*!" I called. Edward just groaned with pain. Then the door cracked, and shattered into pieces.

"Damn, you have a hard head." Pindel commented.

"Shut up you stupid dwelf," Edward growled, "or I'll drop something heavy on you."

"Simmer down, dumb ass." I snarled, "or I'll ask you a trivia question."

"Guys, there's some kind of alarm on this thing. It's going off now." Charlie said.

"Then let's get in, *my* way." Edward said. Then, before anyone agreed, he smashed through the wall. (A). the alarm is *already* going off, and, B). that's going to set off, *more* alarms). Charlie, Pindel, and I exchanged glances,

"Let's not." I suggested, they nodded and followed me through the doorway. We entered a large room with stairs leading downward. When we looked off of the balcony we were standing on, we saw a cage holding Keira and Charity. Vincient was standing in front of it, glaring at Edward, who was standing in front of the very large hole in the wall he had just made.

"I'm stuck! But I managed to pick the lock though!" Keira was shrieking.

"Well that's helpful." I muttered. Finally, Edward seemed to realize that he and Vincient weren't the only two in the room. He ran over to the cage and began to try to get Keira free. But Vincient apparently wasn't going to let that happen without a fight, so he and Edward began fighting, (And yes, Keira is **still** stuck in the cage). She began to twist her hand until, finally, it became freed from the bars.

"I'm free!!" she shouted. At that, I had to laugh. She was such a loser. That's ok though, because she's still smarter than Edward. (Not that *that's* too hard to accomplish).

"I think we should go help. Charity looks scared." Pindel noted. When does she *not* look scared?!

"Fine." Charlie agreed. They began to walk down the stairs, slowly.

"Ok, that's not working for me." I noted, then I jumped up onto the banister, and slid down to the ground floor. "That was fun." I said.

"She's hyper again." Charlie noted.

"Is that a bad thing?" Pindel asked.

"It can be."

"Hey, I *am* still standing right here, you know!" I shouted.

"Yes, I know. It's not like you care anyway." Charlie laughed.

"Good point." I shrugged. They reached where I was standing and we looked over to see what was going on.

Edward was holding on to Keira's wrist and, though I'm not sure, I think he was actually being nice to her. "Are you ok?" he asked. She looked just as shocked as the rest of us. But before she could answer, Vincient interrupted.

"Get your hands off on *my* woman half breed!!" he shouted. (Did I hear that right? Oh, this ought a be good).

"*Your* woman?" Keira shouted.

"Half Breed?" Edward demanded. Vincient carelessly flung Edward aside and grabbed Keira's hands.

"Did he hurt you?" he demanded. Keira glared at him.

"No, actually, he was going to rescue me." she said angrily. At her words, Vincient looked livid. He spun around to face Edward and shouted,

"She belongs to me! Not you, *me*!!!"

"She doesn't belong to you!" Edward snapped. But it was obvious that he immediately regretted his words.

"Then who?" Vincient challenged. Edward looked frantically around the room before replying,

"Uhh…she belongs to Pindel!"

"WHAT!!?" Pindel and Keira screamed at the same time. I heard Charlie laugh. I, myself, was trying not to. (But it was *very* hard).

"I hate her!!" Pindel screeched, near tears. "she scares me!" He added.

"Hey!" Keira shouted. Then she seemed to be thoughtful for a moment. "Charity, come here and give me a bottle of holy water." (Oh shit, we're all in trouble).

"O-ok." Charity pulled a small bottle out of her pocket and walked shakily over to Keira. "What is it that you want?"

Keira held out her hands over Charity's and the bottle and said, "start singing."

"Why?" Charity asked. I took a step back, as did Charlie.

"Just focus your powers into the holy water and I'll do the same, ok?" (Another step back).

"I'll try." Charity grinned. (Two or three steps back).

"Good!"

After a little while of them channeling their powers, Keira let go of the bottle. "Charity, throw it at Vincient!"

"No!!"

"Then hand it over!" Keira demanded.

Once the holy water was in Keira's possession, she launched it straight at Vincient. Then she motioned for us to leave. In about ten seconds we were outside. Then we watched as the entire building collapsed in on itself. Vincient was gone…for now.

Chapter 17
Evil Plan

After we (Temporarily) got rid of Vincient, Edward kept coming up to me and glaring at me.

"What!?" I finally shouted.

"You're evil, that's what!" he snapped back.

"I'm not evil, yet." I said angrily.

"See, *yet*. You will be and I think you should leave. If you don't, your power will become a threat, and I'll have to use force." At Edward's empty threat, I laughed.

"Your stupidity endangers us everyday but you don't see us taking up arms against you." I defended myself.

"But I don't choose to be stupid." Edward said, I would've laughed, if I hadn't just gotten nauseated by a familiar scent.

"It's been a while, hasn't it?" Jezaba asked. "You don't know where I am, but I know where you are." he laughed. I rolled my eyes.

"Hmmm...." I pretended to think about it, "let me guess, you're up in those trees, right?"

"Damn! You're good! And I thought it was such a hard place too!" Jezaba whined, jumping down and standing in front of us. "Well, at least I led them here." he snapped his fingers and we were transported into a building and...my father and Sedrick were standing before us, both glaring at me.

Then, Jezaba glared at me too, as he said, "Because of *you*, you demonic bitch, I have to wear *this*!" he finished, raising his right hand. There, over what I knew to be bone, was a black glove.

"Ok...what did she do?" Edward asked, (why does he have to ask *that* question?)

"This!!" Jezaba exclaimed, yanking off the glove. Keira gasped. Charity, Pindel, and Edward screamed. And Charlie looked at me questioningly. I smiled innocently back at him.

"HOLY FREAKIN SHIT!!!!" Edward shrieked, cowering in the corner. Meanwhile, my dad looked like he was about to rip out Jezaba's lungs.

"Jezaba, put that away…*now.*" he demanded.

"Hey, *I'm* the future supreme overlord of the world! I'm the Alpha and the Omega and you're not so I suggest that you stuff it."

"What?! But I'm the ruler of the- never mind. I suggest that you stuff it before I rip you into a million pieces." (That was really close).

"You know what, I'm leaving. And I'm taking my glove with me!" Jezaba said, and with that, he shimmered.

"I'll be back later." my father threatened. Then with one last glance at Sedrick, he too shimmered.

"Reilly, why do I have a bad feeling that he's not here to tell you he found a cure?" Charlie asked. I was about to answer, but just then, Sedrick spoke.

"Reilly, Dad and I have agreed that it would be best for you to come back to the castle." Sedrick said, his eyes glowing.

"Sedrick, what are you talking about!?" I demanded, he wasn't making any sense. When I'd left the castle, he seemed to be almost back to normal. But now he was talking insanity again. What did he mean by that?!

"I'm saying that all of my theories about him were wrong. Dad never had anything but our best interests at heart." Sedrick replied.

"He doesn't have a heart! You *know* that!" I said, my voice shaking with fury. Then it happened again, my whole body began to tremble. Another seizure, I sank to the ground and hugged my knees to my chest, waiting for it to end.

"Reilly, what's happening!?" Sedrick asked, I could detect real panic in his voice.

"We don't know, they started right after her last encounter with your dad." Charlie explained.

"Why does she look so-" Sedrick began to ask.

"Weak?" I finished for him, finally able to stand. "That's what happens when you turn evil against your will, Sedrick." I glared at him, " of coarse, *you* wouldn't know, considering you were *born* that way." I finished, then

I saw it. The look in his eyes, something wasn't right. Or maybe…it was exactly right.

"Reilly, please I-" Sedrick said weakly. Then it hit me, so I played along.

"You what? You want to ruin my life? Or maybe, you just want to kill me because Dad can't!" I said, but he understood the hidden meaning in my words. Charlie did too though everyone else was still clueless.

"Yes, that's *exactly* what I came to do!" Sedrick snarled.

"Uh…Reilly…why is your brother looking at us like that?" Edward asked shakily.

"Because, he's going to attempt to kill us." I shrugged.

"Oh, is that all?" Edward mumbled.

"Pretty much." I said, turning my head toward him.

"Reilly, watch out!" Charity screeched. I looked back in time to see Sedrick coming toward me. He tackled me, taking us both to the ground.

"Ow." I mumbled.

"Sorry." he whispered, then stood up. "did you not pay attention when I was training you?"

"It's pretty easy to tune *you* out." I said, also rising to my feet.

"You'll regret not listening." he hissed, his hand began to glow and he tried to hit me with it. But I caught it in mid air.

"I didn't say I didn't listen." I growled. Then I let go and shoved him backwards, away from me. He fell a little ways away, and I walked toward him.

"Good, so you did pay attention." Sedrick said, standing.

"Yep." I said, springing my claws out. I 'attempted' to hit him but he caught my hand.

"Ready?" he asked, I put my claws back.

"Uh-huh." I nodded and he threw me upward. In the air, I spun in a circle, shooting fire out of my hands as I did so. Shortly afterward, I heard the screams of the government of the Underworld, who had been watching.

As I descended, I pulled my hands inward and landed gracefully crouched on my feet. Then, as I stood up, I brought my claws back out and leapt toward the remaining demons that now surrounded Sedrick and I. With in minutes, they were all dead. But it was far from over.

Chapter 18
Tragedy

"How did you figure it out? I was trying to give you as many clues as I could but you weren't seeming to get it." Sedrick laughed, I glared at him.

"You aren't as good of an actor as you credit yourself for. *I* was acting." I said.

"No you weren't." Charlie mumbled.

"Shut up." I said, "fine, I didn't get it until you gave me that look."

"What look?" Sedrick asked, confused.

"The one that makes you look like a pathetic puppy who's lost his home." I grinned.

"Oh, that one." Sedrick said, grinning back at me.

"Aw, how touching." an evil voice said.

"Great, not again." I groaned.

"What's wrong, Reilly? Didn't you miss me?" my dad asked, appearing in front of us.

"Depends, if 'miss' means 'wish you were damned to hell,' then I missed you a lot." I said.

"It doesn't mean that." my dad snarled.

"Well in that case, no, I didn't miss you." I said.

"What kind of world is it when a father and his own daughter can't get along?" my dad asked no one in particular.

"The same kind of world where a father tries to kill his daughter." Sedrick hissed.

"Really, Sedrick? And here I thought that all I had were your best interests at heart." my dad laughed.

"See, I told you I could act." Sedrick said to me.

"You win." I sighed, pretending to be disappointed.

"Do you two think that this is a game!?" my dad yelled.

"Did you think it was a game, Reilly?" Sedrick asked.

"Yeah, I thought we were playing Monopoly." I said.

"You mean, we're not?" Sedrick asked, "well in that case, let's kill him."

"The only ones dying here will be you two!" my father shouted, then he added, "how are you dealing with those seizures, Reilly?"

"How did *you* know about that?!" Charlie asked.

"Well it wasn't that hard considering I caused them." my father said.

"What?" I asked.

"Don't you remember what I gave to you?"

"The shot. But what-" I began.

"It was a powerful 'medicine'. To make the stigmata progress faster. It was pure evil. The seizures are from the shot trying to bond with your DNA."

"Sorry I asked." I said.

"You should be sorry, that I didn't do it sooner! I know I am. This way, you'll be evil with in, oh, three months, tops." my dad said.

"See now, that's why everyone hates you so much." I said.

"Not everyone hates me, right Sedrick?" Lieam asked, turning to Sedrick.

"No, I think Reilly's right on this one. Pretty much everyone hates you." Sedrick said.

"I agree." Charlie added.

"Now guys, this is between Reilly and I. You two need to just stay out of it." my dad said, waving one hand through the air, simultaneously I felt paralyzed.

"Uh-Oh." Sedrick sighed.

"What?" Charlie asked, then he added, "I can't move!"

"That's 'what,' *we* can't move."

"Neither can I." I added.

"Us either." Edward called.

"Not important." I muttered.

"That's correct, I have given up on trying to kill your friends as it will do me no good. I think I'll just kill you." my dad said, he was standing right in front of me and as he spoke he turned my head so that I had to face him.

"It might do you good, considering if you kill her then I'll kill you!" Charlie shouted.

"Yeah, I'll help." Sedrick said.

"You do that." Edward muttered. If it's possible to glare at someone without being able to look in their direction, Charlie accomplished it.

"Enough! I haven't even **killed** her yet!" my dad thundered.

"No, but you were talking about it." Sedrick said.

"So you're saying that I should just get on with it, correct?"

"Guys, not helping!" I shouted, annoyed.

"Well, they're helping *me*." my dad laughed, "any ideas as to *how* I should kill her?"

"Well you could-" Edward began, but I think he could sense the hatred that got directed toward him, because he stopped. "Never mind." he said.

"that's ok, I have an idea." my dad said, then he snapped my head sideways, causing me to fly through the air, spinning, and land (VERY hardly,) on the opposite side of the room.

"Reilly! Are you ok?" Charlie called.

"Fine." I said, pushing myself back up to my feet.

"You won't be." my dad said, and I had to avoid another attack.

"Reilly, you can undo whatever he did to us." Sedrick called.

"And how do you propose I do that?" I asked, as my father pinned me to the wall. I kicked him in the stomach and he released me.

"Just concentrate." Sedrick yelled.

"Can she really do that? I mean, she's powerful but is she really that-"

"Edward, unless you want to stay frozen like that forever," I glanced at him, he was frozen in a way that looked like he had been about to fall, " I suggest you SHUT UP!!" I finished.

"Ok." he said. I sighed angrily as my dad tried to kill me with a blast of fire. Then I focused all of my energy on the others. Moments later, I heard Edward fall to the ground.

"Hey it actually worked!" Keira yelled, (All right, ye of little faith. Next time you'll stay frozen!)

"Ow." Edward groaned.

"Hey I did it!" I said, (*I'm* the only one allowed to doubt me).

"Congratulations." my dad hissed, as he punched me in the stomach, causing me to double up. Then he either kicked or kneed me in the face. I heard my nose crack, and seconds later felt the blood run down my face and into my mouth. I spit it out but I could still taste it.

"Well, that's disgusting." I murmured.

"Too bad, deal with it." my father said, grabbing me by the throat and lifting me off the ground. I coughed, gasping for breath, but it was no use. I saw him reach his hand back and extract his claws, but as he moved them forward to stab me, something, or someone, got in the way.

I heard a gasp of pain, followed by my father's maniacal laughter as he let me go and backed away. I fell behind whoever had saved me and looked over to see Sedrick lying motionless on the ground.

"Sedrick? Please be ok." I begged, he didn't move. "Sedrick! Please don't die!!" I was shouting now and my father's laughter grew louder to drown me out.

"Reilly, he's gone." Charlie whispered. He was kneeling beside me and was trying to get me to let go of Sedrick's hand. I hadn't realized anyone had moved, but when I looked around, I saw that Keira, Edward, and Charity were headed toward the door.

"No! he's not, he can't be!" I cried, closing Sedrick's eyes with my free hand.

"Reilly, come on, we should go." Charlie said calmly.

"No! I can't leave him!" I shrieked, tears streaming down my face.

"Yes, Charlie let her stay. She only wants to stay with her brother. This is a family matter, you should just stay out of it." my father said.

"He *is* my family. He and Sedrick and the others. Now, GO TO HELL!!" I screamed, tackling my father with all of my strength. I must have done at least a little damage, because he threw me off of him, stood up, and was bleeding badly. I, too, stood up, and my demon blood was about to spill over.

"Now, now, Reilly. We wouldn't want to do anything, rash, would we?"

"Yes, we would!" I screamed, leaping at him. He pushed me out of his way and turned to face me.

"You can be mad at me all you want. But deep down you *know* the truth, you *know* that it was *your* fault that your brother died." My dad said, then he left with an explosion that sent the whole building into self-destruct mode.

I ran back over to Sedrick's body and sat down beside him, crying once again.

"Reilly, we have to leave now!" Charlie shouted. He was no longer calm, which told me that we didn't have much time before the building collapsed with us inside.

"No! you go!" I shouted back.

"C'mon!" Edward yelled from the door, which caved in. "We'll have to shimmer."

"What?" Keira asked.

"Reilly, come on!" Charlie yelled, "we're leaving!"

"No! I'm not!" I said.

"Yes, you are." Charlie said. Unexpectedly grabbing me and shimmering.

"No!" I screamed, once outside. I tried to run back to the building, but Charlie still had his arm around my waist and he was keeping me from going anywhere. "Let go!" I screamed.

"No, Reilly, you can't go back in there!"

"Why not!?" I screamed.

"Because, you'll die too. Do you really think that Sedrick would want that?" Charlie asked.

"No." I admitted. Then we heard explosions as the whole building collapsed. "it **was** my fault. If I would've just stayed at the castle like my father wanted, then-"

"He would've killed you." Charlie stated, I hadn't realized that I had started to cry again, but now I felt the tears flooding from my eyes.

"Yeah, probably." I said, beginning to calm down.

"Let's get the hell away from here." Keira said.

"Ok." I agreed. I felt my extensive injuries healing, and I also felt the stigmata progress again.

Chapter 19
Guilt

As we were about to shimmer, I heard Keira curse under her breath. I knew what she must be seeing, because I could sense Kara probably as well as Keira could see her. "Edward, don't look." Keira commanded, so of coarse, Edward looked.

"Kara!!" he shouted, but she ignored him completely and walked straight to Keira.

"You." she said, not bothering to conceal the bitterness from her voice. "I came here to **warn** you and, besides that, I have a job for you as well."

"I should've known…" Keira muttered. "And would this job involve Jezaba?"

"Partially." Kara admitted. I rolled my eyes but kept my senses alert. Beside me, Charlie did the same.

"Shit. I don't want the job then, I've had enough of him for one day! And besides, what exactly is this 'job'?" Keira asked, (I think we've **all** had enough of Jezaba. Him, **and** his glove. What a idiot).

Kara glared down at the ground and replied, "I need you to find something for me. It's something important." (Oh dear God, she's going to ask us to find her a brain. Don't you usually go to wizards for that sort of thing. What do we look like, The Great and Powerful Eternally Damned?!)

"And that would be?" Keira pressed. Kara did not look too happy, (not that she ever does,) but after much 'debating internally' she answered,

"The key." she said.

"Ok…WAIT! A KEY?!" Keira screamed. (No Keira, not *a* key, **the** key). "So let me get this straight, I am to look for a key?" (No, **the** key!!!! As in, and I'm guessing here, the one to the Door to the Darkness).

"It's no ordinary key!" Kara snapped, "it is the key to the Door to the Darkness!" man, and here I was hoping I was wrong for a change. "if Jezaba has that and all eight Apostles there's no telling the amount of damage that would be done!" (To what, your ego? Wasn't it your job to guard the damn thing. Why, yes, I believe it was). Kara began to show signs of calming down, "I want you to head back to Desoto, go to the cemetery that's near your stupid school and find the grave of my old friend Erica Adams. In her tomb lies the key. I shall meet you at stupid's house." she gazed at Keira a while before adding, "good luck."

"Whatever." Keira said angrily. Ok, I just lost my brother to my demonic father, I really don't think looking for a key is what I should be doing right now.

✯ ✯ ✯

11:30 P.M (in the freaking cemetery!!!)

*"You can be mad at me all you want. But deep down you **know** the truth*, why didn't we bring flashlights!!!" Keira's demanding voice broke me out of my nightmare. The same one I had been having through all of my waking hours since Sedrick's death. Maybe it had something to do with the truth in them.

"Maybe it's because someone is stupid and forgot them, am I right Edward?" Charlie mumbled from beside me. It was pitch black outside and needless to say, we didn't have flashlights. For Edward, Charlie, and I, it wasn't a problem, but some careless idiot, who shall remain nameless, (EDWARD!!!!!) forgot that Apostles of God and dwelves can't see in the dark.

"Wait! I can't help it that I forgot that Keira and Charity...*All your fault. You know that it was your fault that your brother is dead!*" this time the words echoed loudly in my mind. And, because I wasn't paying attention to anything else, I tripped over a conspicuously laid grave marker. I landed on my back on the ground. But I didn't try to stand. I simply sat up, leaned against the tombstone and declared,

"You know what? I'm staying **right here**!" I said, brushing Charlie away, who had come to help me stand back up. "*All your fault. If you'd have just listened to him, Sedrick wouldn't be dead. All your fault. If you'd have just stayed at the castle, Sedrick would still live. All your fault.*" fine, I'd rather listen to my stupid conscious give me shit anyway. "I can't stand anymore of this, so I'm staying right here and no one can make me move!!!" I shouted. Half talking about the whole 'quest to save the world' thing and half talking about the stupid voices in my head, (no pun intended. There was literally a voice in my head at this point).

Suddenly I heard a crash and saw Keira disappear underground. I saw Charlie, Charity, Edward, and Pindel go down after her and then I was alone. That's when my conscience really started in on me.

"*All your fault, all your fault, all your fault.*" it said, over and over. Like a chant. I couldn't take it anymore, I clamped my hands over my ears and closed my eyes as tightly as I could. The chant only grew muffled, I could still hear every word, "*Sedrick's death, is all your fault. should've listened, now too late. should've stayed, now too late. should've saved him, now you can't. It's all your fault.*" (wow, a conscience sure doesn't have a very big vocabulary).

"*All your fault! All your fault! All your-* Reilly? Are you ok?" this time, it was Charlie's voice the broke me out of my nightmare. I opened my eyes and uncovered my ears.

"No." I answered truthfully.

"What's wrong?" he asked, I debated on telling him or not because I knew what he's say, and I knew that it wouldn't help. But I decided to try anyway.

"It was my fault. And now I can't even fix my mistake, not with it having the outcome I need." I said. Charlie sat down beside me and put his arm around me.

"It wasn't your fault. And even if you would've stayed at the castle, Sedrick still would've tried to save you. That's what he wanted to do, and that's what he told me to do before he died." well that was unexpected.

"Huh?" I managed.

"Before he ran in front of you, he said to keep you safe. And I think that includes saving you from yourself. You can't keep killing yourself over this, that's not why he did it. He saved you to give you a chance, to give us a chance, to save everyone. Including us. So don't give up, not now. " well what do you say to that? If you have any ideas, please, I'd like to hear them. *I* couldn't think of anything. I kind of just sat there blankly, tears forming in my eyes. Charlie obviously could tell that I wasn't going to respond, because he turned toward me and hugged me so tightly that I almost couldn't breathe. "Come on, we'd better go help Keira and the others." he suggested, I just nodded. (Damn, he got me to move!!)

Chapter 20
The Key

We got down into the tomb and saw Keira dragging Edward into a very dark and creepy crypt.

"It would be nice if you weren't dragging and choking me." he mumbled. Keira only tugged tighter. "Jeez! Hold on!" Edward screamed like a two-year-old *girl*. She let him go and they entered the inner chamber, out of sight.

"Now what?" Charity asked.

"Now we wait." Charlie answered her. But I had a feeling we'd have to help Keira. Actually, it was more like a fact, considering Jezaba had just crossed into my senses. (Good, I have a bone to pick with him. He lead my father to me in the first place. Not to mention ripping out Charlie's horns).

"We need to go help Keira." I stated.

"Why?" Charlie asked.

"Because I just sensed Jezaba. Charity, you and Pindel stay here." I commanded, they both nodded and Charlie and I ran toward the next room.

We entered the burial chamber in time to see Edward handing the key to Jezaba! (And *I'm* the evil one?!) Right afterward, Keira passed out from her multiple injuries, caused, no doubt, by Edward.

"Edward!! What the hell are you doing!!?" Charlie shouted. Edward stepped back and blinked several times. But Jezaba had already gone.

"What happened?" Edward asked, still dazed.

"You just gave away the key." I stated.

"Huh?"

"*You* just gave the *key* to *Jezaba*." I said slowly.

"Well what happened to Keira?" he asked.

"She met you." I mumbled. Edward glared at me. "Just go away, Edward."

"No, I can't leave them alone with you."

"She's not the one I'm worried about. What happened." Charlie stepped in, sounding annoyed.

"I don't know." Edward admitted.

"We need to get Keira somewhere less filled with dead people." I said.

"Right." Edward and Charlie agreed.

✯ ✯ ✯

We were all sitting in the kitchen, as we had been everyday since Edward's idiocy almost killed Keira, (which was about three days ago,) when we heard a crash coming from Keira's room.

Edward was the first to reach the doorway and with horror I saw a look of utmost joy cross his face.

"Move Edward." I demanded, pushing passed him to help Keira.

"Bull shit! Where the hell is the key!?" Kara was shouting. She had Keira pinned up against the wall and was strangling her.

"Hey, Kara." I said, my voice sounding **very** demonic. She spun around to face me and I let my fist smash into her nose with as much force I could put behind it. She stumbled, dropping Keira to the floor.

"Damn all of you!" she shouted, clutching her bleeding and, most likely, broken nose. "Especially *you two*!!" she added, thrusting a shaking finger at Keira and I. Well, that went well.

"Hi Kara!!" Edward screamed, almost glowing with happiness. "You look angry." he noted, then he glared at Keira, "what the hell did you do *now*?!" he demanded.

"W-what?" Keira shouted, "you're the asshole who gave the key to Jezaba!"

"WHAT!?!" Kara thundered, then she grabbed Edward by the throat and growled, "what the hell did you do!? Why did you do it? Because of *you* the whole world is probably going to be engulfed in darkness!" she let him go and yelled, "I'm leaving!" then she stormed out the door, slamming it shut behind her.

Wait!" Edward shouted, running after her. Keira stood up and quickly followed them.

"That was interesting." I noted.

"Keira's going to get herself killed." Charlie said.

"Yeah, I know." I sighed.

"We should probably go make sure that doesn't happen." Charlie said calmly, though my anger was beginning to rise.

"Yeah, I know." I said, fighting to keep my voice level. We turned and raced out the door, with Charity and Pindel close behind us.

We arrived at a small clearing in time to see Kara falling backwards off a cliff, (yes!!!!). Edward, of coarse, shouted, "Kara!!!!" as he ran out from his and Keira's hiding place to where *Jezaba* was watching the evil witch-I mean- holy woman fall.

Great, now Edward's gonna go all spastic on us and start screaming Kara's name. He's such an idiot. I should so kill him! (Whoa, where'd that come from?)

Upon noticing my expression of shock at my own thoughts, Charlie gave me a strange look and whispered, " What's wrong?"

"Nothing." I lied, still trying to figure out why I was suddenly so violent. I mean, yeah, I hated Edward with every fiber of my being, but he was Charlie's friend so I'd never actually kill him. But that time it took all I had *not* to.

"Yeah, whatever." he said skeptically. I knew the subject wasn't closed. We followed Edward and Keira, (mainly to make sure that Jezaba didn't kill anyone else.)

"Jezaba." Charlie growled, no doubt remembering his horns.

"Hello, well my work here is done. Oh, Reilly, I am sorry about Sedrick." he said.

"What!?" I snarled, I tried to go toward him, but Charlie held me back.

"No, Reilly, the stigmata." he warned.

"I don't care!" I shouted.

"Goodbye." Jezaba said happily. Then he left, leaving me fuming.

"I need to destroy something," I stated, relaxing slightly. "Where's Edward?"

"Reilly…"

"Ok, fine…where's Pindel?" I revised my plan.

"Reilly! You're scaring me." Charlie admitted. (Was I being violent again?)

"Sorry. I don't realize I'm doing it." I said.

"I know, that's what scares me."

"Kara!!" Edward's agonized yell came from the edge where she'd fallen.

"Oh dear God. The lady dies like every two years or something, you'd think he'd be used to it." I rolled my eyes. Charlie, obviously relieved by my sarcasm, smiled and said,

"Be nice."

"Edward, it's ok." Keira tried comforting him.

"It's no use, Keira. You should've seen him the last time she died." Charlie said.

"Damn it!!" Edward shouted, punching the ground with his fists.

"I don't think I would've *wanted* to see him." Keira said.

"Probably not." someone said from behind Charlie and I.

"Vincient, go away." I said without turning around.

"Reilly, I'm sorry about your brother. It's unfortunate that he died, but at least we still have you." (Does *everyone* know!?!?)

"You don't know what happened, you weren't there!!" I shouted, spinning to face him.

"Ok..." Vincient said, taking several steps backwards.

"Reilly, calm down." Charlie whispered in my ear. He had one arm around my waist and was restraining me for strangling Vincient. I slightly relaxed and let him pull me behind him. He kept one arm around me and turned back to face Vincient.

"What do *you* want, asshole?" he growled, sounding *very* unlike himself.

"Keira!" Vincient yelled, ignoring us completely. Or maybe that was the answer to our question. The latter is most likely.

"I'm gonna go help Edward." Keira said, backtracking toward where Edward still looked miserably over the ravine.

"No." Charlie said sharply. "Jezaba's killed one person, we're not sure if he'll come back and we can't risk losing an Apostle!"

"Well I'm **NOT** going to be submissive and I *won't* listen to you! Who the hell put you in charge!?" Keira shouted. Neither Charlie nor I was listening to her tantrum, we were watching Vincient run to her at demonic speed. Before we could act (though we weren't really *trying* to stop him. Hey, it wasn't like he was going to **hurt** her and she needed to be taught a lesson.) he'd already reached her.

Vincient picked Keira up and dashed toward our campsite. All the while we could hear Keira screaming at him.

"What happened?" Edward mumbled, he'd managed to drag himself away from the ledge and was now walking toward us, Charlie and I exchanged glances, (his said, 'no you can't kill him,' and mine said, 'well can I at least hurt him a little?') then he let me go!!

I walked toward Edward and smacked him in the head. "You idiot." I said, then I turned to Charity, " Go to the Order, don't tell any one anything and don't leave until we come and get you." I commanded, she nodded and headed off in the general direction of the Order. Then I shimmered off after Keira.

When I arrived, Keira was shrieking at the top of her voice, "YOU BASTARD!!" she shouted, punching the barrier around her.

"Just wait! I'll get you! I swear it! I'll-"

"Keira…" I growled, interrupting her. "She spun around to face me and jumped when she saw my demonically glowing eyes. "Shut up."

"I'll just sit here…" she mumbled, meekly. Then something caught her gaze. I groaned. She had reached for a rather large rock and began to *talk* to it. Well alrighty then. Jeez, I knew she was insane but holy shit she's freaking talking to an inanimate object. (Remember that whole, 'she's dumber than a rock,' thing from before? Well I take that back, she has to be at least as smart as one to carry on a conversation with it, right?)

"Keira, why are you staring at that rock?" Vincient asked. She glared at him,

"We're not speaking to *you*!" she angrily shouted.

"We?" Vincient asked, more than a little disturbed. Then I noticed Charlie walking toward where I stood with Keira. He tried to take away the rock, (all the while trying not to laugh, as I was,) when Keira angrily snatched it from his grasp. "it's my Rocky, damn it! Get your own!" (Oh dear God she's named the damn thing. It *that's* what's supposed to save us from Satan and all his works, then, dare I say it? *Heaven* help us.)

"Keira…" Charlie sighed, annoyed, we heard light footsteps coming, and turned around to see Edward slowly trudging to us from the entrance to our camp. Charlie had barely taken the barrier away when Keira raced toward the approaching idiot.

"You waited for me?" he asked, confused. (Well if it had been up to me, we would've been long gone by now. But, unfortunately, yes, we waited for you.)

Keira nodded and smiled at him, but Edward barely acknowledged her. "I at least thought I would find her body…" he mumbled, clenching his hand into an angry fist.

For a second, Keira just stood there, then she took a deep breath and muttered, "I hate seeing you like this." she sounded so sincere! But Edward just walked straight past her. She spun on her heel and stormed over to her sleeping bag. Even a blind man with hearing problems could've been able to tell that she was crying, but Edward completely ignored her.

We headed off again in search of Jezaba. And still Edward continued to avoid Keira. Only Charlie and I understood why though neither of us said anything. (in case you haven't been paying attention, here's a little trivia for you. Keira is the reincarnation of what pain in the ass holy woman? Which means she looks exactly like whom? Ding, ding, ding, Kara!!)

"REILLY!" Keira suddenly thundered from directly in front of me.

"I'm right here." I hissed angrily.

"Oh, there you are!" she sang happily, "We have to talk, *now*!" she grabbed me by the wrist and began dragging me away from the others.

"Hey! Let go!" I angrily protested. She did so quickly and turned to face me. "Ok, what the hell is this about?" I demanded.

"I know you'll think I'm being stupid but this is about Edward…" she sighed.

"What about him?" I asked. The idea that anyone would want to talk about Edward truly intrigued me.

"I-I'm worried about him."

"Really." I said skeptically.

"I know, it sounds stupid! He's different since *she* died! It's like a part of him went down the ravine too! All of a sudden it's like I'm invisible! If only he knew…" no Keira, you're right. He is different since…wait, what was she about to say!?

"What? If only he knew what?!" I asked.

"It's nothing." she stated, but her blush spoke louder than her words.

"Oh, you mean your feelings for him." you know, the ones *everyone* seems to know about but you two!

"Uh…No!"

"Keira, Keira, what are we going to do with you?" I sighed, shaking my head. We walked back to where everyone else was waiting, Keira getting paler with every step.

"Hello young ones." an old man said. I smelled something rotting and turned to see an ancient priest looking at us. He grabbed my wrist to pull me out from in front of Keira, and where he touched me I felt extreme pain. I glared at him but he seemed not to notice,

"I've just come from a village from over the mountain. The villagers found a holy woman who washed up on the riverbed." the old guy said. He was a horrible liar. But the only reason why I kept listening was because I couldn't really detect his heartbeat well. "The woman said that she was injured by a man named Jezaba." Edward gasped, Oh lord.

"It was her!" he shouted. Keira cringed and stared at the ground.

"However," the man continued, "she had terrible wounds and she may've already died." he once again tried to add fake sympathy and sorrow into his voice. But no matter how fake he sounded, Edward still believed him. He sighed and continued to stare sadly down at the ground.

"Go, get things settled." Keira suddenly said. We all stared at her for a couple of seconds, too shocked to speak.

"WHAT!!?" Edward, Charlie, and I finally said.

"What the hell are you saying?" I asked angrily.

"This isn't' a time for hesitating! Go," Keira said, glaring at Edward, "Kara should be waiting for you. GO!"

Edward's eyes widened and for a second he almost looked like he was about to stay. But then he took another glance at Keira and sprinted off in the direction the priest had pointed out.

"Keira, what are you thinking?" a small, squeaky voice demanded.

"Pindel?" Keira asked.

"Yep!" he said, jumping onto her shoulder.

"You heard the whole thing, didn't you?"

"Uh…yeah." he said with a nervous smile. I reached up and smacked Keira in the head.

"Ow!!" she screeched.

"You idiot, why did you do that? It's not like you're the Apostle of Charity!" I said, both annoyed and angry.

Keira turned around to face me and faked a smile, "he has to go. He won't be able to move forward it he doesn't know." Now what I wanted to say was, 'that's a load of bull shit and you know it!' but I decided to keep quiet. I, of coarse, figured she'd be mature enough to live with her decision **without** pissing everybody off. The next day, she proved me wrong.

Chapter 21
Mind Trick

"HE'S NOT HERE!!" Keira was shrieking. She was, as I'd predicted, deeply sorry she'd chosen as she had. "WHERE IS HE?!"

"I knew you'd be regretting your decision." I sighed.

"He's not here! But he should be here! I bet that witch did something to him!" Keira said frantically.

"We have to go." Charlie said, Keira glared at him as he continued, "we can't worry about Edward, he'll be fine. He'll know where to find you."

"Keira, he'll follow your scent." Pindel added. (Great, we sound like bloodhounds again!) Suddenly, the slightest noise caught my attention. I glanced at Charlie, who appeared to have heard it as well. We looked over in the direction we thought it had come from and saw a huge group of about fifty people coming our way. They didn't look like villagers and they didn't look friendly.

"You four," the leader said, "you are under arrest!" As he spoke I caught the same scent of something rotten, but this time, it came complete with the overwhelming stench of Violante.

"WHAT?" Keira shrieked, practically in my ear, "WHAT DO YOU MEAN, 'WE'RE UNDER ARREST!?' LOOK HERE PAL, I CAN'T BE ARRESTED, I'M AN EMOTIONAL WRECK!!!!"

"Um...uh...too bad?" the guy said, shakily taking a step back.

"She's also on crack, apparently." I said, glaring at her.

"SHUT UP!!!" Keira shouted, jumping up and down. I rolled my eyes,

"Dude, you're proving my point." I said, acid dripping from my words. She was seriously starting to provoke my demon side.

"That coward." Keira mumbled, looking around. I, too, had noticed that Pindel had fled at the sight of the army, (for I didn't know what else to call them.)

"I should've known..." Charlie sighed. The leader grabbed us and I felt a sharp, stinging, pain in that hand. I flinched and Keira looked over at me,

"What?" she asked.

"That was painful." Charlie commented. He must've felt the same thing I had. Whatever that was, though I had a guess.

"I've been hurt worse." I said, thinking back to almost a year ago when we'd been trapped on a crashing airplane *full* of mind puppets.

"What!?" Keira yelled again, clearly frustrated. We ignored her.

We were taken to a castle that looked all too familiar to Charlie and I. There was now no mistaking who was behind everything, but we couldn't risk doing anything without endangering Keira, and we both knew it.

"What do we do?" Charlie asked as we were led down a dark hallway.

"Wait."

"For what?"

"My signal." I said, he sighed, annoyed, but he didn't say any more. Ahead of us, we could see that Keira was about to be forced into a room. Seeing my chance, for now most of the soldiers had gone to other areas, I broke free of my restraints and knocked out about three remaining demons before they knew what hit them. Then I glared at the one who had burnt my arm. Before he could blink, he was sent spiraling down a tunnel of eternal darkness. (I didn't even know I could do that! This is so cool, if not a little scary.)

"What did you just do?" Charlie asked as several more troops raced around the corner.

"I wish I knew." I admitted.

"What?!" he demanded, outraged. But I didn't have time to answer, within seconds neither of us could talk because we were too busy trying to kill as many soldiers as we could. We had been fighting for what felt like hours when a quick moving shadow caught my eye. Everything appeared to be under control, so, making sure that Charlie saw me, I followed the mysterious shape. Somehow, it looked familiar.

"Reilly!!" I heard Charlie's voice above the battle. I turned around, expecting him to stop me. Instead, he added, "be careful." I nodded and continued in the direction I was going.

The phantom moved extremely quickly and I found myself running just to keep it in my sight. Soon, however, it stopped in front of a door and looked back at me. I stopped as well and the minute I did so, it flew straight through the door. I had an overwhelming sense that I needed to follow it, so I stepped in front of the door and paused. What if I was wrong? What if this was just another of Jezaba's tricks, or worse, one of my father's tricks? But then again, what if I was right, and this...*thing* was leading me to something important.

I decided to risk it, and pushed the metal door open. To my immense surprise, it was unlocked. Well either that or the shadow had unlocked it for me.

"Reilly!" I heard a faint but urgent whisper coming from inside. Normally my common sense would've told me that was a great reason **not** to enter. But my instincts and my **heart** told me otherwise.

I walked through the door and stepped cautiously into the room. As soon as my feet entered, the door slammed shut behind me, but I didn't really care, because what I was looking at, was far more important to me.

Chapter 22
The Hall of Scrolls

The phantom I'd followed was no where to be seen, but I wasn't overly concerned with that at the moment, because at that point I was staring at possibly one of the largest rooms I'd ever seen. Even in the Castle of the Underworld this room would've seemed massive. More than that, though, was that it was filled with rows upon rows of scrolls. There had to have been trillions of them.

"Hello?" I called, and it echoed off the walls of the huge room. "Hey, I don't know why I'm here." I wasn't really expecting an answer, but I didn't know what else to do. "Couldn't you help a little more, I'm still lost here." I was about to have myself committed for talking to no one, when I saw it. The faint glow coming from the back of the room. I walked toward it and as I got closer, the light got brighter until I reached the area it had originated from and that entire row was lit.

I looked up at the column in front of me but nothing drew my specific attention until I noticed a certain scroll that in itself seemed to be the origin of the bluish glow. I reached for it without thinking or even being concerned that it would burn through my hand or something. The minute my hand touched it, the glow faded and I was left in complete darkness.

It wasn't particularly hard for me to find my way back to the door but it was becoming increasingly more annoying that I couldn't read the damn thing in the dark. Which in itself was odd. But what was even more disturbing was that I couldn't open the door! Then I heard the footsteps outside, not knowing who it was, I kept quiet.

"Reilly? Where are you?" Charlie whispered from right outside the door.

"Charlie! I'm in here!" I said.

"Where's here?" he asked, I rolled my eyes.

"Look to your left." I said.

"There's a wall there." he answered.

"Huh? Well that's weird. I came through a door right here." I said. But now that I remembered I hadn't felt a door handle before. And now that I looked again, there wasn't one.

"How am I supposed to get you out, if you don't know how you got in?" Charlie asked.

"I do know how I got in, I just don't know what happened to the entrance." I admitted.

"Wait, hold on." he suddenly said.

"What?" I asked, alerted by the note of urgency in his voice.

"Stand back, I have an idea." he said, but before I had time to move, the bricks and doorframe came crashing down almost on top of me.

"Jeez, maybe something like, 'hey I'm gonna destroy this wall' could've been said." I said, Charlie laughed as he pulled me out from behind the wreckage.

"I said stand back." he grinned, then his face turned serious, "we have to go, quickly." there was no need to explain, I could already hear the soldiers on their way down the hall. "C'mon." Charlie said, grabbing my hand and dragging me down the hall with him. While we were running, I stuffed the scroll in my pocked, vowing to try to open it as soon as I had the chance.

Chapter 23
Secret Password

We managed to make it all the way outside before the soldiers caught up to us. We, after all, couldn't leave Keira there, (as much as I would've liked to). So we fought off the army while trying to keep from getting ourselves killed. The latter was difficult considering over half of the soldiers were Violante's flesh puppets who don't actually *feel* anything. Eventually, however, we managed to finally destroy all of them.

"So what were you doing in there?" Charlie asked me after the last one fell.

"I was…uh, trying to read this." I said, handing him the scroll.

"What is it?" he asked after looking at it for a couple of seconds.

"Don't' know, I can't open it." I admitted.

"How did you find it?" Charlie asked.

"Well, I'm not positive. There was this, uh, shadow. And I followed it and it led me to that room. But when I got in the door closed and I couldn't get back out."

"Don't you think it's a little weird that this thing just happens to show up and lead you to a room where you couldn't get out?" Charlie asked the question I'd been wondering about. But before I could answer, Edward and Pindel came walking down the pathway toward the entrance.

"Well I guess you two pretty much hate me too I guess." Edward laughed nervously. Pindel said something that caused Edward to smack him and say, "Who asked you?! Besides, we need to go up to that castle and find Keira!!"

Once inside, we went straight to the room where Charlie and I had seen them take Keira. But no one except two dead people were there.

"Great, two of Violante's flesh puppets and no one else." Charlie commented.

The scents were still too strong for them to have been gone long. "We must've just missed them, they can't be too far." I said.

"Well then let's go!" Edward shouted.

"He *still* can't choose between Kara and Keira." Pindel sighed, earning him a smack on the head from Edward.

"Can't you let that go?"

"No." Pindel said, rubbing his wound.

We kept running around the castle, following **Edward** until, finally, he stopped. "This is getting us no where!" Pindel shouted.

"And I'm pretty sure we've been going in circles." Charlie added.

"And I'm positive that you're an idiot, Edward." I said, he glared at me but I continued before he could speak, "if you'd just make up your freaking mind we wouldn't be stuck in Jezaba's castle, running in circles, trying to find a room that-" I broke off, thinking. "A room that doesn't exist. Or isn't supposed to." I said.

"Huh?" Edward and Pindel asked, but Charlie understood.

"I really doubt she's in *that* room." he said.

"Probably not, but one like it." I said.

"I still don't get it." Edward said.

"It's not important, what is, is that I think I know where Keira is." I said.

With me leading the way, we continued to run through the halls. Finally, we reached the place where the wall had been destroyed. But I ignored that and walked back to the end of the hall. Then I heard it, the faint whisper of voices coming from the opposite wall. But there was no door, only a solid brick wall.

"Ok Edward," I announced, "you want to save Keira? Be my guest." I motioned to the obstacle and, without having to be told twice, Edward smashed through it headfirst! "So that's why he's missing so many brain cells. I wonder how many times he's done that?"

"What's that?" Pindel asked, pointing to the splinters of wood among the stone.

"There was a door on this side." I said, recognizing the fragments of a door frame.

"Edward!" Keira screamed, running to him. But she tripped and fell. "About time you showed up!" she shouted.

"Now I understand why Jezaba hates you." Violante noted. I was slightly surprised to find myself anxious to kill someone again. Only now I had a target.

"You people ruined my plan!!" Jezaba shouted, jumping up and down.

"Is he drunk?" I asked no one in particular. Violante answered,

"Probably." she said.

"Violante, I leave them to you." Jezaba announced, and left.

"Why do I get all the crappy jobs?! Can't wait 'til I kill him for good!" Violante said, causing everyone to shout,

"Huh?!"

"You didn't know I was planning to overthrow Jezaba?" she smirked. Then she, too, left. (Well I had a guess, but I didn't think I was right.)

"That was weird." Charlie commented.

"Keira, are you ok?" Edward asked. Keira turned to face him and for a second no one said anything. Then she smacked him across the face. "Owww!" he shouted, "what was that for?!" Keira glared at him.

"Dumb ass." I said, then I smacked him in the head. The overwhelming rage wasn't completely gone, but I didn't' think I'd try to kill him. That is, until...

"You damn bitch!!" Edward shouted, coming toward me. I got my claws out and held them at his throat,

"Say it again. I'm just *dying* to see you dead." I snarled.

"Uh, I'm good." Edward said, backing away. I put my claws away and relaxed slightly.

"Guys, we should probably go." Charlie suggested, noticing, as I was, the slight progression of my stigmata.

"B-but I just got here." Vincient said. (Ah, I knew I smelled something cowardly. Of coarse, I thought it was just Edward.)

"Holy shit!!" Keira said, jumping away from Vincient.

"Come near me with a portal and I'll sent you straight to hell." I warned, Vincient flinched but then said,

"I didn't come here for *you*! I came here for Keira."

"She's not here!" Keira shouted from behind Edward.

"Oh, there you are, Keira." Vincient said, pushing Edward aside.

"No I'm not!" Keira said, staying behind Edward.

"Besides, she said she loved Edward, about time!" I said, remembering back to what she had told me. Technically she hadn't *actually* said that, but she didn't have to.

"WHAT!?" Edward and Vincient shouted together. Then they glared at each other and back at Keira.

"Did not!" Keira protested, I just glared at her. "I didn't' say that! How could I ever say that!?"

"How can you love **him**?!" Vincient howled in disbelief. "he left you for Kara!"

"Hey, she told me to go!!" Edward defended himself.

"But you shouldn't have listened! Women **never** mean what they say!!"

"Excuse me!?" Keira stepped in.

"Sorry sweetie."

"Don't call her that!!" Edward yelled. But something was coming that seriously worried me. The scent had entered so fast, he must be in full form…Oh shit.

"Uh, guys." I said.

"Shut up, Reilly!!" Vincient and Edward screamed, still in the middle of their argument.

"No you! I really think you guys should leave! Do you sense that?" I asked, he was closer. What could he want?!

"Yeah." Charlie said, glancing around nervously.

"Hello daughter dear!" he voice echoed through the walls and something tackled me to the ground. "What did you do with it!? I know you stole it, where is it!?" he whispered, sounding *very* angry. He could only have meant one thing, but I played dumb.

"What the hell are you talking about?" I asked.

"Don't play stupid! I know you have it! The scroll that you stole from the castle is here. How did you get in?!" Now I really ***didn't*** have a clue. I wasn't in the castle, was I? It ***would*** explain why I couldn't get out.

"Why can't I move?!" I heard Charlie yell.

"What's the matter, afraid to fight us all at once!?" I asked, he lifted me off the ground and threw me into the opposite wall. "Ow."

"No, I just want to get that scroll back." Lieam screamed. Deciding that playing dumb wasn't working, I chose to find out more about this, scroll. Namely, how to open it.

"Why? What's the importance of a piece of parchment to…someone like you?" I asked.

"Oh, you mean the ruler of the-" I didn't give him time to finish, I kicked him straight in the mouth, knocking him to the ground. "You little brat!" he shrieked, getting up quickly. He took out his claws and plunged them into my wrist right through the stigmata. The pain was nearly unbearable and I couldn't break free. He jerked his other hand back preparing for the kill, but then he hesitated, "you haven't opened it." he said, it wasn't a question.

"No, not yet." I admitted, he just cackled. I jerked my hand away from his claws, (slicing through my arm as I did so.) Without saying anymore, he left. Just shimmered away without another word. Leaving me with many questions. What was so important about a piece of paper? And why was he so sure I couldn't open it? Unless, he knew I would and wanted me to. Ugh! Too many questions, not enough answers!

"Ha. God I hate him." I said, holding my wrist and walking back to the others.

"When will this spell end?!" Keira groaned. Vincient stood and walked to her,

"I'll carry you." he said.

"No!" Keira protested quickly, "Never! Don't you dare touch me!"

"Then it's true what Reilly said." Vincient accused, "you do love Edward!"

"I never said that!" she denied it. I coughed. "What? Stop giving me, 'the look.' " she said.

I rolled my eyes, "if you would tell them, Vincient would leave you alone." I said.

Everyone stared at Keira as she looked at anything but us, "I-I love… uh…well…um…"

"Spit it out!" Vincient yelled.

"I uh…I love…it's obviously *not* Vincient!" she declared.

"What!?" he cried, "you don't love me!? But I thought you did…"

Keira glared at him, "I tried to be nice about it but you're really getting on my nerves!"

"Keira, you don't mean that! Edward hypnotized you!" Vincient yelled, but even *he* didn't believe it.

"You know what?" Keira cried, "I HATE BOTH OF YOU! Now please, I just want to go home!"

So we headed back toward the order to pick up Charity. But the way my father was so sure of himself pissed me off.

"How are you going to open it?" Charlie asked from beside me. We had been discussing that very problem since leaving the castle.

"Don't know." I said, still holding my wrist. Oddly enough, it hadn't stopped bleeding.

"Do you even have a guess?" he continued.

"Nope." I said simply, he rolled his eyes.

"Are you even gonna try?" he asked.

"I'm kind of afraid to." I admitted.

"But…now I want to know what it's about." he said, I glared at him, debating on whether to agree, or smack him for not being careful. Finally, (after *much* consideration) I chose the former.

"Fine, I have one idea." I said, motioning for him to hand me the parchment. He obeyed and the second the scroll was in my possession, the blood from my injury spread onto it. But not in any natural, accidental way. It was as if it was attracted to the paper. Not only that, but after the blood had soaked through, my wound healed. I was so confused by this that it scared the shit out of me when Charlie snatched the scroll and began to open it.

"Wow, Reilly, that really did work!" he exclaimed, I decided not to tell him that *that* wasn't what I'd had in mind. "Here." he said, handing it over to me, confusion and disappointment clear on his face.

"What?" I asked, taking the scroll.

"It's all in some weird writing." he said. I looked down expecting to see old symbols or weird words. But instead I saw plain, boring English. I was about to point this out when Charlie stopped dead.

"What?" I asked, handing him the scroll.

"Uh…nothing. Can we just hurry?" he asked, then I noticed an odd scent mixing with the air.

"Ok." I agreed, vowing to find out eventually.

We arrived at the road and immediately, Keira turned toward her house. "is there any reason why we all have to go get Charity?" she asked.

"Not really." I said, "I can go and meet you all back at Keira's."

"Uh, no!" Charlie shouted suddenly.

"What do you mean, 'no'?" Edward demanded. Noticing, as I had, Charlie's strange behavior.

"Well I just don't think that Reilly needs to be alone while her dad's around." he said.

"But he's not around." I protested, what I sensed wasn't my dad, but it was something. Just no one I knew.

"Aw, very sweet...let's go." Edward said, turning once again toward Keira's house.

"Go." I said to Charlie, then I turned in the opposite direction, toward the order. But I heard footsteps behind me and turned to see Charlie following me. "No." I said, putting my hands up, "stay." I commanded. I turned and once again, Charlie followed. I rolled my eyes and kept walking. But once we were a little ways away from Keira and Edward, I turned on him. "what is your problem?" I demanded.

He stopped and immediately put on an innocent expression, something I had to fight not to fall for. "nothing." he said, I glared at him, waiting. "Really," he assured me, "nothing."

"Whatever," I said, then I pointed toward Keira and Edward, "go." I said.

"Why?" he asked.

"Because Edward's an idiot, I have to go get Charity, and you're the only one left who can protect Keira."

"But..." he began, but seeing that I wouldn't give up he sighed. "Fine." he agreed, turning. Then he hesitated, turned back, and closed the short distance between us. Taking me into his arms, he leaned forward and kissed me. Then he whispered, "be careful." and pulled away.

"Uh...K." I said, stunned and highly confused. He shimmered then and I decided to do the same, (it's faster than walking.) I was still trying to figure out his strange behavior.

I arrived at the order seconds afterward, except a strong barrier kept me from entering the grounds. I rolled my eyes and pushed the buzzer on the gate. Upon looking at the sign above the gate I realized it actually had a name. 'The Order of the Archangels.' it read, and underneath, 'demins beware.'

"Ha!" I laughed out loud.

"Go away, demon. can't you read?!" a nasally voice that I could barely recognize said on the intercom.

"Actually, contrary to popular belief, yes, I can. You spelled 'demons' wrong." I stated, smirking.

"Oh it's you. Very well, you may enter." Sister Elizabeth answered, and the gates opened.

I walked in and headed for the main building. Several nuns and monks walking by stared at me with faces filled with horror. Anger, I was used to from people like them, but fear? That was new.

I reached Sister Elizabeth's office and barely opened the door when Charity tackled me in a hug. "Oh thank God you're here!" she shouted.

"Charity, thou shall not use the Lord's name in vain." Sister Elizabeth said angrily, as if they'd been over that particular commandment a thousand times. I'd taught Charity well.

"Help me." Charity mouthed, I laughed.

"Have no fear, I have come to rescue you from this nightmarish prison." I laughed again and Sister Elizabeth gasped. I looked up, not to see anger, or even annoyance, but fear.

"You…but…Oh dear holy Mary. I must alert the-" she began shakily, but as she picked up the phone, I pushed the button on the cradle, hanging it up.

"You don't want to be doing that." I said, she continued to stare at my wrists, her eyes wide with terror. "Sit down." I said gently. She obeyed, her eyes not leaving the markings on my arms.

"Reilly, let's go." Charity said, tugging on my arm. "Reilly, come on!" she shouted when I didn't move. I realized that my eyes were glowing only when she screamed and backed away.

"Sorry." I said, smiling weakly.

"Get out." Sister Elizabeth commanded, standing up. "Now. And don't think I don't know what those symbols mean, because I do!"

"Well you should ignore whatever you *think* you know." Charity said firmly, causing both Sister Elizabeth and I to look her way. At first she coward back, but then she took a deep breath and continued, "I'm not positive about those markings, but I *do* know Reilly. And she has done nothing but good for so long!" I was utterly shocked. But, strangely enough, extremely grateful. However, before anyone else could speak, a nun came running in.

"Sister, we've detected a demon just outside the barrier." she declared, to my surprise, they all looked at me. The only thing I sensed was that same unfamiliar scent.

Upon realizing what they were waiting for, I said, "I don't know who it is." then something occurred to me, and if I was right, Charlie's strange behavior would've also been explained, "But I'm pretty sure they're after me."

"Oh, well, I guess you should leave." Sister Elizabeth said, then a softness overcame her features, "Do be careful, uh, for Charity's sake." I nodded and we left the grounds.

As we walked toward Keira's, Charity started staring at the stigmata, and I waited for her inevitable questions.

"What do those markings mean?" she finally asked, (Damn, she sure doesn't waste any time getting to the point, does she?)

"Nothing good." I said evasively, not wanting to scare her.

"But **what**, exactly?" she persisted.

"They mean…" I began, but something crossed into my senses. It was the same scent I'd noticed before the others left and again before leaving the order. "Charity, I don't want to scare you, but you're going to have to be ready to run."

"Why? What is it?" she asked, her voice already raising in panic.

"Nothing good." An unfamiliar voice said from behind us. I spun around and got between the stranger and Charity. He was definitely demonic, and his scent matched that of the one I'd been sensing all day.

"Hello Reilly, you're just the demon I wanted to see," he grinned, "alone."

"She's not alone." Charity squeaked.

"Charity, shut up and start running." I said, but before Charity could move, the unknown demon snarled in a fearsome voice,

"If you tell anyone, Reilly will be dead before you've had time to finish the story." he said, I laughed.

"What makes you so sure about that?" I asked.

"I have an advantage." he said, but before I knew what that was, he was right in front of me. "This ought to really piss Charlie off." he said.

"Huh?" I stuttered, but before I heard the answer, an electrical charge filled my body and knocked the breath out of me. The last thing I heard was the evil bastard threatening Charity not to tell, then blackness.

Chapter 24
More Secrets

I woke up and immediately knew that I didn't know where I was. (Seriously, I had no clue. All I could see were the bars of a cage.) I felt unusually weak and I couldn't figure out why. Even if the guy had stabbed me, I still shouldn't be this weak. What bugged me the most, however, was the chain around my neck. It wasn't really a collar, but it was as tight as one and where it touched my skin it burned. I reached up to pull it off and was granted a severe shock to my hands and neck.

"You really shouldn't do that." a now familiar voice warned.

"And why is that?" I asked defiantly.

"Because it will only kill you faster. (Oh, faster, that's a comfort.)

"What will only kill me faster?" I asked, not bothering to hide my irritation.

"The miasma. That chocker is filled with it." Well that explains the stinging, but not the 'why the hell am I here!?'

"Who are you? What do you want and what does it have to do with Charlie or I?" I asked, I turned to face him and saw his look of shock. "Yeah, I remember. You're little trick wasn't that effective."

"You're stronger than I thought. My name is John." he said.

"Ok, John, I really hate you and you've greatly underestimated me if you think that these bars are going to stop me from ripping out your throat." I sad fiercely.

"That's why I'm not relying on the bars. It's the necklace that will stop you. " John said confidently, ignoring my earlier comment, (You know what, the worst part is that he's right, I can feel my strength ebbing.)

"You're really annoying!!" I shouted angrily after several minutes of trying to get out of the cage. Which was made impossible by the miasma necklace at my throat.

"Why? Because I want revenge? It's not *my* fault that Charlie was evil. Yet *I* had to pay for it. Actually, no, *I* didn't. Amelia, she-" he stopped talking. As if he was afraid he'd already revealed too much. He was right, of coarse, I knew roughly what happened.

"Did Charlie kill Amelia?" I asked, afraid of the answer but knowing I had to know what happened.

"Yes, slowly, painfully, and right in front of me." he said, then he grinned wickedly, "So I'm going to return the favor." Ok I *almost* felt sorry for him there. But then he had to go and ruin it.

"When are you going to kill me?" I asked, more out of curiosity than general concern.

"When he gets here." he shrugged, as if we were discussing the weather. I sighed. "you have to know that it's nothing personal. You just happened to be with the wrong demon at the wrong time." I looked him straight in the eye,

"What, I just happened to fall in love with the wrong demon at the wrong time? Go to hell." I snarled. As soon as the words were out of my mouth, an alarm sounded.

"That can't be him," he muttered, striding to the door,

"he wouldn't be that stupid." while I had to agree, I knew three people that *would* be that dumb. And at the moment, they were being escorted into the room by several soldiers and John.

"Put your weapons on the table." One soldier commanded, Keira glared at him. "Now." he added, grabbing Charity by the hair. I sat up and put both hands on the bars, my eyes glowing. I knew I wasn't getting out, though, I was too weak.

"Can that be optional?" Keira asked.

"No." I growled from the side.

"Don't kill me!" Charity squealed, placing a small bottle of holy water on the table the soldier had indicated. He let her go and she stood off to the side. Edward followed her, looking confused. He placed his sword on the table next to the holy water and then stood by Charity. And then there was Keira...

"Do I have to?"

"Yes you do."

"Please, can't I just keep one?"

"No."

"C'mon, just one?"

"No, set them all down."

"A half of one!?" if I hadn't felt so horribly nauseous, I'd have killed them both.

"No."

"Yes."

"No."

"Yes!"

"NO!"

"YES!"

"NO!" the soldier said with force. Keira sighed in defeat and slumped to the table to empty her bag. This was something I found no interest in. FINALLY, she was finished, they were all led into the cell I was in and the door was locked.

"I need to go re-set the alarm," John said, glaring at Edward, Keira and Charity. "I'll be back."

"Reilly!!" Charity said, trying to run toward me. Luckily, Edward held her back.

"Miasma." I warned as Charity glowered at Edward. Even my voice sounded drained.

"Oh." Charity said, and sat with the others, which was as far away from me as Edward could get.

About ten minutes had gone by when John came back into the room. He was with three soldiers and had the keys to the cage in his hand.

"Good news Reilly, we're moving you to a different cell. I didn't think you'd want your friends to watch you suffer." he said, grinning widely. I rolled my eyes, an act that was becoming increasingly more painful the longer the necklace was in place. I was **not** looking forward to when it would become impossible.

"Whatever." I said, sounding like I had a hangover, and feeling worse.

We walked a little ways down the hall and stopped in front of a large, metal door. John unlocked it and I was led into a windowless room with steel walls. "This should be pretty hard to get out of...or into." John commented. He wasn't talking to me but I replied,

"But not impossible." he rolled his eyes and walked out of the small prison.

I sat alone for what felt like hours, all the while feeling the necklace draining me of my power. Then, a piercing alarm went off, it sounded as though it was coming from the room where the others were. It was shut off as fast as it had sounded but now I could hear footsteps rushing past the door.

"Great, now what?" I sighed as I heard the lock click open. The door was shoved aside and John came rushing through it, holding two keys. One, I knew, was for the door, but the other one I'd never seen before. He ran behind me and unlocked something on the necklace, I knew he was messing with the chain because he had it pulled back to the point where it was strangling me. After he released it, he stood and vanished into the shadows and I was left wondering what the hell was going on.

My eyes were closing without my permission when I saw someone enter the room. I opened them again, wider, and saw Charlie running toward me. But then I remembered where John had slithered to. I knew I had to warn Charlie but wasn't sure if I could speak. So, instead, I pointed a shaking finger toward the darkness off to our right. He looked up in time to see John slinking out of his hiding place, a triumphant smile plastered on his face.

Chapter 25
A Miracle?

"What did you do?" Charlie growled, in a deadly tone. He was sitting next to me now, and had moved to where he was in between John and I.

"Aw, you sound mad. But are you as mad as I was?! I doubt it! She'll be dead in, oh, twenty minutes, tops." ok, I agree that he's 'mad' but I'm thinking more 'insane' than 'angry'.

"She had nothing to do with that! WHAT DID YOU DO!!?" Charlie shouted, looking **very** angry. Then he looked over at me and the anger vanished, replaced with sorrow. "Come on, Reilly, snap out of it."

I couldn't say anything so I just touched the necklace, hoping that would be enough to explain what was going on. Immediately the pain I'd grown used to intensified, and I think he understood. But John stepped in anyway.

"It's miasma. The necklace is filled with it. It's killing her and you're helpless to stop it. How does is feel?" he said, I was experiencing tunnel-vision and he sounded like he was speaking through the wrong end of a megaphone. Once again, my eyes closed, and this time I couldn't open them. My breathing became shallow and it was becoming increasingly harder to get air.

"Reilly! Oh God, Reilly wake up!" (If I'd have been able to talk I would've said something like, 'I'm awake stupid.' to Charlie. And trust me, I'd have had a few choice words for John as well.) Charlie sounded so far away but I could feel his hands on my shoulders. John started laughing and I sensed something that both shocked and terrified me. Charlie had gone into full form. Panic over took me as I remembered what that could do.

No matter what I did I couldn't break free of the unconsciousness that overtook me.

When I awoke, the sounds of fighting had died down but a horrible scream, that I hoped was John, rang through the silence. Then soft footsteps were approaching. Faintly, I thought I sensed that it was Charlie, but I wasn't positive until I heard his voice. It was right next to my ear and he was whispering, with sorrow in his voice. And, though I couldn't see his face, I could also hear how guilty he felt.

"Reilly, I'm so sorry. I should've told you when you asked me what was wrong. Now you're paying for my mistakes, but I swear, I'll get you out of here. I'll come back for you but first I have to go help the others." I couldn't move or talk and I was terrified that when he came back it would be too late. I felt tears escape from under my closed eyes. "It's ok, Reilly, I promise I'll save you and tell you everything." he promised, then, gently, he touched his lips to mine. I heard him leave and more tears poured from beneath my closed lids.

"Reilly, get up." a voice I thought I'd never hear again commanded. His words were inside my mind and I figured my traumatized brain had decided to give me one last shred of hope before death. Until Sedrick spoke again. *"Come on Reilly, you know you can. Dad wouldn't want anyone to kill you unless it was him. He would've given the curse some way to fight back."* he continued, and I understood what he was saying. Partly because I could already feel every ounce of my strength returning.

"Thank you, Sedrick, for everything." I said, finally able to talk. Then I tried opening my eyes and standing. That I could also do, though I was still a little dizzy. Looking around revealed a mangled heap of bloody skin and bones that could've only been John, (or, rather, what was *left* of John.) I didn't even blink, instead I started shakily toward the room where the others had been fighting.

When I finally reached the door, it was obvious that the battle was still going on. But I desperately needed to speak with my boyfriend. So, hoping I had enough strength to do so, I flooded the room with fire. Making my friends immune.

I'd barely crossed through the doorway when a wave of dizziness struck and I nearly collapsed. I leaned against the doorframe for support and gazed across the room at all of the dead soldiers until I saw them, the small group of four, (Not counting the dwelf,) standing off to the side.

"Reilly!!" Charlie shouted, practically sprinting toward me. If I hadn't been a half-demon, his bone crushing hug probably would've killed me.

As it was, however, I was just happy to be there. "You're alive!" he said, clearly relieved. 'Well, not for long if you don't let go,' I thought, but didn't say anything as I was just as relieved as he was.

"Yeah." I said, "look at this." I pointed to the stigmata on my left hand where some of the miasma still lingered, but it was quickly disappearing. I wasn't finished speaking but he leaned forward and kissed me before I could. Which normally would've annoyed me considering how many questions I had. But I was so happy that *he* was alive, that I didn't care. But as soon as it was over I continued, "I forgive you." I said before he could apologize again.

"Thank you." were the words he was speaking, but what he was *saying* was, 'I don't deserve it but thank you.'

"It's **not** your fault and I forgive you." I said, he smiled. Then my newly re-acquired senses detected someone approaching.

"Kara!!" Edward shouted, seconds after we reached where they were standing. I still had to lean against Charlie to keep from falling but soon, I knew, I'd be able to stand on my own. Which was good, considering who was about to arrive.

Chapter 26
Kara's Final Words and The Real Evil Villain

I'm not an expert on 'the good of this world' or 'those that belong to the church' but it seemed to me they aren't supposed to be seething with hatred or giving off murderous vibes. Kara, the lovely little witch, was doing both. For about five minutes, Keira and Kara glared at each other, neither one willing to break the silence. Finally, Keira decided to be the mature one, (Now isn't *that* a scary thought?!)

"What are you doing here?!" she demanded, Kara began to laugh.

"Why do you say that, Keira? After all, you brought me back from the dead." She did **WHAT!!?** Jeez, I leave for like a day and all of a sudden people start popping out of their graves. Aren't there *laws* against that sort of thing!? If there's not there should be. You know, eternal *after*life and all that.

"Thank you Keira!!" Edward shouted, gleefully. He gave her a hug and continued, "You brought her back! Thank you! Thank you!"

Keira, looking more than just a little pissed off, shoved him away. Then she stood over him looking for all the world like a crazy ax murderer. Kara pushed her aside and helped Edward up. "look, the only reason I came was to tell you that I know exactly what Jezaba *and* Violante are plotting, and I know how to stop them." she paused, letting that sink in. I hadn't missed the fact that she'd emphasized the word 'and'. "Jezaba's moronic minions began to pursue me, but I escaped. It's Violante I'm worried about…she-" Kara stopped dead. Quite literally actually, as a sharp blade stuck out from her chest. Kara howled in pain and Violante pulled out her sword, smiling all the while.

"There, that ought to shut you up for now." Violante laughed, standing over Kara with an approving expression.

Edward rushed over and grabbed Kara in his arms. Also, his demon blood rose so rapidly that it was difficult *not* to smell it. "How...dare... you...YOU BITCH!!"

"EDWARD STOP IT!!!" Keira shouted, "don't make me use a cross barrier on you!" she added. Edward's eyes stopped glowing and became filled with tears. Which he immediately tried to hide. Once she was sure Edward could control his rage, Keira turned to face Violante. She pulled out a handgun and aimed it at Violante's head. But before she could pull the trigger, a shift in energy told me that Violante had something else in mind. Sure enough, Keira vanished, probably off to see Jezaba. It figures that *she* would get to deal with the idiot, while *I* got stuck with the true 'wizard behind the curtain'. For now I was positive that Violante had finally seen how little she truly needed Jezaba. Things were about to get *very* interesting.

"I sense miasma." Violante said with a grin in my direction. "had a few problems?"

"Not really." I shrugged and took a half step toward her. Charlie kept my hand in his, refusing to let go.

"It smells like it."

"It was taken care of."

"You look horrible." Violante's grin widened as we began to circle each other. I'd finally freed myself from Charlie's grasp and was ready to destroy her.

"You sure you're not looking in a mirror?" I asked, her grin faded, replaced with a scowl.

"You really shouldn't provoke a demon you don't have the strength to fight."

"Oh I will *find* the strength to kick *your* ass." I said, completely alert and strong enough to kill her if I had to. Which, eventually, I knew I would.

My less than subtle taunt had done it's job. Violante's energy spiked and she lashed out, catching me in the right shoulder and knocking me back a few feet. I shot back with my own energy, sending her flying though the air and skidding to a stop on the opposite wall. "Was that much power necessary?" Charlie asked, something in his voice made me turn to face him. Whatever he saw caused him to ask, "Are you ok?"

"Yes." I said, my voice sounding like the hiss of a snake.

"You don't sound ok and your eyes are glowing." Edward whimpered.

"Are they?" I growled, turning to face him.

"Uh…yeah…" he stammered. I laughed at his fear, surprising myself with the sound. It didn't sound even remotely human.

"Reilly, snap out of it." Charity begged. I took a deep breath and closed my eyes, focusing on my demonic energy and calming down. But a sharp stab of icy pain yanked me out of my meditation. Violante's sword was plunged deep into my torso and she was laughing. I rolled my eyes and stepped forward, the sword slid out from my upper body and the wound healed instantly.

"How did you…wait a second." Violante said, staring at my wrist. She didn't' say anything else but after seconds, she began to laugh. "I see." she finally choked out, wiping tears away. "Things will become *very* interesting over the next few weeks." she declared, then she shimmered away as if nothing happened.

"That was close." Charlie muttered, coming toward me.

"You're telling me! She could've **killed** us!" Edward shouted.

"Yep, Violante did look-"

"Violante!? Who cares about Violante, I'm talking about **her**!" Edward thundered, cutting Charity off and pointing a shaking finger at me.

"Edward…" Charlie said sharply.

"What!? You saw the way she looked at us, she wanted to kill me! You too, and if we're not careful, she'll kill us all." Edward shouted.

"Edward!" Charity screeched. Pindel, for once, was being silent.

"Guys! Edward is correct. At least on two accounts." I sighed.

"W-which two?" Edward stuttered. I grinned,

"The first one, except that I *always* want to kill you. And…the last one." I admitted.

"Reilly…" Charlie reached out, took my hands, and pulled me into his arms, "you know I trust you. So trust yourself. We'll figure this out, together." he promised.

"We'll see." I said, and he hugged me tighter.

"I still think she's our greatest threat." Edward mumbled. With a sudden stab of pain, I realized he was right. The worst enemy we had, and possibly the most dangerous, was me. Well shit, that's something I'm *definitely* gonna have to change. Even if it kills me.

Chapter 27
Taste of Darkness

We left the room in a hurry, following the lingering trails of Violante's power, tracking Keira. Shimmering hadn't been too difficult, except for the fact that the miasma necklace kept sending jolts of electrified pain through my body. Finally, I reached up with both hands, grasped firmly on the metal chain, and yanked with all of my strength. It shattered under my grip and I felt as if a weight had been lifted off of my shoulders. I also felt my senses sharpen.

"We need to hurry." I said when we appeared near a large cliff. Then I shimmered to the top, the others right behind me.

We appeared in time to see Keira fall (or rather, *jump*) off the cliff. Jezaba stood inches from the edge looking down,

"Damn," he muttered, "I needed her."

"Oh God," Edward moaned, "Oh God, this isn't good. Not Keira too, Oh God."

"Edward!" I snapped, causing him to look at me, startled, "go get her." I commanded. What I meant was, 'shimmer to the bottom and save her,' but Edward, instead, took a running leap off the edge. "Idiot." I muttered.

"*You!*" Jezaba shouted, pointing at me. "You did this!" he accused, holding up his gloved hand. "And now everyone laughs at me! I will get even with you for this, soon. But now, I'm leaving!!!" he shouted.

"We should probably go after Edward and Keira." Charity said. Pindel glared at her for half a second before reluctantly agreeing.

"Fine." I said, grasping Charity's hand and shimmering. Charlie followed with Pindel tagging along, no doubt arguing and coming up with many reasons why we should just leave. We reached the bottom and found Edward pacing at the base of a waterfall. It fed the river that passed down the remainder of the hill and into the valley.

"I lost her and the river washed away her scent so I can't even track her." he admitted.

"Well *that* sucks." I said, everyone looked at me, "because now we have to look the *human* way." I elaborated.

"Which is…?" Charlie asked, not sure where to start.

"We split up. Edward, you and Pindel go that way." I began, pointing across the river, to the other bank.

"Why do I have to search with *him*!?" Edward and Pindel both demanded, followed by, "Hey, what's wrong with me!?"

"Just go!" I commanded. They both jumped and then rushed to cross the river. "Ok, now Charlie, you take Charity and go that way." I said, pointing down the river on the opposite bank.

"But-"

"Don't start." I said, interrupting his complaints before he could start making them.

"Fine, call me if you get into any trouble." he said, I grinned.

"I'm *always* in trouble." I said, he laughed and then shimmered to the opposite bank with Charity.

I sighed, "this could take a while." I said, then I headed off down the bank, following the river.

✷ ✷ ✷

It had been about an hour when I finally saw her. She was lying, crumpled into a pile, on the bank just barely out of the water. I sent out a mental signal to Charlie and Edward and then headed toward her.

"Keira?" I asked, she didn't respond.

"Keira!!" Edward's horrible shriek filled the air. He rushed down to her and I sensed Charlie and Charity's appearance.

"When did you find her?" Charlie whispered as we watched Edward basically hold a vigil next to Keira.

"Like two seconds ago." I replied.

"She's dead!!" Edward shouted from beside Keira's mangled form. Mangled, but not motionless. I walked over to her and felt for a pulse, detecting a faint, fluttering heartbeat.

"She's not dead-"

"Yes she is!!" Edward cut me off.

"No, she's not." I said, calmly. He looked at me, confused. "Edward, she's still breathing." I stated, he looked down then said,

"Oh…I knew that."

"Sure you did." Charlie mumbled, Edward glared at him. I was about to laugh, until I sensed a presence near. It took about a nanosecond for me to figure out that it was Keira. There was someone, or something, else though. I shuttered when I realized who it was. The Angel of Death, Uriel.

"What?" Charlie asked, noticing my discomfort.

"The Angel of Death is standing over there with Keira." I said. If you're not sure, the Angel of Death is neither good nor evil. His sole, (no pun intended,) purpose is to ferry souls from one world to the next. No matter where they're headed, if you know what I mean.

"Should we tell Edward?" Charlie asked.

"Nope." I said. Uriel left and Keira approached where we were standing. The look on her face made my senses immediately alert. I began building energy and sure enough, Keira tried to possess me! My mind was too powerful for her to enter and it sent her sprawling to the ground. I glanced down at where she had landed, "Nice try Keira." I said. She got up and went toward Charity, I rolled my eyes. What was she gonna do, *sing* Edward to death? Charity's powers were for healing, not destruction. But, no matter how much of a waist of time, Keira tried it anyway.

Edward, being the idiot he is, shouted, "But Keira's dormant, can't' we just put her soul into Kara's body?!"

"Edward," Charity began, then she stopped and blinked several times as Keira took over. "How about you die and go to hell!?" she shouted through Charity. In Charity's soft voice, the words were a little more unnerving. Everyone stared at her with shock except me. I watched Keira slip out of Charity's mind with a bored expression. (She does know that possession is a sin, right?)

Edward was now cowering behind Pindel, so Keira possessed him next. Pindel grabbed a handgun and muttered, "Hey Edward." he turned to face 'Pindel' and all the color drained from his face.

"WHAT THE HELL IS GOING ON HERE!?" he shouted.

"It's me Edward." Keira said.

"Kara!?" Edward asked, hopeful.

"NO!!" she screamed loudly, "Keira!"

"Oh," Edward sighed, disappointed. "I knew that. Why are you in the dwelf's body, then?"

"Well, Edward, my soul has been separated from my body because I ***almost*** died. To make a long story short, someone has to put my soul back into my body." she said. Edward thought for a minute, (wow, Edward thought, that's new,) before saying,

"Why did you possess Charity and Pindel?" well maybe it had something to do with your whole, 'hey lets find Keira's soul and bring Kara back!' idea.

Keira/Pindel laughed nervously, confirming my theory. "Well...sorta said something...Kara...I...got really mad." she muttered.

"I don't remember." Edward lied, the look on his face told us that he clearly ***did*** remember.

"YOU SAID IT A FEW MINUTES AGO!!" Keira shouted. Then, quieter, she added, "just put my damn soul back ***now***. Or I'll haunt you for the rest of your miserable existence."

I grabbed her wrist and drug her from Pindel's body, flinging her back into her own. Her eyes snapped open and she began coughing up water. I watched as Edward rushed to help her and she smacked him. Then I looked over at Uriel, who was watching me. I wondered briefly why he was still here, until he held up one bony hand and tapped his watch, staring straight at ***me***. Oh, ***wonderful.***

☆ ☆ ☆

It seemed as if we'd been walking for hours, but we hadn't gone very far. Partly because Edward and Keira hardly stopped arguing and when they ***did*** stop, Edward wouldn't stop whining. "Kara, why did you have to die...again!!" he cried, making me want to kill him. A feeling that wasn't easily kept under control. I had to fight not to strangle him right there. Finally, Keira stalked over to him with clenched fists, and punched him! Edward just whimpered more, so she kicked him. "Leave me alone!" he shouted, curling into fetal position and motioning for her to leave.

"No!" Keira screamed, "last time you obsessed over Kara dying, I almost got taken over by Jezaba! You dumb idiot! Screw this, I'm finding my way out by myself." Keira turned without another word and stomped into the forest...***alone***. You'd think that after everything that happens to her when she's not with us, she'd learn to stay close.

"Edward..." Charity sighed, he looked up with a puzzled expression.

"Look, Charity, you wouldn't understand. So just leave me alone, ok." he said softly. That really pissed me off,

"No, Edward, it's not ok! Why don't you just admit it already? You love Kara! You also love Keira! Just say it already!!" I screamed, "and pick one, you two timer! On second thought, pick Keira, she's cooler! And, Oh yeah, she's not *dead*!!!" I finished, everyone stared at me. Then Charity slowly nodded and Pindel muttered a silent agreement.

"Reilly, you're eyes are glowing." Charlie whispered from beside me. I clamped my eyes shut and sighed,

"I'm gonna go walk around for a while. Could you stay here and make sure no one…*dies?*" I asked, he chuckled then said he would. I opened my eyes and headed in the opposite direction of where Keira had gone, deeper into the darker part of the forest. Once I was quite a ways away, I stopped and sat down, thinking.

"Reilly! Fancy meeting you here." a painfully familiar voice said brightly a few minutes after I'd arrived.

"What do you want, Jezaba?" I asked as he appeared a couple feet in front of me. Apparently my eyes were still glowing, because he kept his distance as he spoke.

"Well, actually, I was looking for Keira. But you'll do." he was lying and grinning wickedly, but refusing to come any closer. Which was actually smart on his part because I was way too tense to approach safely at that moment. Which was probably why what he said next I actually believed. "You know, if you'd just be who you naturally are, no one else would have to get hurt." he said.

"Shut up, Jezaba." I said, tiredly. "I really don't care what you think."

"But do you care what *you* think?" he asked, then added, "you really do believe I'm right. I can sense it. Even though you're fooling everyone else, we both know that you really want to be free of the stress that fighting the stigmata has caused you." he said. I glanced up at him for the first time, acknowledging his words. My will power was starting to falter, and we both knew it. His smile widened and he commanded, "stand up, help me kill the others, and I'll free you of this burden that you didn't ask for." he promised. "don't you remember how happy you were when you worked for me? Before life got so complicated? I can help you remember how good it felt to kill, to take away the lives of unsuspecting weak minds. I can give you the chance to feel that way again, powerful and unstoppable. All you have to do is agree." his words were registering in my mind and before I could think about it, I was nodding and saying,

"I will help you." To my horror, I knew I would. But then a fog of darkness clouded my mind, I slumped to the ground as a shrieking voice commanded, *'what do you think you're doing?!'* the words echoed in my mind and threatened to shatter my eardrums. *'if you listen to Jezaba everything you've worked for would be for nothing!'* the voice was sounding even more familiar by the minute and I struggled to place it. *'it's not important who I am…you have to fight him! Don't listen to his commands!'* suddenly I knew who the speaker was. Not a name, but a face, a woman who used to come to my father's castle and help with… with what? I couldn't remember much. Only that she and many others would be in the labs of the castle designing…designing…Oh who cared?! The point was that no matter what she'd done before, her words were truthful enough now. And I did what she instructed. I was about to attack when one final echoing thought entered my mind, *'he has Keira… save her and then open the scroll…read it and find me…before it's too late for us all…hurry…'* well what could that mean? I know I have to save Keira, (when *don't* I have to save Keira, though?) but the rest doesn't make sense. I'll know soon enough I guess. But for now, I need to make Jezaba believe he has control over me. "Take me to the others, I will kill them…I will kill everyone." I said, my voice becoming a trancelike drone. The fog lifted from my mind and again I had to fight for control. Ignoring Jezaba's commands wouldn't be easy, but I would try.

Chapter 28
Captive

Walking back toward the others was a nightmare. Between trying to block out my demon blood and listening to Jezaba's ranting about God, I would've been happier if he'd have just killed me. Finally, we reached the campsite, and saw Keira standing over Edward with a gun! She definitely looked like she was about to kill him…sweet. (I mean, no! killing is bad…but it *is* Edward…wait, stop! Killing, bad. Friends, good. Just, not Edward. Crap, this is going to be harder than I thought.) Anyway, Keira's gun going off snapped me out of my internal dilemma. I looked over and saw that she'd missed!! "How could you miss?! He's right in front of you!!" Jezaba screamed from in front of me. Keira appeared to be struggling with the darker part of her mind a while before lowering the gun. "WHAT. IS. GOING. ON." Jezaba shrieked.

"I- I can't kill Edward!" Keira said, I grinned, my demon blood getting the better of me briefly as I growled,

"But I can." I stepped away from the concealment of the shadows and into the open.

Keira must've realized that anything I'd do to him would be far worse than a gunshot, because she abruptly re-aimed the gun. Then she muttered to Edward, "Pl-please don't hate me." she started to squeeze the trigger, then added, "I'm really sorry it had to end like this!" she shouted, then closed her eyes and shot the gun. (Yes, she fired a powerful weapon with her eyes closed, don't you feel much better knowing *she's* gonna save your future?!) this time, the bullet found it's mark. Edward crumpled to the ground, lying motionless. Past experience told me that he wasn't really dead, but it was still fun to pretend that he was. (Wait, no. It **wasn't** fun, it was bad.) Jezaba walked over to Keira and put his arm around her, "See?" he pointed at Edward, "There is nothing to live for now. That is, unless you care about your sister." he grabbed her hand, "Shall we go?"

it had begun to rain and the cold air was snapping me out of Jezaba's control. I glanced at Charlie, and found that he was looking at me.

"Reilly!" Jezaba's angry voice snarled in my mind. "Come on." I shook my head and took a step toward Charlie, Charity, and Pindel. "Now." he snapped , and darkness flooded my mind again. I walked to where he was standing and he clamped his hand around my arm. "You're on thin ice." he warned, his grip tightening, when I didn't reply, he shimmered Keira and I to his castle.

※ ※ ※

Violante waited for us at the gates, a triumphant smile on her face. She glared at me and I returned the favor, causing her to look questioningly at Jezaba. He nodded and her smile widened as she let us in.

As we entered the castle, I noticed that nothing had changed. the theme was still, 'Jezaba.' "...As you can tell, there's another-"

"SHUT UP!!" Keira, Violante, and I shouted. It was bad enough fighting him taking over my mind without listening to him talk about himself.

"Is there anything that doesn't have you on it?!" Keira shrieked. Jezaba paused before answering,

"Nope. Well, then again, there's this tiny picture of Violante, but that's it." he said, we all exchanged annoyed looks. "Reilly," he continued, "would you help watch for any intruders? Keira and I have much to discuss." he said. Glad that it wasn't *me* he was talking about, I headed back down hall.

On my way to the doors I noticed that everyone I passed seemed to recognize me. (Which, in case you haven't been paying attention, isn't a good thing.) I finally reached my destination only to have to turn and sprint back down the hall. Violante, over the shriek of an alarm, was screaming my name. I reached the doorway and stopped dead, leaning against the wall.

"You bellowed?" I said, she glared at me and then explained,

"Charlie and the rest of those *ungodly* creatures you keep company with are-"

"Technically, Charity *is* godly. She's an Apostle." I corrected, she glared at me.

"Well, they just broke in…" she paused as a wide grin spread across her face, "Well, actually, they just ran through the front door." she laughed.

"What do you want me to do about it?" I shrugged, "it's not my problem."

"Oh yes it is. You're-"

"**Not** legion. Do it yourself." I interrupted. She looked like she was about to blurt out a few words one might not normally hear, but then Jezaba and Keira walked into the foyer.

"Sir, the demons…and a dwelf and the final Apostle, have-" Violante rushed to explain, but Jezaba cut her off.

"I'm sure our little break in is nothing my two most powerful allies can't handle." he said.

"Great, I get to work with the angel." Violante moaned, but Jezaba shook his head,

"Terribly sorry, Violante, but I was referring to **Reilly** and Keira. Not you. Maybe you'll get to work with one of them in later times."

"Well…I…but…Ugh!!!" she shouted, and stalked off down the hall.

"Run along, now." I called after her, thoroughly enjoying myself.

"Be nice, Reilly." Jezaba said. I shot him a glare that made him take a few steps back as he added, "alright, off with you both, now. You have intruders to deal with."

"Fine." Keira and I said, as we headed off in the direction of the commotion.

We reached the entrance hall where all of the fighting was and saw everyone I expected. But there was one person there, that Keira never expected to see again. As soon as she spotted Edward she nearly fainted. I only had two words for her,

"**Hello**, demon." I said, before leaping into the chaos. As I joined the battle, the first person I saw was, of coarse, Charlie. A large group of soldiers separated us but he defeated them easily and was soon standing right beside me.

"What are you doing?" he asked.

"What do you mean?" I asked, punching Edward in the face. He'd stumbled over into my reach. I assumed he was running from Keira, but I couldn't be sure. Charlie's eyes widened at my complete lack of remorse.

"I mean, **that**!!" he said, indicating my blood covered fist. I'd shattered Edward's nose, and even though it healed two seconds after it had broken, I still felt better. I didn't really feel like talking anymore, so I just shrugged. Then a sudden calm moved through my mind, replacing, for good, Jezaba's dark energy. I blinked several times and stumbled backwards. "Better?" Charlie asked as he caught my outstretched hands, keeping me from falling.

"Yeah, what did you do?" I asked, still slightly dazed.

"I didn't do anything." he admitted, "You did, I think. Doesn't matter though, now we can leave." he started toward the door but I stopped and shook my head.

"No," I said, "I can't. if I leave with you, who will watch out for Keira?" I asked, then I heard Edward shout with pain and anger. "And Edward." I added.

"Good point, then I'm staying." he said, "capture me." he added, holding out his wrists. I rolled my eyes and walked him, with the others, to the dungeons. (which consisted of Charity, Pindel, Edward, and Charlie. Jezaba's dungeons aren't the busiest places. Mostly, anyone who cares to break in gets out with out being caught.)

Right after we got everyone locked up, we heard Violante and Jezaba approaching. I let enough of my demonic energy surround me so that I still appeared to be evil. (which, judging by his expression, freaked Charlie out.)

"Oh, so you were successful. Good job." Violante said, sounding like she thought it was anything but.

"Well done." Jezaba congratulated us. "Now, bring Charity with us, Keira. Reilly, you go with Violante to help her with some final arrangements." at this, he and Violante exchanged a look that I didn't' miss. I decided it was a pretty good idea to escape sooner rather than later, and in my mind I already had everything worked out. Little did I know that I wouldn't be leaving the way I'd arrived. None of us would.

Chapter 29
The Apostles' Purpose

Violante led me up a narrow staircase and through a long hall. Both of which were completely deserted. All the while I was trying to figure out how to get away from her without immediately raising an alarm. Finally, she stopped at a door and motioned for me to follow her inside.

"Now or never." I muttered.

"What?" Violante asked, turning to face me.

"Nothing." I smiled, then pointed at an imaginary distraction across the room, "Oh my God!!"

"What?!" she shouted, spinning toward the direction I'd pointed in. I looked around for a heavy object and found that, conveniently enough, the door was made of steel. I yanked it off it's hinges and swung it around, smashing it into the back of Violante's head. She dropped like a ton of bricks and I turned and raced back toward the dungeons.

When I reached the bottom of the steps I saw what would have been a hilarious sight if it hadn't been for the murderous soldier about to kill Pindel. The latter was standing in front of the locked cell door in his shortest form, holding a key that was almost bigger than he was. The earlier mentioned soldier was standing behind him about to bring down a sword over his head. Deciding that it was a pretty good time to step in, I silently moved behind the soldier. Then, in less time it took for him to even think of crying out, I put my hands on either side of his neck, and jerked it around, snapping it at the top of the spinal cord. He was dead even before he fell heavily to the ground. Then I took the key from an astonished and terrified Pindel and unlocked the door.

No sooner did I have the door open then Edward was in front of me demanding, "Where did they take Keira!?"

"I don't know…maybe the-" I began, but he didn't give me time to finish. He rushed past me and flew up the stairs.

"Reilly…" Charlie said, "your eyes are glowing.

"They are?" I said, closing my eyes for a few seconds then opening them again. I hadn't even noticed, which kind of worried me.

"They were."

"Well, nothing we can do about it now. What we *can* do is go get Charity and Keira before Jezaba carries out whatever the hell it is he's planning." I said, Pindel agreed quickly but Charlie glared at me. (I just wanted to not think about my lessoning ability to control my more unpleasant side but I definitely wasn't ready to admit *that* yet.)

"If we *don't* do something about it, *you're* going to wind up getting yourself killed."

"You got a point?" I inquired.

"Don't start talking like that!! You dead will *not* help us. Besides, I'd really prefer it if you'd *not* be suicidal, please." he said, his eyes still wide with shock.

"I know, I'm sorry. I just…never mind." I really didn't know how to describe how I felt at that point. Luckily, thanks to Edward's shriek of terror, I didn't have to.

"Let's go!" Pindel shouted, already halfway up the steps. Charlie gave me a look that said something to the extent of, 'don't think you're off the hook yet, we'll talk later,' and then we both raced after Pindel.

We reached the top in just enough time to see Edward sprint past us and down the hall. Keira was no where to be seen at that moment, but she couldn't have been too far behind. "Run, Edward, run!!" I called. He sped up until he banished from sight completely. At least for weaker eyes, to Charlie and I he was more of a blur.

"You gonna go tell him he's going the wrong way or should I?" Charlie asked, trying not to laugh.

I sighed, "I'll do it. You go toward the throne room. Look in every room you pass and try to find Charity or Keira's scent." Great, back to being bloodhounds.

"Ok, hurry and be careful, there's got to be guards posted everywhere by now." Charlie said, then he and Pindel headed off in the opposite direction as Edward.

I didn't even try to catch up with Edward by running, (though I probably could've,) instead, I shimmered down the hall, somewhere in front of him. It wasn't' long before I sensed, and **heard**, his approach.

"Edward!!" I shouted, causing him to come to a dead halt just ahead of me.

"What!?" he demanded hurriedly. He head a panicked expression on his face.

"What are you doing?"

"The voices…in the walls…I must obey them!!" he shouted, shifting back and forth on his feet.

"Uh…what are they telling you to do?" I asked, slightly annoyed. I had a feeling I knew who his 'voices' were.

"RUN!!" he shouted, then he took off. Apparently, shouting at Edward when he can't see you causes him to go all, 'schizophrenic'…well that's nice to know.

"Damn it." I muttered as Edward, once again, became a blur as he raced down the corridor. This time, I *did* sprint after him. When I caught up, I slide tackled him, causing him to trip and go sliding about a yard and a half.

"What was that for?" he shouted, sitting up and turning to face me. I stood up,

"We have to go save Keira and Charity, so if your done playing tag with your imaginary friends then get up and lets go find them." I said.

"But the wall people-"

"There are *no* wall people!" I shouted, grabbing his arm and yanking him to his feet.

"But I heard-"

"***Me*** making fun of ***you***." I said.

"Oh…hey!" he stammered.

"Just go." I said, pushing him back in the opposite direction. Soon we were both racing back down the halls in silence. Well except for Edward's grumbling about how mean and evil I am.

We arrived back in the hall where I'd left the others and it was completely deserted. Same as every other hallway we'd been through so far. So we continued on through the castle and still, no one. "Where are all the soldiers?" I muttered to myself. Surely Violante had alerted **someone** by now.

"Uh...out for lunch? You know, union break and all." Edward said, I glared at him out of the corner of my eye, "what? It could happen."

"Not here." I said. Then we heard the talking. "this way." I said, and led Edward around the corner into the next hallway. There, down the hall from us, a light shone through the doorway. We reached it and found everyone inside. But we weren't in just any room, nope, we were looking at a freaking *chapel*!

"Ah, our final guests have arrived. Now we can begin." Jezaba greeted us from the center of the huge circular room. We were shoved from behind and stumbled forward. I heard the door slam behind us and about a million locks of many kinds clicked shut. We weren't going to be getting out that way, that was for sure.

"I'm beginning to think maybe this was a trap." Edward said.

"You *think?!*" I snarled between clenched teeth. I felt someone's hand grab my arm and gently pull me backwards, away from Edward. I didn't have to turn around to know it was Charlie,

"Calm down, Reilly." he whispered, clasping my hand in his.

"I can't believe you tried to trick me!" Violante shrieked from beside Jezaba. She looked like she had a concussion, which, judging by how hard I'd hit her, she probably did.

I shrugged, "I can't' believe you fell for it." I said, finally getting control over my demon blood. Violante glared at me and sighed with frustration. Then the door burst open and Keira and Charity came in. Keira looked around nervously and muttered, "uh...hi."

Charity wasn't as quiet, she waved frantically and shouted, "Hi!!!" so loud it echoed.

"Welcome my friends, but mostly enemies. You shall all have front row seats to my taking over the world!" he shouted, his eyes glowing with pleasure at the idea. "But first, I must have a little fun while I finish my preparations!" he summoned an army of legion and added, "harm anyone but my Apostles, have fun!"

He departed and we were left facing an entire army of legion. "Damn it." I heard Charlie growl. I didn't have time to see what was wrong, however, as most of the legion had recognized me and were now on their way over to where I was standing.

"Reilly, behind you!" I heard Charity squeak from somewhere near me. I turned just in time to avoid the point of a legion soldier's sword. I grabbed his wrists and drug him closer to me where I could reach him to be able to shove his nose into his brains. Not the best idea considering that doing so only made my already fragile control slip farther. I more or less went on a rampage, killing dozens of legion before I finally calmed down.

"Well, well, what have we here? Is someone's self-control evaporating?" Violante asked me as she stepped down to stand in front of me. "Good, I'd hate to think you were holding back. Then my killing you wouldn't matter."

"First of all, I could kill you with one hand tied behind my back. Second, I would *never* hold back when fighting you, anyway." I snarled.

"Why do you keep fighting on that side? Why protect a race that's destroying itself anyway?" she asked, I answered immediately.

"Because they can't protect themselves. Not against us. Yes, the humans *are* dying off. And yes, they will eventually wage too many wars and pollute themselves into extinction. But they deserve to make that choice themselves. Besides, what's the point in fighting a species that never stood a chance in the first place?"

"Because it's *fun*!!!" Violante shouted, and she began to charge toward me, sword outstretched. At that moment everything seemed to happen in slow motion. I could see her getting closer but it was like I had ages to move. When the point of her sword was about a foot in front of me, I stepped to the side, grabbed the handle of the sword, and yanked it out of her hands, sending her flying passed me.

"Hmmm, that was interesting." I commented, balancing the sword on my pointer finger. Violante just stared, wide-eyed, as I stood the sword on the ground and cracked it into two halves.

"You...I...my...NO!!" she shouted, grasping the two halves in her hands. "Why?! Why the sword!? You could've broken *anything* else. Why go for the sword!?" she shouted.

"You were too far away for me to reach your neck." I shrugged. She seemed to regain some of her control before replying,

"You will pay for this...as soon as I get a new sword. Jezaba!!!" she called, "get your ass back here, I need you!" she paused, then added, "Well, actually, I just need a new sword." I rolled my eyes, and turned back to fighting the few remaining legion.

"Ok, ok, ENOUGH!!" Jezaba thundered, he looked around sadly then whimpered, "you killed all my legion. Now I have to get *new* legion. Do you know how hard that is?"

Don't worry Jezaba, I can take care of them for you!" Violante shouted, but Jezaba just ignored her.

"Never mind that, look at what I can do!" he shouted, snapping his fingers. The minute he did so, Violante began to float toward him.

"Whoa, what are you doing?! Jezaba, put me down!!" she shouted, Jezaba agreed reluctantly.

"Don't you get it!? Now none of the Apostles can escape! They don't have a choice but to help with my plan!" he shouted gleefully.

"Uh, well, technically, I'm only *half* Apostle so…see ya." I said, backing toward the door.

"Oh no you don't." Violante said, blocking my exit and shoving me forward. I would have retaliated, but Jezaba snapped his fingers and I was thrown backward, landing next to the other Apostles, who were already in place.

Jezaba looked around the room excitedly, "Do we have them all?"

"Um, Jezaba, last time I checked there were *eight* Apostles, not six, you dunce." Violante hissed angrily.

"Oh…I knew that." Jezaba said after counting us.

Violante looked like she was desperately trying not to kill him, (or else just trying to come up with a fun way of doing it,) when she sighed, "Just hurry up."

"But, Violante, I think I lost the other two." Ok, first of all, he's an idiot. Second, now would be a good time to disappear!! As Violante and Jezaba continued arguing, I edged farther and farther out of sight. When I reached the far edge of the platform, I jumped down, landing silently on the ground. Figuring that if I came back in through another entrance I could surprise them and get everyone out safely, I raced to the door. I'd just grasped the handle when Keira shouted,

"If I have to be here then you have to stay, Reilly!!" at first I couldn't believe what I'd heard. Shocked, I turned to face her, but seeing that now everyone was looking at me, pissed me off. I glared at her as I hissed through clenched teeth,

"I'm going to *kill* you Keira!! Do you have *any* clue what that door leads to!!" I shouted. Knowing full well that she had no idea, (I myself, only had a guess.) Before she could reply, Jezaba snapped his fingers and I flew back onto the platform, right next to Keira. Because I was couldn't kill her, (though I **wanted** to) I stood there, tense and seething.

"Oops?" she muttered, I turned stiffly toward her, fighting every impulse to attack, and gave her a nasty glare. "You know," Keira said, turning toward Jezaba, "just because we're all here, doesn't mean we're going to cooperate."

"She's right, you know." Violante said, but not in a very convincing tone. "Unless…" she didn't finish. And, because I already felt the drastic increase in energy, she didn't have to. As the energy level grew, Violante waved one hand through the air, causing Charity to vanish.

"Damn it." I hissed, "fine, Violante, you win."

"What!?" Keira demanded. Charlie and Edward protested as well.

"Reilly, you can't use your Apostle powers." Charlie pointed out.

"We don't have any other options. We have to go along for now and fight back later." I insisted.

"I can't talk you out of this, can I?" Charlie said, I smiled at him sadly.

"God I wish you could." I said. Keira sighed,

"Ok, Jezaba, do your worst." she said. For the first time since knowing her, I admired her for thinking of someone else. She turned to me, everyone did, and waited.

"Bring it on, asshole." I said.

Jezaba held out his hand toward us and I closed my eyes. About three seconds after I shut my eyes, I felt an icy pain shooting through my veins. I was determined **not** to show how much it hurt, so I gritted my teeth and fought against it. I heard Keira scream and tried not to do the same. I opened my eyes then, and found that I had fallen to my knees. Violante wasn't anywhere to be seen, and when I did finally locate her, she was **behind** me! Not knowing what she was up to, (and not caring,) caused me to do something that, considering the circumstances, could've killed me. I lashed out at Violante with my demonic energy while my Apostle powers were re-awakening. I heard her scream and then I heard the crash as she smashed into one of the pillars holding up the platform. It tilted and then crashed to the ground.

But none of the Apostles fell with it, we were all held aloft with our newly reacquired wings. Without really realizing it, we moved into a formation none of us had ever seen before. Keira and I were at the top, with Charity and Brittany slightly below and to the outside of us. Then two other Apostles and after them, then the last two.

Being a demon, I can sense energy, and the amount radiating from us eight was immense. But I didn't have much time to think about it, because the icy sting in my blood became a throbbing pain. Then I heard Charity cry out, and all knowledge of my own pain vanished.

"Keira...we...have...to save...them." I choked out. Every illusion vanished and realization struck me. We were going to die!

"Reilly...are we gonna die?" Keira asked.

"Not...if...you...help me." I managed, talking was becoming difficult. Keira didn't reply, but I saw her stretch her hand toward me. I did the same and the tips of our fingers barely met. The second they did, however, the energy level doubled, then tripled, then quadrupled, until my mind was swimming with power. Together, Keira and I redirected the energy toward a small opening in the delicate balance of time, that had appeared during the ritual. It slammed through the small rift and evaporated into nothing, closing the hole as it went.

Once everything was back to normal, (or at least, *our* normal,) I saw that Keira and I had also managed to save Charity, Brittany, and two others. The final two, however, weren't as lucky. There was no trace of them, but we knew they'd been destroyed.

Jezaba's excited shouting snapped me from my thoughts, "Excellent!! Oh wonderful, Violante, look! I did it!!!" he shouted as he skipped, (yes, *skipped*,) gleefully over to a giant, black, door. He put the key into it's place, and then turned to face us. "Now, I will be the ruler of the--uh...ah!"

"Uh-Oh." I muttered, as Jezaba fell to the ground.

"No, *I* will be!" Violante said, putting her sword away.

"Hey, how do you rule an 'uh-ah'? and what's that red stuff?" Edward demanded. I sprang my claws out and advanced toward him, but Charlie held me back.

"No. Stigmata." he warned, I relaxed slightly in his arms, and waited for Edward to make an even bigger idiot out of himself. Which, of coarse, happened.

"The red stuff is Jell-O, Edward." Keira said, sounding as drained as I felt.

"Really!? Oh, I want some!!!" he shouted, running to where Jezaba had fallen.

"It's not Jell-O, Edward! It's blood, Jezaba's dead." Violante shouted, halfway between angry and amused.

"I knew that! So, why did you kill Jezaba?" Edward asked. Did he seriously not know?

"Because now that you Apostles have opened the door, I can raise an army of dead demons, impossible to defeat. Then, I will kill all humans, so the world can be used for *my* demonic empire."

"There's somewhat of a problem here, Violante." a horribly familiar voice said. Causing Violante, Charlie, and I to tense.

"Wh-wh-what would th-that be, y-your h-highness?" Violante choked out. (She didn't just say what I think she just said, did she?)

"What did she just call him?" Edward asked, looking suspiciously at me. He, too, must've realized who it was lurking just beyond the light.

"Not now, Edward." Charlie said.

"They're going to find out eventually." I sighed.

"I know, but *now* is not a good time." he said, which was a good point.

"Enough. *I'm* the center of attention here, not you!" Violante shouted. (doesn't that sound vaguely familiar? But who said it…Oh yeah!)

"Wow, Violante, you have acting like Jezaba down. What's next, are you going to cower in fear and suck your thumb?" I asked.

"NO!!" she protested. Too quickly in my opinion.

"Violante! Summon your legion so I can finish what I've started!" my father ordered. That can mean one of two things, and I'm pretty sure he's not talking about rebuilding the dungeons I destroyed, so he must mean…shit. Charlie's arms tightened around me, but I stepped away.

"I *have* to do this." I said, and I knew it was true. If I backed away from a fight now, someone I loved would get hurt and it would be my fault. One of us had to die, and I would try my damnedest to make sure it was him.

To my surprise, Charlie agreed. "Ok," he said, "just be careful. I don't want to lose you."

"Aw, how sweet! Too bad you don't have a choice!" my father shouted.

I spun around toward his voice and he appeared in front of me, smiling wickedly. Before anyone could say another word, he reached forward with a speed that would have put a Puff Adder to shame, and grabbed my wrist in a vice-like grip. Then he shimmered, forcing me to go with him. (nothing hurts worse than being *forced* to shimmer, especially because I couldn't use my own powers. Something he could only prevent because he was in full form.)

All I managed to say before we were in a new location was the protest, "hey!", then everything changed.

Chapter 30
Free At Last

"You'll never kill me! NEVER!!!" Lieam shouted.

"What makes you so sure?" I inquired. I remembered Sedrick's cold, lifeless eyes and every other thing he'd done to others throughout his life and felt a surge of demonic energy coarse through my veins. Fueled, no doubt, by the anger I was forcing under control.

"You're not strong enough to actually finish me. If you were, you would've killed me at Mt. St. Helens." he laughed. I thought back, he was right. It would have been so easy to end his life that day. He was, after all, weakened to a point of almost Legion status.

"You're right, I should've killed you then." I admitted, then I looked up at him, hoping he could feel every bit of the hatred I felt for him. "But better late than never." I snarled, diving toward him. Because he was in his full form, and I wasn't, he was much faster than me. (Which I would've counted on if I hadn't been temporarily blinded by my rage). He avoided my attack easily and knocked me aside with a kick that caught me in the shoulder.

"You can't defeat fate, Reilly. Sedrick learned that lesson and so will you." I cringed at the mention of Sedrick. I still felt guilty despite Charlie's many efforts to make me understand that it wasn't my fault.

"I *can* kill you. I *will* kill you." I said, rushing toward him again. This time, he tried to turn and fly. I knew if he got air born, I'd be dead. So, out of sheer desperation, I reached out and grabbed his wings, one in each hand. Then an idea occurred to me. Before he could free himself from my grasp, I put both of my feet on his back, between his shoulder blades. Then I pushed of, flipping backwards in the air. I heard the ripping and crunching as his wings detached from his body. But I didn't really realize what I'd done until I had thrown the useless wings aside and was watching him frantically try to feel the bloody gashes that had been left.

"You...little...half-breed...brat!!" he shrieked, turning to look at me with a hatred I could almost feel burning my skin.

"What's the matter dad? Am I a little bit more willing to kill you than you thought?" I asked, watching him closely. I knew that I couldn't let him catch me off guard, if that happened then I was doomed.

"I knew that making you queen was a bad idea. But I thought you were smart enough to figure out that those so called 'friends' of yours, not to mention the whole world, would be better off without you." as hard as I tried not to, I flinched at his words. He noticed this and continued, making his speech sound more and more like snarls rather than actual words. "You know it's true, you know I'm exactly right. Deep down you truly believe that staying with them is selfish. Have you told them what you're turning into? What you will soon become?" he took a step toward me, and something like a smile spread across his face. Making him look like Satan himself. (Whom, I believe, is closely related).

"They know." I said, my voice betraying me, revealing some of the fear I was beginning to feel.

"Do they? Have you told them, *everything?*" As the word left his mouth, he took another step forward. Making it so that he was almost directly in front of me.

"Yeah...mostly." I said, taking a quick step back. He followed.

"Mostly. You mean you're lying to your beloved friends!? Lying to your precious Charlie?!" He laughed, as if it was a stupid care I shouldn't be concerned with. (OK, first of all, I don't consider Edward a friend, or even an acquaintance, he's more like the person I'm forced to be nice to. Second, I'm not lying, exactly. I've told the truth, just not all of it).

"I-I told them almost e-everything." I stuttered, backing away again. And again, he followed. "Charlie knows everything, we just haven't told the others yet and why am I telling you this?" I asked myself out loud, suddenly aware that his attempt to distract me had worked. (I wasn't exactly scared of him. But with every word he said, he was giving me a horrible realization that he was right. And every time he spoke the way he had been, it brought back terrifying and painful memories that had taken me years to forget). "I really need to kill you." I said, again, more to myself.

"Have it your way." he said, standing directly in front of me. He seemed to be…glowing? Oh shit. Too late did I realize that he was building up energy. The following explosion sent us both flying backwards to opposite sides of the small building. It also caused the ceiling to fly upward, into the sky. But, unfortunately, what goes up, must come down. Seconds later, the marble-tiled roof came crashing back to earth with the full force of gravity pulling it down. I dove to the ground and covered my head, but that didn't make the impact any less painful. I really thought I was going to be crushed to death.

When the crushing, smashing, and utterly painful, stones had stopped falling, I attempted to stand up. Only to find that I was buried beneath about ten feet of rock. "OW." was all I could think of to say. I couldn't figure out what was more frustrating, the fact that I was in immense pain, or the fact that, somewhere in the room, my father was probably still breathing. I sighed out of annoyance and tried to pull myself free of the rubble. Once I had succeeded, I looked around and confirmed my suspicions of my father's survival. He was completely unharmed, so I was confused when I saw the look of horror on his face.

"How the hell did you survive that!?!" he demanded, only confusing me more.

"You made a building fall on my head. I do that on a daily basis." I shrugged, but the look of terror seemed to be frozen in place.

"You don't get it, do you? You actually didn't even *feel* it!?" now he was starting to creep me out. (Well, more than usual anyway). **What** didn't I feel?

"Would you care to explain?" I asked, trying not to reveal how much he was actually starting to scare me at that point.

"The Miasma!!! It was everywhere, I made sure of it!" as he screamed, he also began to circle me. As he did this, he stared at me. It was as if he thought that by my appearance he could figure out what had happened. (Which I, myself, now wanted to know). I heard him gasp, but when I turned to face him, he was laughing.

"What?" I asked, confused. Then I noticed the stigmata on my hands and arms for the first time since I'd been captured by John. And, as they had been then, they were 'bleeding' out the miasma. I felt my mouth drop open as I began to realize what was going on, "I'm immune to miasma?" I asked, the question was more of a rhetorical one, but my father's outraged answer came anyway.

"What?! You dare to assume you have that kind of power? Cocky little half-breed." his words made my shock vanish. It was replaced with an anger so fierce that I could feel it boiling just below my skin. It was *his* fault that I was turning into a monster. *His* fault that I would eventually kill everyone I loved…and Edward. (Not that killing *him* would be a bad thing).

"Do you have a better explanation?!" I asked, letting the anger flow through my words. For the first time in my entire life, my father seemed to be speechless. True, that only lasted for half of a nanosecond, but it was enough to give me at least a little self-confidence. Clearly what he didn't want me to know, was what I'd figured had been the case. That was twice, now, that the curse he'd bestowed on me had become a blessing. But I still had to find a cure.

"I'm going to make sure you don't leave this place alive. Whether it kills me or not!" (Great, now he's suicidal). "Do you remember what happened to your mother? I killed her, burned her alive." he smiled at the memory that had haunted me since it happened.

"I know, I was there, remember?" I said.

"Do me a favor when you enter hell," my dad said as he prepared to attack, "Say 'hi' to Sedrick for me." at this, my heart nearly stopped. My throat closed off and I couldn't breath. But I couldn't figure out whether it was my dad, or my own guilt that was killing me. Soon it didn't matter, however. About three seconds after I was being strangled by *something*, I heard a nasty crunch.

The shriek that followed was loud and almost inhuman. Which is why it scared me so much to know that it was mine. But the reason for my scream was the white hot pain flooding through my arm. I wasn't sure what he had broken, but it was almost enough to make me lose consciousness. I fell to the ground, gasping for air as the pain rocketed up to about a fifty on a scale of one to ten. I didn't have time to look at the damage, though. Because I was being pulled to my feet by the arm that, I was sure of it now, had every bone in it shattered. I inhaled sharply as the pain swelled when he grabbed my arm

"See, you can't win." My father whispered in my ear.

"If I'm going to hell…so are you." I gasped. The whole left side of my body was starting to go numb. My dad laughed at my threat. (It really didn't sound like much of one, considering I wasn't very far from going under). He let me fall back to the ground, and for the first time since the battle had begun, I realized that we weren't alone. Violante stood watching a little ways away from the edge of the platform. (When the ceiling fell, so did the entire north wall. Behind it was a straight drop off into nothingness).

"Last chance, Reilly. Come with me to the castle. Take your rightful place at the throne." My father said. He glanced at Violante, who looked as if she would've rather been being ripped to shreds by wild animals, rather than watching someone *else* kill me.

"Thanks but no thanks. I'd rather be dead than the ruler of hell." I said.

"And why is that. Why are you so against your destiny?"

"Because, being evil is too easy. I mean, where's the challenge in getting everything you want?" I said, my voice getting stronger. The pain in my arm was ebbing and I was finally able to stand without getting dizzy. I rose to my feet and at the same time, Violante shifted so that she could be ready to attack more easily. Lieam gave her such a look that I actually thought he was going to forget about me for long enough to kill *her*. At his glare, she relaxed reluctantly.

"Patience, Violante." Lieam said in a soft voice. Then he added to me, "You've made your choice. Now you'll have to die with it." about three things happed at the exact time he was finished speaking. The first was that Violante crouched forward, ready to attack. The second, was the wave of heat that over came me. And the third were the images that flashed through my mind before everything went black.

The pictures I saw in my head as I was flying through the air and into the southern wall, (Which fell backwards upon my impact and revealed another large hole,) were of things I both remembered, and figured that my subconscious had made up. They were things both horrible, and comforting. The first thing I saw, was my mother. But not as I remembered her, her face distorted with pain. Instead, she was smiling, looking down at me from a place lit up so much it would have shamed Las Vegas. The next thing I saw was my dad, laughing at my pain, *exactly* as I remembered him. Then, the final illustration in my head, was of Charlie.

He was happy, but at the same time sad. It was as if he was trying to find the good in something very bad that had happened. He was speaking, but the words made no sense. "Not yet, Reilly. You can't die yet. You have to keep fighting." before I could figure out what his words meant, I was dragged back to consciousness, and to my own crippling pain.

I heard my father and Violante's laughter before I ever saw them. I could also feel the many burns and cuts and bruises that I was, now, probably covered in. "You might want to hold the celebrations considering I'm not dead yet." I growled, struggling to stand. Once I was up, I could fully see the shock and disbelief that colored Violante's white face. But Lieam looked like everything was going as planned.

"It's the 'yet' you should be focused on." he said. (Now how the hell do you not get surprised when someone who's heart was surely stopped, suddenly comes back to life).

"Even if you do kill me, I won't be going to hell. I'll enter heaven, and Sedrick and mom will both be there. And I'll laugh at you from the sky. I'm an angel remember!?" I said. (Ok, so it was a long shot, but whatever I let myself believe now didn't really matter much at this point).

"You're not going to heaven, Reilly. You may be an angel, but you're an angel of darkness." My father said, and though I didn't want to. I heard the truth in his words.

"Well, I might as well go out with a blast." I announced, letting every ounce of the demonic energy inside me rise to the surface. Then, I directed it all at my father, as he did the same toward me. Just before the super nova, I saw Violante shimmer. Then there was a flash of heat, followed by a blinding light. It was as if I was being separated from my body. I really wasn't sure if that was the case or not until I landed, barely alive, on the ground where I had been standing.

When I finally had enough courage to open my eyes. I saw that I was the only one who survived. (Well, not counting the one who ran away). My father was definitely gone this time. There was nothing left of him, he'd been completely destroyed. I was sure of this only because I could still faintly sense his presence, his soul was still occupying the area. Fighting not to lose the battle against Satan. Then, as if he had never lived, his soul was dragged down to the fiery depths of his eternal home. And I shimmered back to those with whom I truly belonged, with tears of relief in my eyes.

Chapter 31
Enter into Hell

When I got back to the 'chapel', it looked like a bomb had gone off. Debris was every, and so were bodies of legion.

I wasn't surprised to hear Keira explaining herself, "well…I just happened to 'find' it in Jezaba's weapons room while looking for…uh…Charity."

"Why were you looking for Charity in the weapons room?" Edward asked.

"Um…she was lost too?" Keira shrugged as Charity and the other Apostles came over.

"Who was lost?" Charity asked, Keira glared at her.

"You were, now be quiet." she said.

"Keira, stop talking, you're digging yourself in deeper." I said, walking over to them. Slowly, as all of my more serious injuries hadn't healed yet. Charlie rushed past the other and ran toward me, "uh-oh." I muttered, before he gave me a huge hug. Every one of my injuries screamed in protest but I ignored it and hugged him back.

"Are you ok?" he whispered.

"Actually, yes." I said, and for the first time it was the truth.

"Sorry to interrupt," Violante said, she was standing in front of the Door of Darkness. "But I have an empire to build." she turned the key and opened the door. "with this gateway, I should be able to get exactly what I need. Bye!" she said, she made a quick movement with her hand and I saw her slip something into her pocked. Something rolled up like a…Oh shit. Like a scroll! She must've taken it when I was focused on my father. Before I could do anything to stop her, Violante disappeared into the portal.

"I've got a plan to stop her!" Edward, of all people, said. This ought to be good. " I think Reilly should go through the door while we just go home." actually, that made sense.

"NO!!" everyone but Edward and I protested.

"I'll go." I shrugged, Charlie looked at me, actually, glared. "Someone has to go! It might as well be me." I said, then I shimmered over to the door, and stepped inside.

I hadn't been inside the door two seconds when Charlie came in behind me. "yeah, I figured you'd follow me." I said, he shrugged,

"Do you care?"

"Nope." I said, staring out at the vast wasteland.

"Where are we?"

"Not sure, but if I had to guess, I'd say purgatory. Or somewhere like it." I said, Charlie looked at me quizzically,

"Purgatory?"

"Or somewhere like it. Right now we're in between worlds. In between hell and earth." I said, before he could say anything, Edward came stumbling in. I caught sight of a dark shadow moving toward us from across the wasteland as the door closed behind him.

"Don't worry, I-"

"Why did you volunteer Reilly!?" Charlie demanded suddenly.

"Because she's evil." Edward shrugged.

"Edward, I'm going to kill you!" Charlie shouted.

"But, I told Keira that we'd come back safely." he whimpered.

"Edward, I'm pretty sure you lied to Keira." I muttered as the black force field got closer.

"Why? What is that?!" Edward demanded.

"It's a portal." I said.

"That leads where?" Charlie asked, coming to stand next to me.

"Hell." I replied.

"Shit." Charlie and Edward mumbled, then the portal sent us flying through darkness.

The End

Reilly's story will continue in **Reilly, Angel of Darkness Volume 2 :** *Ruler of the Fallen* and *Heaven or Hell*

About the Author

Amanda Boyer is 16 years old and a sophomore in high school. She began this book about 2 years ago. Amanda is active as a soccer player, cheerleader, a member of the Art Club, and sings in both the school choir and the church choir. Amanda is also the artist of the outside cover art of this book. She lives with her parents, younger brother, a fish, and one dog in Missouri.

About the Inside Cover Illustrator

Hello, I'm Katelyn Gettner, but all my friends call me Moosey. I was lucky enough to illustrate a few covers for my friends, the authoresses, Amanda and Ellen. For this book, I did the inside cover before Angel of Darkness. So here's a little about me…I have three dogs, not including my brother, and I'm sixteen now. I live with my parents. My work ethic is extremely lax. Concept doodle, to the rough image, to the outline, then add a little art magic and *poof* finished picture.

LaVergne, TN USA
27 September 2009
158962LV00005B/11/P